HAVANA BLOOD

MAX RAY

Cover design by David Gagne

Published by Cabbage Palm Publishing

Edited by David Ray

ISBN: 1502466880

ISBN 13: 9781502466884

Library of Congress Control Number: 2014917060

CreateSpace Independent Publishing Platform

North Charleston, South Carolina

Foreward

I was fortunate to have formed and maintained a lasting friendship with, perhaps, the last man on earth who truly personified the warrior discipline and mentality as exemplified by the samurai of feudal Japan and especially the post-feudal era of Miyamoto Mushashi, et al. When the samurai culture lost its raison d'être as the feudal lords and their parochial fiefdoms were replaced by larger Kingdoms with a more organized military. Though the culture died out, the remnant discipline of these unusual warriors morphed through the centuries and reappears now and then in a few modern submission wrestlers, boxers and mixed martial arts combatants the world over. Pockets of sword and knife fighters, foot fighters and a plethora of aggressive-defensive devotees also have kept the samurai discipline alive … barely!

Karl Gotch, nee Istaz [1924-2007] was the real deal! Big, aggressive, skilled beyond belief in hand to hand combat [weaponless], and absolutely dedicated to the code of the samurai and the rigorous training, mental and physical, needed to attain and maintain its perfection … for a lifetime.

Gotch told me on many occasions that when you quit learning or think you know it all, you are dead meat. He was humorless in combat, merciless in his regard for the truth and absolutely fearless in expressing his opinion. He was as organized in his personal life as he was in his professional one; his private life imitated his art … totally defeat your adversary and never stop learning.

Karl Gotch feared no human on God's earth.

Karl was also enamored of pit bull dogs as they represented, to him, the true character of a combat warrior. In that particular class of canids, he found no willful submission or anything resembling 'quit', once engaged.

I have always been intrigued by the warrior culture, especially as personified by the Japanese Samurai and their code of Bushido. I do not think that any man in Western life, or lore, quite matches this extreme test of personal courage and the discipline necessary to nurture and enforce it. Exploring the mentality needed to attain this level of self-sacrifice, given the catered modern youth, is next to impossible. How does a man go to battle for another, with the unshakeable will to fight and not consider his own mortality and self-preservation?

I have spent many years reading and considering the circumstances of cultures that promote this unseemly, unnatural behavior among this certain class of men. I have yet to arrive at a reasonable conclusion ... I am unable to overcome, or rationalize, my innate distaste for self-sacrifice at that level, and, therefore, cannot objectively explain it.

This changes, however, when I consider the warrior characteristics of the canine. I have spent over fifty years attending the medical needs of animals, particularly the dog. I have hunted with them, lived with them, and admired them; therefore, it was only natural for me to explore the warrior concept in these fine animals.

Of the many breeds of dogs, I came to realize that one breed stood out as the possessor of the warrior mentality, to a degree I felt matched, or surpassed, that of the feudal Japanese Samurai. That breed is known, casually, as pit bulldogs - among which are several creative varieties, all guilty of possessing this unshakeable characteristic that continues to puzzle me in my fascination to understand it.

It is with this in mind that I wish to take my readers on a journey into the modern world of canine warriors and how that remarkable quality, so basically anti-social and self-destructive, can result in heroism, self-containment in its expression and a wonderful human-canine relationship.

Havana Blood takes you into the world of warriors, with the canine versions being two American Pit Bulldogs; the human ones, two highly trained, self-assured American private operatives. One, Samson Hercules Duff, has been gifted with the smelling ability of a Bloodhound and has bonded with his American Pit Bulldog, JunkYard. These two are true warriors. This narrative is not for the faint hearted and I do not wish to offend anyone – nor do I wish to apologize for this Samurai version of reality in the world of Pit Bulldog Bushido.

I want to thank my family for supporting me when my writing interfered with our precious time together. Special thanks to my son, Dan and his company, Cabbage Palm Publishing, for making the dream of Havana Blood a tangible reality. Thanks to the staff at Beach Park Animal Clinic for putting up with me all these years. I am a very fortunate veterinarian to have been placed among such fine people, and I trust that readers will judge this book on its own merits and that it contributes to a better understanding of the blessings that dogs bring to mankind.

I wish to dedicate this novel to the last real warrior whose friendship and council blessed me for more than three decades: Karl Gotch, nee Istaz … R.I.P.

Preface

Gator Moon recalls the story of a self-disciplined man with significant physical abilities and his American Pit Bull Terrier known as The JunkYard Dog, or JY.

Samson Hercules Duff, possessed of extensive law enforcement and counter-intelligence experience was working independently on a case in a central Florida county with his partner and best friend, Charles 'Skeets' Kirby, when a rogue Miccosukee Indian beat him half to death with a baseball bat.

Taken to a local hospital in the small central Florida town of Centra, Sam's life was saved by a brilliant, albeit unorthodox, surgeon who replaced his traumatized brain tissue with that of a bloodhound. Dr. George Martinez' creative surgery not only saved his life but gifted him with the smelling ability of a mature bloodhound.

Considering his patient a homeless drifter, the innovative surgeon was ill prepared for the forthcoming influx of FBI agents, law enforcement personnel and least of all Samson's partner, the volatile, barely controlled sociopath, Skeets Kirby.

His professional 'hideout' at the small Centra Hospital was mercilessly dragged into the limelight, as was his past credentials causing his amorous relationship with the beautiful, dark-haired nurse Elise Jones to take a wrong turn.

Samson recovered and had little time to adjust to his newly acquired sense of smell before he was sucked into the mysterious

River of Grass; the mighty Everglades of Florida … Pay-Hay-Okee, as the Natives called it. The postsurgical swatch of white hair dividing his thick black mane only added to his newfound mystique.

The man who beat him, Joe Billie Bloodtooth, was slowly drifting towards insanity and broke with his corrupt, scheming Greek crime boss, Gypsy Jack Papadoupoulis and kidnapped prominent rancher, Can Martin, and his new private nurse, Elise Jones after savagely murdering all of Martin's domestic help.

Plunging into the vastness of the Everglades as if his backyard, the murderous Miccosukee dragged his hapless captives through the green hell with the threat of horrible death as expectant as the ubiquitous swamp mosquito.

Sam's friends in the FBI came to investigate and help but they had no answer for successful hostage retrieval from the deranged Joe Billie as long as he stayed in the formidable River of Grass. Senior Agent Bob Long along with Ralph Woodham, former associates and lifelong friends of Duff and Kirby, had been assigned the case and bluntly told Samson that there was no way to bring the two hostages out alive, much less even find them in the green hell of a battlefield chosen by the malevolent Miccosukee.

Samson Hercules Duff's nascent attraction to the dark-haired nurse was weighing heavily on his psyche and the thought of her being ravished and probably clubbed to death was not something he could live with. Abruptly taking JunkYard, his Randall knife, 9mm pistol and scant supplies, the determined pair soon cut the renegades spoor and the chase was on.

Havana Blood picks up in the life of these adventurers after their Everglades showdown. Welcome to and enjoy Havana Blood!

Chapter ONE

Big Jaxe squinted as he strained and tried to muffle his porcine grunts, covering his ears with his mitt sized hands to filter the sounds. Jaxe had been uncomfortable for hours, and now that relief seemed a few grunts away the confining cubicle seemed to mock his effort for relief.

'Dammit', he thought, 'These public crappers are so small there's no way I can get comfortable ... shit, I'd have to step out just to change my mind!'

Jackson Larry was a big man and had been given to morning toilet duty as long as he could remember, so when a meeting took him away from home the disruption with this morning ritual became apparent: Big Jaxe got grouchy - seriously grouchy! The meeting was in Orlando and he had brought his grandson, Gherrie, and his academy friend, Benito, since they were spending two weeks at Jaxe's Marion County thoroughbred farm, VentureQuest, and Orlando was only an hour drive from the Ocala farm.

Gherrie Larry was 13 years old and the only son of Big Jaxe's only son, Jackson Larry, Jr. Big Jaxe and his wife, Dolly, doted on young Gherrie and when he wasn't away at an exclusive school or camp was a welcomed visitor at VentureQuest.

Feeling another spasm, the straining man positioned his elbow on his right knee and rested his forehead on his fist, his florid face mirroring the urgent contraction. 'Ah, relief,' he thought, as his purged mind reviewed the morning meeting. He hoped the kids weren't too antsy waiting in the conference room lobby because Big Jaxe wasn't into restroom hurry-up; the electronic games should keep them occupied, as Gherrie and Bennie were into these new-fangled gee-gaws. In fact, Jaxe had noticed a small, pager-sized device the olive skinned boy carried on his belt. He figured it for a compact Japanese made radio, but could care less as long as the boys got along.

'Strange kid,' Jaxe thought: 'Good manners. Same age as Gherrie. Expensive clothes. Damn curly hair, looks like finger painting. Sure 'nuff strange kid.'

Gherrie had called from The Island, as Big Jaxe called the exclusive boys academy where Gherrie spent the last two summers, and asked if he could bring a friend. Of course he could and since then Bennie, short for Benito, had been a frequent companion of Gherrie's at VentureQuest.

Big Jackson Larry had been locked in conference all morning with a small, start-up Biotechnology Company from the west coast, near Clearwater, that had developed a potent immune modulator - but what the hell, so had a dozen other companies if you believed all the biotech gossip. Anyway, he didn't give a rat-turd about their brilliance, just whether he could turn a buck or two – million – off their products. 'Fuck brilliance,' he thought, as his face puckered: 'Bullshit walks, money talks - and always will!'

Larry, Winans, Puck and Gore knew this as they had stepped in and reorganized many brilliant but poorly managed start-up companies, throwing them a financial lifeline baited with patronizing platitudes and money - and a very sharp hook to be set at the right moment, leaving the entrepreneurs flopping like fish out of water as their Company gets reeled away.

The big man smiled and rested his chins on his other fist. There was a jerk scientist that got mad some years ago when Jaxe's group diluted the original partners' stock, forcing them into a minority position and making them market their technology prematurely; boy, was he pissed! What was that guy's name? He was the real brain behind their research and technology.

Jaxe's face relaxed as his rigors melded with relief and he managed a grin as he recalled the young biochemist he had manipulated 3 years ago. Transforming his fist into coned fingertips to support his head, Larry rolled his globular eyeballs to take in the nondescript booth with its Spartan paper holder designed to discourage overuse as much as thievery; the shiny, easy to clean walls with the simple bar latch barely holding the door closed given the one inch gap it had to span between door and facing.

Quentin Burgaard - the Third! That was his name. The big man laughed as the scientist's name tumbled from his clouded mind. Yeah, what did the guys call him? ... QB-3? ... QB cubed? ... Dr. Cube? ... What a trip he was. Mucho macho, brilliant, ambitious ... and unscrupulous!

It was ambition that did in Quentin Burgaard, III. It made him vulnerable to the venture capital lifeline bullshit as the young genius spent money like a lotto winner. Jaxe squinted as he recalled QB-3: Thick, curly hair with a decided reddish tint covered his oversized skull like a wild weed covering a rock. His garish red beard, punctuated by well formed lips glistening from saliva left by his tongue in its quest to keep the curls from his mouth. Six feet tall, Jaxe remembered, with thick forearms and meaty hands remindful more of a blacksmith than a scientist. A noticeable paunch jutted over his custom tooled leather belt, and the glint in his eye demanded interpretation ... Impossible to read.

When Larry, Winans, Peck and Gore came to their rescue, Quentin took the money and ran – straight to the gun shop, the boatyard, the adventure outfitter, the limo service and started living it up. It wasn't long before the founders had a falling out over their leader's excesses allowing Jaxe's group to take over, with two of the founders sent packing – QB-3 being one of them. The last word Big Jaxe heard about the good Dr. Cube was that he was aiming his talent at computers. 'Well,' thought Jackson Larry. 'Fuck

him and the theory he rode in on. He shouldn't have been so easy
to compromise. Computers, huh – more power to him!'

Larry, Winans, Peck and Gore made a bundle when they took
the Company public and sold out before the technology had time
to develop. The founders, including Quentin Burgaard, III, made
zip, and it was this that fueled the beefy smirk on Jackson's florid
face as he shifted his beefy body inside the restricting lavatory.

Impressed by his own ingenuity, Jaxe's thoughts were a long
way from the small cubicle and he did not notice the thin metal
tube lift the bar latch through the gap in the door facing, causing
the door to partially open as gravity acted on the uneven hinges.
Looking up with, "What the fuck do you ..." as the small tube spit
45 grain lead pellets with the unconcern of a woodpecker tapping on a tree trunk. Discreet marks appeared on the forehead
of the stunned man and seemed decorative until they reddened,
and blood spewed from the nine holes. The thin, blue veined arm
never wavered as a slender finger squeezed the trigger twice more
after the initial nine, as much reflex as encore, before withdrawing
to allow spider-like fingers to close the stall door and secure the
latch.

Jackson Larry died wedged in the small crapper, his slack jowls
channeling bloody slobber down his chins where it dripped, like a
leaky roof, onto his lap.

• • •

Thirteen hundred miles to the north, in the Finger Lakes area of
upper New York State, Rick Smithson was playing catch with his
three children: Stacie, age 3, Audry, age 6 and 13 year old little
Ricky; also playing was Ricky's friend, Jacques. Rick was Jackson
Larry's protégé and right hand man, shoved into the venture
capital group by his late father, George, Big Jaxe's closest friend.
Rick was serving an apprenticeship and took every nuanced
business maneuver of Larry's as gospel.

An ex-marine officer, Rick cut an impressive figure with his athletic 6' 2" frame, Italian silk suits highlighting his abundant dark hair; the very essence of the All-American boy-man and the reason for his bitter divorce. Prior to the marital split, Rick and Cynthia had been jet-setting, albeit doting, parents and farmed their kids out to the best boarding schools money could buy.

Young Ricky was a friend of Gherrie Jackson and the two attended the same exclusive camp on Hoostra Island in the Bahamas, between Cuba and Marathon, Florida. Myrmon Academy was the 'in' camp for young men 7 to 15 years of age with very selective admittance standards - also expensive. It was at Myrmon Academy that Ricky met Jacques, a very strong, athletic, hawk-faced boy a year younger than Master Ricky. Ricky had Jacques as a visitor several times and Big Rick liked him, as his mannered style contrasted vividly with the spoiled kid attitude of the Smithson offspring. In fact, Rick wondered how the self-controlled visitor tolerated his volatile friend Ricky. Maybe the small gadget Jacques fiddled with had something to do with his mild demeanor, or just a toy he used as a distraction. Anyway, Jacques was a nice young man and his native French was a big help in Ricky's attempt at language diversity. Young Master Ricky needed all the help he could get!

The sun was low when Smithson called a halt to the game. The maid would be preparing dinner within the hour and Cynthia would be picking up the kids shortly after, so Rick hustled the youngsters off to bathe and dress while he headed for the outside shower by the empty guesthouse. He stepped into the cubicle and tugged at the sweat soaked tee shirt clinging to his torso like Velcro. With the ivy covered slats provided privacy, Rick dropped his shorts and stepped into the cooling stream, turning his face into the pulsating jets of water as they cooled and cleansed his body.

Relaxed in the bliss of the moment, Rick didn't notice the dark blue tube that materialized between the slats at precisely chest level. The first three shots were barely noticed and he casually rubbed the oozing dots that appeared on his lower torso, stepped away from the stream of water as the next three 45 grain pellets entered his chest, staggered against the wall and half turned as the final three lead pellets entered the back of his thorax at heart level.

An incredulous focus settled in his eyes. An unblinking stare, as if Rick Smithson was not in his vented body, its lifeblood escaping from nine tiny dots like air leaving a punctured balloon. The stricken man's mind was functional enough to fool his body – as brains are apt to do – and as Rick Smithson slid down the water slick wall in terminal distress, his brain whispered that it was someone else dying.

• • •

Samson Hercules Duff winced as the aroused stallion mounted the permissive mare, impatiently accepting the manual guidance provided by the sterile gloved attendant before thrusting his turgid, arm-sized penis deep into the receptive equine, forcing her to widen her stance and squat to withstand his lustful assault. Three, four, five, deep, purposeful thrusts and the spent horse slipped off the tensed mare and offered only token resistance as Clax O'Steen milked the last of the pearly ejaculate from the softening organ into a gelatin capsule and inserted it in the mare's vagina prior to putting her into her bridal suite stall. Carpeted outside and floor-covered with fresh straw, her droppings hardly hit the straw before a tee-shirted, rubber booted attendant scooped them into a hand woven basket with rope handles and carted them away. Ultra violet insect traps snapped and crackled at each end of the barn as flying insects fried themselves as reward, or penance, for succumbing to these alluring sirens; no Circe here to wax their ears or offer caution. This was first class horse breeding: Indeed, VentureQuest was a first class thoroughbred horse farm.

"Well, Sam, what do you think?" The question failed to penetrate the fog of Sam's concentration, so Clax O'Steen shrugged his shoulders and turned to the gloved attendant. "Leave the mare's tail wrap on until you feed …"

"What? What did you say, Clax?" Sam's Orphan Annie eyes were sighted now and locked onto the Irish blues of his friend. "What do I think of what?"

"About that horse, man ... a Graded Stakes winner, and I will own two shares in him ... part of my deal if I can make this farm profitable again. The last manager couldn't handle old HighandMighty and was running this place into the ground, so old man Larry really sweetened the pot when he came calling. Heck, I was tired of training anyway and looking for a place to roost."

Sam turned his head, testing the air, as the wafting aromatics of horses, disinfectants, cleaners and a myriad of pungent aromas hammered his heightened olfactory system. "Hell, Clax, you for sure found a cushy place to set and ruffle your feathers. Sure does keep my sinus' open." Sam forced an explosive "ah-choo", and grinned as his friend responded to the ersatz sneeze by giving him the finger. The suddenness of the mockery caused a movement against the far wall, as a smooth, muscular head rose up and deliberately covered the room with its one eye before returning his chin to sinewy outstretched legs. The crimson leather patch covering the dog's left eye did little to detract from the angular symmetry of the pit bulldog's head and neck. Unless needed, or summoned, JunkYard remained a shadow.

It had been six months since the gallant dog had his left shoulder broken and lost his left eye in the deadfall set by the misguided Joe Billie Bloodtooth. The bone pins had been out for months and the sturdy animal had worked his lithe body back into shape, thanks to the treadmill that Claxton O'Steen had put at Sam's disposal. Except for the eye patch, JY was the same as before - only wiser and tougher.

"And I like the stud, Clax. Seems like a sweet deal. You still have those mares?"

"Yep, Sam, I do." Clax replied. "Got two of them here on the farm and I hope to use my shares this breeding season."

Claxton Shamus O'Steen carried his 175 pounds stretched evenly over his 6' 1" frame, the knotted muscles sticking to his bones like fat leeches as testimony to handling 75 pound hay bales and 50 pound sacks of grain; throw in the half ton two year olds in training that jerked him around the shed row a dozen times a day and before long you have a workout.

Clax's thick red hair had thinned during his twenties and at 35 was conscious of his thinning pate, though his arms were thick with carpet-like, sun-bleached coils of reddish-blond hair. Un-athletic, but tough as a Texas tom turkey, Claxton O'Steen was a real stud and his recently noticed hearing problem only a minor inconvenience. Raised by Irish horse people in a proper equine environment, young Clax never considered a lifetime involvement with anything that couldn't raise its tail and produce horse manure, ergo his disenchantment with the FBI and eventual resignation.

Clax's upbringing included pit bulldogs and fighting cocks, a gimme on Southern horse farms and racetracks. He didn't drink hard liquor, smoke, or believe in divorce, rationalizing his womanizing in that sanctimonious manner which men have subscribed to for eons – he loved his wife and these opportunistic sexual escapades would never jeopardize his marriage…. no big deal! Don't worry, honey…

Clax seldom cursed and never took God's name in vain. Fighting dogs and chickens were horses of a different color and the lean Irishman had quite a reputation as a pit dog man. His Silver Nugget line of American Pit Bulldogs was well known throughout the South and Cuba, Puerto Rico, and anywhere dogs were pitted. Many hombres had been known to plunk down five grand for a weanling Nugget dog-pup, almost as much for a bitch. It was this mutual interest in pit bulldogs that cemented the friendship between the two men even though Samson had zero tolerance for dog fighting; although he acknowledged the heritage that produced this remarkable breed of dog.

It was at the University of Florida Veterinary Medical Teaching Hospital that Sam and Clax renewed their friendship. Clax had cause to be there while JY was being treated and the two met in the reception area with the result that Sam and JunkYard were invited to stay at VentureQuest.

Clax had been running a public racing stable for the past five years and Jackson Larry had taken to the hard working Irishman since he took a pair of ill-tempered two year old colts and broke their maidens in their first starts, when all the pundits were telling him to geld them. The VentureQuest farm manager job came next since the daily routine at his public stable resulted in run ins with his wife's veterinarian lover; one flake too many to add to his volatile Irish dander. Goodbye racing stable - hello VentureQuest. Claxton O'Steen never looked back.

Sam smiled as he listened to his friend. He was happy for Clax and hoped these good times lasted, though he doubted they would. Cynicism was an integral part of Samson's fiber since his beating at the hand of the Miccosukee half-breed and his experiences in the Centra County hospital, coupled with his ongoing relationship with Skeets. Again, Sam smiled. Charles Kirby. What a friend to have - if anyone could rightfully make that claim.

Sam ran his fingers through his hair, its blackness highlighted by the distinct silver streak that appeared following his surgery. His thoughts wandered to his first meeting with Skeets after his rescue in the Everglades. He chuckled as his mind projected the image of the Skeeterman's apoplectic look when he insisted that Skeets fly his injured pit bulldog to the Veterinary Hospital in Gainesville – immediately – or he could forget talking. The gaunt Samson Duff was not to be denied and even the cold rolled Kirby knew to back off and tend to Sam's gallant companion. He did as asked, and only then did Samson give in to the enormity of his experience with the malevolent Joe Billie Bloodtooth and the treacherous Pay-Hay-Okee.

Thinking of Skeets brought Sam back to the present as he turned toward the narrow stairway leading to the cozy loft apartment. He threw a "See you later, Clax. I need to make a few calls and see if Skeets got my messages ..." The languid dog got up, stretched lazily and silently followed the man.

● ● ●

Chapter **TWO**

Athens was at war with Crete and Cephalous, King of Athens, hurried to the island of Aegina to beg assistance of his old friend, King Aces.

"I have men enough to keep my kingdom and spare you such a force as you may need," Aces replied, whereby Cephalous rejoiced and replied. "I am in wonder at the hosts of youths I see surrounding me – all apparently of the same age. Yet I know none of these minions. Where are the many individuals I knew and respected previously? I look for them in vain, pray what has become of them?"

Aces groaned and replied with such sadness, "I have been meaning to tell you and will do so now that you may see how from the saddest beginning a happy result sometimes flows. Those whom you formerly knew are now dust and ashes! A plague sent by angry Juno devastated the land. She hated it because it bore the name of one of her husband's favorite females. While the disease appeared to spring from natural causes we resisted it as best we might, by natural remedies but it soon appeared that the pestilence was too powerful for our efforts and we yielded."

"At the beginning the sky seemed to settle down upon the earth and thick clouds shut in the heated air. For four months together a deadly South *wind prevailed. The disorder affected our wells and springs; thousands of snakes crept over the land and shed their poisons in the fountains. The force of the disease was first spent on the lower animals: dogs, cattle, sheep and birds. The luckless ploughman wondered to see his oxen fall in the unfinished furrow. The wool fell from the bleating sheep and their bodies pined away. The horse, once foremost in the race, contested the palm no more but groaned at his stall and died an inglorious death. The wild boar forgot his rage, the stag his swiftness, the bear no longer attacked the herds. Everything languished; the dead lay in the roads, the fields and the woods – the air was foul by them."*

"I tell you what is hardly credible, but neither dogs nor birds would touch them, nor starving wolves. Their decay spread the infection. Next the disease attacked the country people and then the dwellers of the city. At first the cheek was flushed and the breath drawn with difficulty, the tongue grew rough and swelled and the dry mouth stood open with its veins enlarged and gasped for the air. Men could not bear the heat of their clothes, of their beds, but preferred to lie on the bare ground. But the ground did not cool them, on the contrary, they heated the spot where they lay. Nor could the physicians help for the disease attacked them also and the contact of the sick gave them infections, so that the most faithful were the first victims. At last all hope of relief vanished and the men learned to look upon death as the only deliverer from disease."

"Then they gave way to every inclination and cared not to ask what was expedient, for nothing was expedient. All restraint laid aside, they crowded around the walls and fountains and drank till they died, without quenching thirst. Many had not strength to get away from the water, but died in the midst of the streams and others would drink of it notwithstanding. Such was their weariness of the sickbed that some would creep forth and not strong enough to stand, would die on the ground. They seemed to hate their friends and got away from their homes, as if not knowing the cause of their sickness, they charged it on the place of their abode. Some were seen tottering along the road as long as they could stand while others sank on the earth and turned their dying eyes around to take a last look, then closed them in death."

"What heart had I left me during all this or what ought I have had, except to hate life and wish to be with my dead subjects? On all sides lay my people, strewn like over-ripened apples beneath the tree, or acorns under

the storm shaken oak. You see yonder a temple on the height. It is sacred to Jupiter. Oh, how many offered prayers there, husbands for wives, fathers for sons and died in the very act of supplication! How often, while the priest made ready for sacrifice the victim fell, struck down by disease without waiting for the blow. At length all reverence for sacred things was lost. Bodies were unburied, wood was waiting for funeral piles, men fought with one another for the possession of them. Finally, there were none left to mourn; sons and husbands, old men and youths perished alike – unlamented."

"Standing before the alter I raised my eyes to heaven. O Jupiter, I said; if thou art indeed my father and art not ashamed of thy offspring, give me back my people or take me also away! At my words I heard a clap of thunder. I accept the omen, I cried; oh, may it be a sign of a favorable disposition toward me! By chance there grew by the place where I stood an oak with wide spreading branches, sacred to Jupiter. I observed a troop of ants busy with their labor, carrying minute grains in their mouths and following one another in a line up the trunk of the tree. Observing these numbers with admiration I said, give me, O Father, citizens as numerous as these and replenish my empty city. The tree shook and came a rustling sound in its leaves, though no wind agitated them. I trembled in every limb yet I kissed the earth and the tree. I would not confess to myself that I hoped, yet I did hope. Night came on and sleep took possession of my frame, oppressed with cares. The tree stood before me in my dreams, with its numerous branches all covered with living, moving creatures. It seemed to shake its limbs and throw down over the ground a multitude of those industrious grain gathering animals, which appeared to gain in size and grow larger and larger and by and by to stand erect, lay aside their black color and superfluous legs and finally to assume the human form. Then I awoke and my first impulse was to chide the Gods who had robbed me of a sweet vision and given me no reality in its place."

"Being still in the temple my attention was caught by the sound of many voices without; a sound of late unusual to my ears, while I began to think I was dreaming, Telemann, my son, throwing open the temple gates exclaimed; father, approach and behold things surpassing even your hopes! I went forth; I saw a multitude of men such as I had seen in my dreams and they were passing in procession in the same manner. While I gazed in wonder and delight they approached and kneeling, hailed me as their King. I said my Vows to Jove and proceeded to allot the vacant city to the newborn

race and to parcel out the fields to them. I called them Myrmidons from the ant {<u>Murex</u>} from which they sprang. You have seen these persons; their dispositions resemble those which they had in their former shapes."

"They are a diligent and industrious race, eager to gain and tenacious of their gains. Among them you may recruit your forces. They will follow you to war, young in years and bold in heart."

The Myrmidons were to be the soldiers of Achilles in the Trojan War – jealous, fierce and at times unscrupulous, belying their laborious, but peaceful origin.[1]

• • •

Charles Kirby's fingers drummed on the white linen tablecloth covering the rickety table in the small booth at Lela's deli in the French Quarters in New Orleans. This was neither a display of nervousness nor impatience – merely a mannerism honed from years of impromptu meetings; some for pleasure, more for business. Anyway, Skeet's Kirby wasn't nervous – just hungry.

Skeet's sloshed the coffee dregs around the bottom of the overworked ceramic cup and scanned the room looking for the waiter, abruptly locking eyes with the expressionless FBI agent, Bob Lang, as he pushed through the glass door. Skeet's quieted the cup and half rose as the FBI agent extended his hand. "Hi, Kirby, good to see you again."

"You ready to eat? I'm just a mite hungry, myself." Skeet's reply did little to alter the blank look on the FBI man's square face as he shed the trench coat and sidled into the narrow booth with a "Fine."

"Skeet's, how did Duff and his pup do after their Everglades thing with that bad ass renegade. I heard they both got pretty bent – the dog lost an eye or something ..." The agent focused on the one page menu as he spoke, softly, before blurting out. "Hot pastrami on rye, mustard, pickle ... Heineken draft," to the waiter who suddenly materialized.

---

[1] *Bulfinch, Thomas, "The Myrmidons", THE AGE OF FABLE, Mentor Classic [August 1982], 129-132.*

"Same for me but bring Stella instead of the Heineken. Throw in a few chips." Skeet's leaned back as the waiter fished the menus and empty cup from the table with a "Coming right up, guys."

"Samson and JunkYard are doing fine now, Bob, but they were, you might say, sort of rearranged a little; especially the dog – yea, he did lose his left eye and had a broken left shoulder that required surgical stabilization. Sam had a god-awful snake bite wound on his arm and that crazy Indian clubbed the shit out of him but Sam's tough. He's healed and they're down in Florida at one of those fancy horse farms managed by a friend of his, recuperating: Swimming. Fishing. Jerking off … you know - all those good things you do for R and R."

"I've been holding the fort since then, but I think Sam's straining at the bit to get back to work. Anyway, what've you got?"

The amused FBI agent smiled as he thought – 'so much for small talk from the Skeeterman … cut to the kill!'

"Skeets, there's been a few killings of low profile political activists. The Bureau was only recently called in and what was thought to be random backyard murders may not be so random. The regional Bureau called last month and gave me carte blanche to go after this thing for some perspective." Agent Long paused as the waiter approached.

"It goes like this, Skeets: A few ex-patriot Cubans have been killed in Dade County over the past six to eight months – wealthy, anti-Castro - but not zealots. Then, a few high powered business types were iced – Tampa, Jacksonville, Atlanta – with zero leads. Two months ago a young detective from Tampa was investigating the killing of a local attorney and started analyzing modus operandi and running various unsolved murders through a new computer program, and wouldn't you know, he found a common thread running through these seemingly unrelated jobs. So, we looked at his data and I think there is a link, but we're not exactly sure what it means."

"Why us, Bob?" Skeets had eaten while the agent was talking and threw down the last of his draft beer as Lang picked up his sandwich and took a bite, wiping his mouth repeatedly as the warm, mustard colored juices dribbled down his chin. Skeets' quieted fingers began to drum the table edge – slowly at first, but picking up steam as Agent Lang continued to chew, trying to devour the aromatic pastrami–mustard–pickle pellet as fast as he could since hyper-salivation had rendered meaningful conversation impossible. Thus, it was only a few seconds before Bob Lang's mastication movements were in sync with Kirby's finger tapping.

● ● ●

Between the Florida Keys and the island of Cuba stretches 90 miles of open water, its dazzling sameness broken by forbidding outcroppings called cays. Uninhabitable, these moonscape rocks harbor no fresh water or mammalian life, only marine birds and crustaceans indigenous to the area. Foliage is sparse, stunted, and grossly abused by the relentless elements. Unshod human trespass is impossible! The infinite pounding administered by the gin clear seawater has resulted in under-cuttings and tunnels, with openings at the end of some called blowholes, where wind and tide driven waters slosh out and up in a frothy gush as if from a pod of giant whales turned to stone as they spout.

A few of the larger cays display emerald green pools carved out from blowhole beginnings, and are reachable from the sea by underwater passages that can extend a distance through the rock before reaching the pool. The surrounding reef drops off sharply, tapering out to 80 or 90 feet depths before dropping, wall-like, to depths of over 700 feet. These purple depths along sheer, under water cliffs are home to a variety of marine life: Abundant. Big. Voracious!

Away from the walls the reef bottom is pockmarked by sink holes of various size and configuration, resulting in a vivid reef bottom interrupted by the inky blackness of a sinkhole – some plumbing 300 foot depths, some two or three times that. Each hole has its signature and over the years visiting SCUBA divers have given them names like The Black Hole, The Blue Hole, Wayne's Shark-Hole or The Gruesome Grotto. Due to location and the brutal unfriendliness of the area, visitors are limited to sporadic dive boat charters, a rare billfish sportsman, and more commonly, fish and lobster poachers from Cuba or the Bahamas in their leaky boats with emphysematous Hookah rigs puffing while they ply the depths trying to be predator instead of prey – not always succeeding.

It is totally isolated. Most maps do not show these cays and the hardy souls that visit call the largest collection of them the Salt Keys, or Cay Sal.

• • •

The bone white, 25 foot Mako center console rose and fell in synchrony as it acquiesced to its anchor tether and nodded fore and aft as the silky swells passed with math-like precision. Three men were aboard. One was pulling things from a dive bag while the other two, smaller, dark complexioned, adjusted a SCUBA dive vest to a fluorescent yellow air tank. The larger man was pulling a skin suit over his ample frame while sweat streamed down his red-bearded face like foam down an overfilled beer mug. Wrinkling his face as the sweat balls hit ticklish skin, the big man's countenance resembled a fuzzy faced clown trying to suppress a sneeze. Trapped in his Farmer Jones wet suit top by his rounded shoulders, Quentin Burgaard, III, growled at one of the dark skinned men, who forced the reluctant neoprene over his shoulders. Fishing his dive mask from the bag, QB-3 applied No-Tears shampoo inside the mask as he stepped to the stern, leaned over, and rinsed it – he didn't like spit – didn't work as good as the No-Tears.

He donned a facemask, slipped into the readied dive vest, pulled on his swim fins and using the "man overboard" water entry, fell backward into the aqua sea. One of the men pushed a large bag over the side, allowing it to sink before tying it off at 40 feet.

Entranced, the man stared into the depths, watching the shadowy figure retrieve the bag and turn toward the anchor rope.

"Hey, man, wake up'n hep me with this top. The Doc don't need no hep – I does."

The second man reacted by grabbing the straps to the blue Bimini top and forcing the snaps into their davits. It was hot.

QB-3 followed the rope to the anchor, securely snagged on a coral head on the rim of the inky hole. A myriad of fish scurried around the rim edge as the diver went over and dropped down twenty feet, coming to rest on a sandy shelf where he adjusted the dive vest to neutral buoyancy and began to tap a peen hammer on a conch shell: Tap – tap – tap … quite oblivious to the two large barracuda lined up above him like silver sentinels, or the coppery shimmer of the French angel fish as they gave berth to his intruding bulk.

One hundred yards across, the sinkhole plumbed seven hundred feet, its vase-like configuration providing an awesome diving experience, especially for novice divers. Schools of reflective margate patrolled the rim as competing numbers of Bermuda chub darted in the dark depths, scattering thousands of fluorescent glass minnows like reflective shards of shattered crystal.

Tap–tap–tap–tap; the persistent monotone penetrated the depths as a dark form separated from the shadows, pointed its wide head upward and effortlessly moved in the direction of the sound. As he tapped, the diver opened the bag and spread its grisly contents on the beach white sand of the ledge: Two small legs, two arms, small torso, and head adorned by tightly curled black hair. QB-3 knew the message sent by the exposed flesh would reinforce the slow Pavlovian reaction to the tapping and the great beast would quicken its approach.

Hastily, he pushed off the ledge and swam back to the boat, folding the empty bag as he went. On occasion, he would lie on the rim and watch the great hammerhead feed, but of late it seemed more aggressive and Quentin Burgaard, III, didn't want to push his luck.

• • •

The aqua blue seawater was clear save for the particulate matter that gave it a milky appearance at the six hundred foot depth, belying the storm ravaging its surface thirty miles north of Cuba. The sunrays didn't penetrate this depth and the varied denizens were oblivious to this weather tormenting the surface.

Sphyrna mokarran, the great hammerhead shark, eased his eighteen foot, silver gray body southward along the Cay Sal wall, his neuro-sensors alert, but the forty pound chunks of blue marlin stuffing his gut dampened any interest in direction or purpose – he was not on the muscle.

The thousand pound marlin was played out when the big shark hit, causing quite a stir aboard the thirty six foot charter boat as the two crewmen cheered their gut wrenched client to pump and reel. The second time he hit the beleaguered fish, the great hammer-head cut it in half, changing the marlin into dead weight and the fisherman into cursing goddam sharks to hell while he blew sweat and struggled with the remnant of his once-in-a-lifetime trophy.

Entering his home territory, the gray beast eased up the wall to sixty-five feet and slipped like a torpedo over the reef, the emerging sun penetrating this depth to produce an eerie shadow as his muted form passed. Abruptly, the sleek eating machine changed direction and picked up speed as its neuro-sensors picked up erratic movement in a sea creature, drawing the scalloped headed beast over the reef bottom with deadly intent.

The door-sized eagle ray knew better than to get close to the overhang of the cay, also knew he was in dangerous water and that discretion should be safer than valor. Reaching the end of the funnel coursing under the shelf, the big ray found the exit to be too narrow to allow passage, and sought to escape this inconvenience by thrashing his way to deeper water – just over the rocks – the idea of backtracking never came up. Flopping on the surface like a spotted bat, the beautiful eagle ray tried to breach the barrier before the receding tide stranded him. Once, twice, thrice he struggled from the receding water to land short of freedom and slide back into a more shallow prison. The forth attempt was his best – and last - as the jaws of the great hammerhead met him as he flopped into the deeper water, seizing half of its left wing and shaking like a Jack Russell worrying a rat until the tortured chunk gave way and the big predator slipped back into the sea while he devoured the glabrous chunk.

The mortally wounded ray flopped in a watery dance as its life-blood spewed like smoke from the grievous wound, safe from everything but its own mortality.

Away from the cay, <u>Sphyrna mokarran</u> swam lazily to the urn shaped sinkhole, slipped over the rim and eased his two thousand pound bulk into the dark depths. This was home and he was stuffed; he wasn't hungry when the eagle ray's signals enticed him – he just couldn't help it!

● ● ●

"The reason is, Skeets, that two days ago, one Jackson Larry was snuffed in a public shit stall and later that same day his protégé, Rick Smithson, was iced at his home some thirteen hundred miles north, as if by the same shooter." Agent Lang swallowed hard as the pungent pastrami aftertaste threatened to drown him.

"So, Bob, why us?" Skeets voiced disinterest as he waited while the agent sipped water.

"Because Jackson Larry owned VentureQuest thoroughbred horse farm in Ocala, and that's where Sam is staying, right? Right."

"Right you are. I might have known you would know where old Samson was. Christ, Bob, do you guys ever do anything but snoop?" Skeets tone was penetrating, but the twinkle in his eye belied his caustic retort. "Let me guess what you want us to do. Find out if this Larry fellow had connection to any of the others wasted in a like manner, and spell it out for your guys so you can ride herd on them and brighten up your white hats just a tad more."

"Right Skeets …" The agent nodded as Skeets cut him off.

"And don't go by the book like you would have to, but take shortcuts and death defying chances, as to solve this thing in a hurry. But …" Skeets eyes narrowed as his voice took an edge familiar to Bob Lang. "if we get caught, you never heard of us – right? Right! The rights were thrown in, amazingly, like Agent Lang had voiced them, causing the staid FBI man to force a smile resembling a crack coursing across a pane of glass.

"Right, Skeets, right. You can contact me at this number, day or night. And don't worry about your fees – we will pick up the tab – no problem. Tell Samson 'hello' for me. Any clarification, just call …" With that, Agent Bob Lang stood and extended his hand.

"Aw shit, Bob, why not? Right." At the last 'right,' both men broke into a wide grin and Skeets Kirby grasped the extended hand.

● ● ●

Thirty minutes after weighing anchor, the white Mako throttled down, eased into a narrow inlet and glided along a sheer rock wall, wake-less, its motor gurgling in contentment as it neared a deserted dock. Quentin Burgaard, III, stepped quickly onto the planking and headed for the electric cart parked at the water's edge.

Entering a sprawling, ranch style building, QB-3 paced down the dimly lit hallway, affecting a limp as he entered a large office Spartanly furnished, with computers and electronic gadgets competing for space on every desk and table. A myriad of books, some opened like blank stares, and some with bookmarks protruding like paper tongues adorned the chairs, except the one behind the main desk in the corner of the room.

"How'd it go, Quentin?" Roderick Osler leaned against a wall cleaning his fingernails with a penknife. "Any trouble? Did the big boy show up alright?"

Affecting more of a limp, QB-3 crossed the room and slouched in the chair behind the desk, wiping sweat from his fuzzed face. Rod Osler bookmarked and closed the two books on the chair next to the desk, placed them on the floor, closed the red handled penknife and shoved it into his pocket as he sat down.

"Like clockwork … no problemo. Any word on those three new ones from Brazil?" As he spoke, Burgaard's fingers were busy at the computer keyboard and as the upper case green letters spelling MYRMIDON flashed on the screen his cocked index finger tapped the 'enter' key.

• • •

Chapter THREE

The sleek head with flared nostrils pointing straight up identified the glistening stallion as he tried to look over the restraining wall between his paddock and the mares' barn. He worked up a lather as the horse transport van disgorged its contents of female horseflesh – for him - and patience was not one of his virtues; he had no virtues save foot speed and honest conformation. He was aware of neither.

One mare was flagrantly in heat and the burnished chestnut horse was advertising his interest concerning this matter. His fully extended member spasmodically spanked his belly with each prancing step, providing credible witness to this interest.

HighandMighty was royally bred and his genetic blend was dynamite. He had looks, speed and endurance but his disposition was loutish. He had won fifteen graded stakes races, including five grade ones, at every distance and was retired, racing sound, at five when Jackson Larry bought him. His chestnut coat with the perfect star on his forehead, and four white socks, gave him more chrome than a horse had a right to, but beneath this shiny image lurked a genuine equine libertine.

The big stallion hated anything with a dick: Dog, man, cockroach – whatever. Many a tough dog had found out the hard way that the jaws and hooves of the twelve hundred pound stud were not to be trifled with, and the shortcut through the stallion paddock should be avoided in the future – that is, if there was a future.

HighandMighty had been at VentureQuest four years and his handlers were used to him, but he never gave in to them. He could be caught and haltered, but woe to the groom who looked away until the nose chain or muzzle was in place. HM, as he was called, or SM, more affectionately, did exhibit sadomasochistic tendencies; he would strike, kick or savage anything within reach when the wafting aroma of an estrus mare crossed his diligent nostrils.

Clax O'Steen had been hired to break and race-train the recalcitrant stallion's get – no small feat considering the prepotency of Sir HighandMighty!

"Hey, Charlie … bring HighandMighty. The farrier is here and we need to get him trimmed. He's working on a toe crack in his near forefoot. Be careful … those mares we just unloaded got him all worked up – I think one of 'um's horsing a little."

Clax O'Steen ambled to the economy size pick-up parked on the asphalt entrance to the stud barn. A wiry, middle aged man was bent over tying the bottom of a heavy leather apron to his thigh, his thick fingers, wrists and forearms bearing witness to years spent under a horse using back, shoulders and arms to offset the brute strength of his weighty customers.

Trimming and shoeing horses is hard work. Thoroughbreds make it harder. Thoroughbred stallions make it suicidal.

"Say, Howie," Clax spoke as Howie Slaughter began unloading equipment. "The big guy has a toe crack starting. But don't cut him down too much, he's got a lot of work to do and I don't want him high stepping on ouchy feet."

"Whatever you say, Clax. The less I do on that orn'ry son of a bitch the better I like it." The lean blacksmith had long tuned out owners and trainers when they tried telling him how to do his job. Howie Slaughter kept a sharp knife and cut every horse's foot the same – to the quick! You could bet the mortgage on HighandMighty walking like the floor was hot for a week after the trim job, if he could walk at all. But … his feet would look good.

Nostrils flared and neck arched, the grand horse pranced from the stall as his whinnies pierced the air like sonic booms. Looking up, Howie noted the breeding readiness of the big horse and hollered. "Hey, Charlie, that old boy thinks he's coming out to get a little and since I'm the only warm body here, forget it! You better put that goddam chain under his lip."

Charlie knew he was in trouble as soon as he put the halter on the testy animal but usually the libidinous stallion knew what was expected and halfway cooperated. He knew when the muzzle was used and two men led him out that he could expect receptive mares; one man with a chain shank meant other things, and he allowed handling with minimal complaint as long as everyone remained alert. Not today!

Rearing, the devilish equine struck the groom with the force of a jackhammer, driving him to the floor like a dropped sack of oats. Wheeling around, ears pinned to his foxy head, he lunged at the hypnotized farrier and struck like a mythic snake horse, grabbing the man by the shoulder and giving him a ragdoll shake as horse powered jaws sank, vice-like, into flesh.

Reaching the end of the barn alleyway, the equine beast lifted 150 pounds of man meat and broke into a trot as his feet welcomed the soft grass. HighandMighty trotted off with the blacksmith in his jaws!

• • •

"Did you ever get in touch with Skeets?" Clax's voice penetrated the pre-dawn quietness like a rock through a plate glass window. The sun had thirty minutes before being tardy and the two men sitting in the portico drinking coffee had been in pensive quietude for the fifteen minutes it had taken to perk and pour the black brew. Samson Duff's wonderment at the smells wafting on the pre-dawn air was as intense as when he first became aware of his strange power; this gift resulting from near death, miraculous reconstructive and transplant surgery and finally, in his opinion, resurrection.

"Yep, there was a message from him last night and he'll be driving in late this evening." Sam whispered in deference to the morning hush and sudden attack of introspection. He stifled the urge to tell Clax that HighandMighty just pissed, and that he could identify each stallion by smell when the wind currents opted to advertise their spoor. His brain had finally adjusted to odor identification and he was not unsure as he was in the Everglades. Samson could now process differing smells without bewilderment plying his face like a nonuser-friendly computer screen.

His eyes no longer reflected confusion.

"Sam … hey Samson, wake up!" Clax raised his voice, trying to get the pensive man's attention as the sun breached the eastern darkness. "Listen, I've been invited down to Lakeport next month, to a big deal pit dog contest …"

"Shit, Claxton, you mean a goddam dog fight. You know what I think 'bout those."

Nervously, Clax cut him off, well aware of his buddy's distaste for dog fighting. "Listen just a goddam minute, will you? This is a big contest. Probably the best pit dogs in the country will be there. Aw, you know I'm not going for the money fights. I just want to roll that young Nugget dog. Man, this will be the-e-e chance to test that little shit's grit! And you could go if you weren't so frigging pig-headed – just to see some of the young dogs duke it out. It's a ways from the main pit to where they roll the pups and you wouldn't have to be anywhere near the money fights."

"Look, Clax, no! That's it, and that's why I wouldn't let you use JunkYard for stud 'cause I know you sell most of your pups to those fools that fight them" As Sam voiced the name, the pit bulldog raised from his position by Sam's chair and yawned, lazily, before settling back on the rug.

Sam stopped speaking as he scented the Irishman's nervousness and saw his ruddy face turn a shade deeper. He remembered

26

his vaporous fear when George Martinez, the surgeon responsible for saving his life, explained what he had done, surgically, to Samson Duff.

Skeets had been there, had arranged the meeting, and Sam clearly remembered the detachment displayed by the doctor as he detailed the procedures and the putative outcome: Sam would have the olfactory ability of a mature bloodhound. A lot of things could interfere with this phenomenon, but not predictably. He had to let experience dictate the scope and boundaries of his ability.

Sam was nervous about the immune system stimulating drug Martinez had given him to use intravenously monthly to avoid infectious disease, especially influenza or the common cold. Any upper respiratory problem could compromise Sam's ability to smell. The resolute Kirby had stiffened during this discourse but Sam agreed and pretended to understand. Since taking the injections, he had not experienced any cold-like symptoms or upper respiratory problems, though exposed to them. Whatever, it seemed to be working, and if he ever had health problems he was going to holler for the good Doctor.

Clax rinsing his coffee cup brought Sam's thoughts back to real time as his ebbing memory signaled his monthly injection. Clax spoke. "Well, hell, Sam, how about old Skeets. Think he would go to those fights with me?"

"He'll be here tonight … ask him. He's a hardwired son of a bitch. There's been times when I thought he would pay to see his Granny fight one of those dogs - and bet on the dog!

• • •

Rod Osler left the computer room and walked back to the dock where QB-3 had moored the Mako. A fitness buff, the fifty two year old disdained the electric carts parked at various points on the bleak volcanic upcropping. Paste white hair and sun crinkled face belied the strength in his athletic, one hundred seventy five pound body as he picked his way along the unsympathetic path.

Osler had been moderately successful in business in Salt Lake City before running afoul of the Securities and Exchange Commission, and in absconding with sufficient funds to fuel his passions ended up in the Bahamas with Quentin Burgaard, III, – whose very brilliance bespoke a certain brand of insanity.

Osler had never met anyone with the mental agility of Burgaard. If Osler, or any of his associates mentioned new technology or unusual application of existing technology, QB-3 would finish their sentences; read their minds, it seemed.

Quentin Burgaard, III, lived on the edge. His common denominator was gluttony - mental, physical, sexual, or whatever: Meta-physicist. Trencherman. Satyr. When dining, it was two of everything: Best wine, biggest porterhouse, extra side dishes and sumptuous desserts, ravenously devouring a few mouthfuls before pushing back and cheerleading his guests into porking out. If fellow guests were reluctant to participate, the cheerleading darkened to goading. Osler disliked dining with Quentin Burgaard, III,.

"Hey, Raul!" Osler's snort alerted two dark-skinned men lounging on the sun washed dock and the large one stood and started toward the Australian pine tree struggling to exist fifty feet from the dock.

"Ahh, Señor Rod, how are you today?" Raul Pena was polite, hiding whatever bias he harbored beneath a silky exterior of politeness but beneath the satin skin of the thirty five year old Cuban ran a steel cable toughness and venality rarely found among the proud island people.

To accommodate use of the scant shade provided by the stunted tree, the men were only inches apart, so Osler's strident voice was barely a whisper as he acknowledged this intimacy. "Dr. Burgaard wants us to take the Mako to Myrmon ... he's staying the night, more computer bullshit. I guess you can send Armando to babysit, but tell him to be seen and not heard – you know how crabby QB-3 can be when he gets interrupted."

Rod Osler's use of the acronym brought a visible grin to the darkly handsome face of the Cuban machismo, an effect noticed by the Myrmon Academy headmaster. He rarely spoke of his business partner except in terms of high regard: Dr. Burgaard, or Professor Burgaard, of which he was neither.

Quentin Burgaard, III, had been squeezed from medical school one year before graduation due to his off-the-wall bacteriological experiments and talent for conning anyone necessary into supplying time, knowledge, materials and even monies for this extracurricular work. He started a biotech company to study the effects of certain bacteria and their cellular components in stimulating the human immune system, duping a Florida philanthropist into providing seed money. His experiments proved fascinating and attracted several farsighted physicians, among them George Martinez, M.D., resident surgeon and medical visionary at a Tampa hospital.

Putting together a multi-disciplinary team of world-class scientists, Burgaard refined his basic bacteria derived immuno-modulator to be effective in nonspecific enhancement of the mammalian cellular immune system. This would be a vaccine against any infectious disease: To prepare the body to repel foreign virus or bacteria that may invade, regardless of type. Medical practitioners like George Martinez, taken in by Burgaard's enthusiasm and legitimate knowledge of immunology provided credibility to the company's research resulting in venture capitalist investment by the venture firm of Larry, Winans, Puck and Gore.

"Also, compadre, have you heard anymore about that street dog in Havana?"

"See, Señor Rod, I think we will get him in short time. My cousin, Humberto, he say he know the old man who maybe own him and if nothing else I will just one day go and take him."

"You think he's as tough as they say?"

Roderick Osler had recently been told of this putative pit bulldog, a stray living in downtown Havana and a terror to any canine unlucky enough to attack him. The word on the street was that this dog never initiated a fight and if confronted would leave, never running, just trying to avoid a conflict. Osler knew that most stray dogs were not pit bulldogs and wouldn't have a fart's chance in a storm to best a pit bull in a fight on the street, so the Havana dog's reputation may be just street-talk.

Osler had been interested in this dog since Raul mentioned its growing reputation as a street fighter in his cousin's neighborhood in Havana, and how his cousin had taken the dog to a pit fight. Raul reiterated Humberto's vivid account of this interlude in the street dog's life.

"Raul, baby, I go to these old man who supposed to own these dirty old dog and I ask him to let me have the dog. He say 'No, go away', so I ask him to sell to me these dirty dog and he say 'No, go away!' – so I get Carlos and we trap these dirty old dog with food in a wire cage. We look in the cage and he just stand with his head down and his tail down, but his body, it shake like Aunt Delores' vibrator up his rear. Carlos says, 'Umberto, this poor dog a sissy. You gone lose your bony ass if you fight him.'

So I, Umberto, said to Carlos. "Load him up in my car since we went to all these trouble to get him."

"And Raul, you won't believe this som bitch when we get to the pit. Sanchez was there with his Two Shot dog … he sees me with these cage with these dirty old dog and he right away runs up and pokes a stick at these dog through the wire and these dog, he jump and squat and jiggle so the stick never stick him, hardly, but never once do these dirty dog raise a lip or growl. Sanchez, he laughs and pulls a wad out his pocket and says, 'I cover you dog against my Two Shot, now, pronto – any amount. This dog belong at home turning over your garbage can or playing with little bunny rabbits.' And Raul, Carlos, he whisper in my ear: 'Umberto, do not do this fight, especially do not do this with Sanchez' dog. Umberto, your dirty dog is a coward. Sanchez will let his dog kill this dog of yours – he will not break him off,'"

"So I said, Carlos, why do you give a shit for. Is not your dog or your money. I said I know something about this dirty alley dog you or Sanchez don't know about. Anyway, cousin, I tell Sanchez put his money where his mouth is, and Carlos and we put two loops on these bastard and he just stand and quiver. Everybody laugh and make way. We drag him to the pit and he just drag along, and shiver, and shake. In the pit Carlos afraid to touch him so I begin to wash him and I tell Carlos, this som bitch won't bite a man – you better believe me when I tell you this. Only, well, he bite the shit out of a dog!"

"So, you guessed it, Raul. Sanchez, he turned Two Shot loose just as I finished the rinse and the poor alley guy, he try to get loose from me but he don't never bite at me but Two Shot bite anything, I know, so I turn som bitch loose and damn if he don't try to climb out of the pit. Holy shit, Raul, Two Shot caught the alley guy by the back leg, high on the hip, and I was so close I could hear these dog's teeth working in poor guy's meat. Carlos, he cried out loud and Sanchez, he laughed, tinkly, like a foot tickled whore, but only one laugh these time 'cause dirty guy twist around like nothing I have ever seen and latch on to Two Shot's face and eye and crunch so hard I have never seen. I hear bones break and Sanchez, he turn white as a grouper belly and start screaming out loud, but Raul, it is all over and Two Shot is hanging limp as you granddaddy's weenie and Sanchez' not a whole lot better 'cause his dog just as dead as that granddaddy weenie!"

Raul chuckled as Umberto finished the story and recalled the climactic ending where the stray dog stood quivering as Sanchez dragged Two Shot's carcass from the pit, and how when the pit door opened, the wounded beast bolted, knocking Sanchez down like a spared bowling pin. Five days later the Havana stray was back on familiar streets with the old man tending his wounds, no worse for the wear.

"Raul, do you think he's really game? These fights at Lakeport aren't for pussies, you know." Osler's query brought Raul back to the present and he responded smartly.

"Yes, yes, he's a game, tough son of a bitch with the hardest bite we have ever seen, or heard of – Umberto and me. Don't worry, we'll do okay at Lakeport even if we have to go with old Ranger. By the way, Señor Rod, does that friend of yours – O'Steen? – have any pups for sale?"

"I don't know, compadre. I haven't seen Clax in weeks but I did call him last month to invite him to the Lakeport doings, but pups never came up. Let's get to Hoostra." Rod Osler started to the dock with Raul in lock step.

"Hey, Armando, get to the lab. Dr. Burgaard's staying the night and remember, campesino, be quiet and do what you are told." Arising languidly, the squat Brazilian ambled up the path as Osler boarded the Mako and began squeezing the gas bulb. Armando knew that Raul calling him a peasant was only poking fun because he had to wet nurse Dr. Burgaard … but … then?

Raul cast off as the 200 Mercury coughed and spit before settling into a spurious purr. Jumping aboard, Raul Pena wondered whether Roderick Osler or Raul Pena liked pit dog fighting more.

• • •

Chapter FOUR

Quentin Burgaard, III, studied the computer screen with the focus of a hunting tiger. He suspected that sending mild electric current through certain nerve cells in mammals could stimulate ductless glands to secrete hormones that initiate body functions such as sexual desire, aggression, fright, thirst and blood sugar variations - among others.

He knew that photoreceptors in the retina could convert light impulse into cyto-chemical reactants, thereby stimulating certain responses beyond the beneficiary's conscious control. The conversion of light to cell chemical created an electrical potential and Burgaard wasn't sure if the chemical or the electrical differential was the ultimate stimulus. The pheromone driven sexual reaction in moths was still an enigma to the bulky scientist. Did the female moth's attractant work through cyto-chemical stimulation or did the chemical set up an electrical potential that triggered the male moth's response?

Burgaard knew the response of creatures like the frog and chameleon to light and color variations in their environment: Their chromatophores reacted to the light stimulus and their skin color changed – but was it totally beyond conscious volition? And could this be initiated by computer signal mimicking the animals' own electrical activator?

What about the ubiquitous <u>Elasmobranch,</u> the shark, able to home in by virtue of neurosensors located in its skin that are capable of picking up the erratic movement of sea creatures without the classical stimulus of blood-in-the-water. This reaction had to be mediated by nerve impulse alone, or in concert with chemicals released by the nerve cells with no ductless gland involved. Burgaard was sure of this.

Many authorities involved in neuro-chemical and neuro-hormonal research agreed that the hypothalamus worked in concert with the pituitary gland in orchestrating these irrepressible, often violent, reactions - necessary for all species survival and reproduction.

Dr. Cube chuckled with the irony that he would be the one to flex the muscles of the computer and show those ivory tower nerds what the little electric box was all about!

The MYRMIDON menu splashed across the screen and REPTILE was briefly highlighted, to quickly morph to a sub-menu with the word, ANOLIS, highlighted. The intent man hit the enter key and the screen transmuted into a montage of medical terms highlighting a graphic model of the American Chameleon, its body organs in finite detail and a neurological network to be envied by the real thing. A flick of the enter key transformed the display into various sections with cutaway views, both transverse and longitudinal.

Pausing to refer to a scientific journal, Burgaard barely acknowledged the low growl reverberating throughout the room and without looking up, spoke sharply. "Goar, shut your stupid face. I hear him."

His master's words unheeded, the rumbling, one hundred eighty pound lump of muscle arose slowly and turned his soccer ball of a head to display a pair of eyes the devil would envy. Simultaneously, muted footfalls could be heard, increasing ever so slightly in intensity as Armando ambled up the hallway toward the computer room. The throaty rumble moved up a notch as the bandy legged Latino stopped at the door and waited.

"For Christ's sake, Goar, stop your bellyaching. That goddam Brazilian is scared to death of you as it is!" The heavy journal, thrown as QB-3 spewed his directive, hit the mastiff on the shoulder causing him to jump sideways and though still defiant, slink to the corner and lie down. "Okay, Armando, come in. I've got the asshole quieted."

Armando Montedinegre opened the door slowly and scanned the limited area. He hated the mastiff and sensed that Goar felt the same.

QB-3 had purchased Goar as a pup and the apricot brindled coat set off by a black mask that extended to his ears gave credence to his royal pedigree. When ten weeks old, Goar's ears were cropped and his flews trimmed. With his upper lips gone the pup had a perpetual grin easily interpreted as a snarl. Grown now, Goar was the incarnation of everyman's bête noire.

Now three, the mastiff was on the cusp of sexual maturity and his pugnacity was more evident every day, especially dog aggression. His nocent master went to great lengths to insure that the big dog would not develop social graces by weaning him at an early age and isolating him from inter-dog contact, depriving the pup of the canine interaction and discipline needed to moderate dog aggression and temper his bite: Goar had a hard bite. Goar hated dogs. Goar hated people. Goar hated!

Armando could not remember how many housecats he had thrown to the slavering dog, the results akin to dropping a live frog into a running food processor. He suspected the experiments Dr. Burgaard performed on the beast did little to improve his disposition; however, the transplanted Brazilian had never witnessed this, only hearing rumors.

One incident he knew first hand was when Goar killed Raul Pena's old pit-dog under highly questionable circumstances. The aged warrior spent his day lying in Raul's quarters, going into the small, fenced backyard through a doggie door to attend his excretory needs which were quite demanding since his age battered kidneys required him to drink more water resulting in more trips to the yard. Two months ago, Raul found his old pal dead in the yard with a snarling Goar worrying the carcass like a schoolyard bully and had to call Burgaard so he and Armando could retrieve the gory remains.

There were no breaks in the fence. Burgaard had to put on the head halter before he could control the adrenalized animal and his comment to Raul was thinly veiled insolence. "Well, compadre, at least he didn't die in bed!"

"Hey, Hombre. I want you to take the big boy for a walk. I don't have time ... here, I'll put the halter on him." Bending over the unsettled beast, QB-3 avoided the evasive head maneuvers and buckled the head halter, snapped the heavy nylon leash to the muzzle band and handed it to Armando. The head halter allowed the mastiff to be controlled and Burgaard was the only one that could put it on. Training him to accept this indignity, QB-3 had encouraged participation but Goar culled those stout hearts leaving only Raul and Rod Osler, other than Burgaard, able to apply the effective device. Once agitated, Goar-dog would allow only Quentin Burgaard, III, to apply the halter.

"Walk him for an hour then go to the yard and let him pull the sled for fifty or sixty meters. I put 500 pounds on it yesterday so you don't have to fool with it ... and be careful of his feet. If any of his booties come off you better goddam put'em back on because if he comes back with cut feet it's gonna be your ass." QB-3's warning came as he tied the layered chamois booties on the mastiff's feet and patted his overdeveloped hip. "Get going, Sport-Model, and don't eat the hired help!"

Burgaard returned to the computer, stopping at the twenty-gallon terrarium to turn on its light and remove the black cover. The American chameleon sat statue-like as the light illuminated the tank. The lizard's dark hues blended with the shadowed rocks adorning the terrarium floor but with sudden brightness the lizard's skin color began to lighten until it blended with the brighter environment. Pushing the tank closer to the computer the scientist highlighted: PHOTOCHEMICAL–PHOTOELECTRIC–RETINAL–CHROMATOPHORE on the graphic display, tapped the enter key and watched as the eyes on the computer model began to blink and spider-web-like nerve pathways leading from retina to brain to skin began to pulsate with light, and a barely perceptible hum exuded from the computer like perfume from warm skin.

The fevered man typed in: DARK GREEN FOLIAGE–SHADOWS–LOW FILTERED LIGHT and hit the enter key.

Fidgety, Quentin Burgaard, III, shuffled to the tank and with a sigh looked at the unconcerned lizard. A somber cloud glazed his eyes as the American chameleon, bathed in bright light, slowly darkened in color.

• • •

Rod Osler and Raul Pena had been unable to talk during the choppy ride to Hoostra Island so the solitude of the Myrmon Academy headmaster's office offered needed opportunity.

Myrmon Academy stood alone on the 125 acres island, and the manicured grounds bespoke opulence usually associated with the grand manors of European landed gentry.

The buildings, plain and white, were neat and trim. The main edifice housing Osler's office was the largest and the first structure encountered upon entering the main gate from the dock; in fact, the gate partitioned the shoreward fifty feet of the heavy planked dock. Positioned around an adjacent four acres were five dormitories, each housing ten boys with a roomy central house providing plush living space for Burgaard, comfortable quarters for Osler, Raul Pena, plus three academy assistants. Groomed playfields dotted the area with a central pool nestled among three tennis courts.

In the basement of the main building was a trapdoor disguising a blowhole that connected via its natural tunnel to the main docking area. At low tide the tunnel would be half full of seawater and a swimmer could exit the basement without SCUBA gear or underwater swimming but at high tide the tunnel was filled with the implacable seawater.

Burgaard's spacious den housed a state of the art computer, a master bedroom plush and mirrored where more than one wealthy matron had been lustfully entertained by this genius of excess while scoping out the suitability of Myrmon Academy for an irksome scion.

"So, compadre, we will get the Havana dog in time for the Lakeport fights ... you think?" Osler's query was interrupted by a blinking green light on his desk phone prompting a rapid response. "Yes ... yes ... okay, we'll be right there." The flinty headmaster cradled the phone and flashed a morbid grin. "Let's go, compadre. Trouble on the big field."

Raul turned the blue and gold golf cart into the large soccer field within minutes of Bud's call and aimed at the small group of boys gathered at one end of the field. Jumping off, Osler sprinted to the knotted group, pushing aside those that didn't give way as he strove to gain the center.

"Okay, Bud, what's the story?" His pointed request targeted the athletic Bud York, a Myrmon assistant and conditioning instructor who was straining to hold an agitated, thirteen years old Hispanic boy with one hand and his cell phone in the other.

"This one is the initiator. Ronnie, there, is the submissive defensive ..." Bud's stacatto response was punctuated by exertive grunts as he struggled to hold the contentious Cruzo Dominguez.

"Okay, okay. Bud, let Cruzo go – you, Ronnie, come here!" The headmaster grabbed Ronnie by the arm and jerked him toward the glowering Cruzo. "Okay Ronnie, tell me what happened." Osler had no sooner spit out the request than the crimson-faced Cruzo blurted. "That stupid motherfuck ..." Like lightning from a shattered bottle, Osler backhanded Cruzo with such force he went to his knees, disbelief spreading across his face like a bloodstain.

"Your name Ronnie, smart-ass?" Osler's words were measured as he locked eyes with the shocked thirteen year old, turned and in the same breath repeated his request to the ashen faced Ronnie." I ... I ... don't know ... I mean, I guess ... nothing ..." Tears leaked from the boy's squinty eyes as he tried to act the man, but afraid of the aggressive Cruzo his resolve evaporated in the glare of the acerbic headmaster.

"Don't know, huh … don't fucking know, is it! Well, dumb ass, I'll see you in my office in one hour!" Neck veins bulging, Osler motioned to the kneeling Cruzo. "Okay, Mr. Three-fingers – your turn. What started this crap?"

The flushed face of Cruzo Dominguez had undergone a sea-change following Osler's slap and his coal black eyes glowed with the intensity of flowing lava, neutralizing the reference to his mutilated hand.

"Well, let's hear your story." The brittle command hit the boy's countenance and shattered into meaningless word fragments. Coolness settled over Cruzo as he faced the riveting gaze of Osler who swore he detected a grin on the rebellious face; the boy's muteness being self-control – not fear. A shiver scurried through the headmaster's lean body as he turned to the coach. "Bud, I want these two yahoos in my office in one hour. Go on with your game, just let these two sit out … see you later." Turning, Rod Osler motioned to Raul and headed for the golf cart, purposely avoiding eye contact with the uneasy young men.

"Well, compadre, what do you think?" The headmaster's words greeted Raul as he eased behind the steering wheel. "That Cruzo kid seems ready, don't you think? You see the way he looked at me when I ruffled his feathers? I'm going to recommend to Burgaard that he be transferred to Myrmex Terminus, if a slot is open – he's ready to explode and we sure don't want him whacking Ronnie or one of the paying kids. It's dicey enough having to get rid of a deficient conscript, so we sure don't want to have that problem with a legitimate student. That hammerhead's fat enough as it is!"

Raul nodded, his crooked smile more an indicator of highly focused introspection than of agreement with his boss. Cold hearted as he was, the Cuban dandy had little stomach for Myrmex Terminus.

• • •

Seen at a distance, the shadowy dog trotting absentmindedly through the garbage festooned alley appeared to be just another unfortunate Havana stray. His amber colored, bird-of-prey eyes were set wide in the muscular, somewhat sloping head displaying as much depth through the head muscle mass as width through the overdeveloped muscles of his angular jaw. The piercing eyes in his relaxed head seemed not in focus, yet the determined metronomic rhythm of his powerful, though somewhat stilted gait seemed to belie this insouciance, as did his uncanny avoidance of the cans and debris marking his path like an obstacle course. The frequent flicking of his head did not add to, or subtract from, his shrouded resolve as he traversed the short alley. Purposefully went this dog.

The sun was lowering to the western horizon and the shadows were lengthening as the fibrous animal turned from the alley onto a wide street still within the sanctuary of the shadows. Filtering sunlight bounced from his fine hair coat as he crossed an open area highlighting his lean, compact body with muscle definition rarely seen in dogs. The determined pace showcased this muscularity, and given a quick eye one could have counted the synchronized muscles as their harmonious contractions propelled his eighty five pound body. Silently he went.

Two blocks from the alley a large, thickly wooded field interrupted the buildings and storefronts and the unwavering dog turned off the street and crossed a sun-drenched clearing as he aimed at a worn path at the far edge of the open space. Exposed to the full lighting effects of the setting sun, the phantom dog took on color and his thin, greyhound like skin fairly rippled as the sun-rays played off his unusual brindle coat. The once rich, black background now sun-bleached was totally compromised by the bleak, mahogany colored vertical stripes interspersed with tufts of gray hair and slathered on like apple butter on burnt toast. The hand-sized white splash on his chest contrasted starkly with this plain décor and a casual observer would conclude that this grizzled beast was in dire need of a bath. He did look dirty.

Gaining the wooded path, the sedulous animal twisted his head to protect his torn ear from the foliage and continued his trek to the humble dwelling of the old man called Pedro – Dom Pedro - the only human the dog was tolerant of. The Dirty Dog, as he was called, did not fear men. He did not know fear. He simply did not like people. He retained faint memories of the boys who trapped him two years ago and tried to geld him, he not even struggling until the two larger boys forced him onto his back while a third, smaller boy ran a single edged razor blade across his scrotum causing his testicles to pop out like jacks-in-the-box. The electric latency between searing pain and adrenalin surge in the mutilated pup's body produced a reaction so quick and potent that the boys holding him felt fused to a hirsute bubble filled with rattlesnakes and they could not let go ... it burst!

Eyes blank and unseeing, Dirty Dog's torpid muscles reacted as if stung by high voltage as he kicked loose, turned in the air and caught one of his tormentors by the hand as stagnant human reflexes delayed the boys' response and caused the razor wielder to slice the other's arm to the bone in his frenzied effort to back away. Pit bulldog karma and bestial strength turned the passive pup into a demonic nightmare and the slender boy-hand cracked like so many chicken bones under the ever increasing bite pressure and suspended weight of the dirty looking dog. The dog-caught kid's screams didn't stop until the tenacious beast pulled the ring and little fingers off the mangled left hand and the boy fainted.

Approaching the beat down, rusted wire fence marking the old man's yard, Dirty Dog stopped and checked the air currents for unfamiliar spoor before stepping through a gaping hole and approaching the back steps. Sensing the old fellow to be home – alone – the cautious dog coursed lightly up the two back steps to the back door and scratched the weather worn bare wood door, retreated to the edge of the tiny porch and lay down.

"Ah, there you are, Señor Sucio Perro. What did you do this fine day? Did you teach any lessons to the dogs and cats that want your basura in the big alley, no? Well, is the tomcat that tore your ear still courting his queens? If he is it is due totally to your wonderful tolerancia, my combustible friend."

With each sentence the quiet dog subtly moved his panther like tail as his flinty eyes relaxed, causing a puppy-like expression to spread across his chiseled face. Dom Pedro sincerely loved this dog and wanted to pet him, being naturally drawn to this time honored act of affection between man and dog but he also knew that the dirty looking dog, Señor Sucio Perro, was not similarly disposed, and out of admiration for this magnificent beast he gladly substituted verbal for physical contact, for with the exception of a few unfortunate animals no one knew or appreciated more the awesome power of this dirty looking dog.

The old Cuban chuckled and absentmindedly shook his head as he thought of the dog's unfathomable tolerance for dogs and cats – and people. Totally out of character, but el Sucio Perro was not dog or cat aggressive and Dom Pedro had witnessed many occasions when the dog refused to bite a person. Even when provoked. But woe unto the animal or person that actually hurt the big fellow; his rebuke could be permanent!

Dom Pedro did not know how the botched castration occurred, having found the gaunt young dog with exposed and infected testicles. The fevered dog had offered no resistance, in fact seemed passive when Dom Pedro lifted him from under the brush pile and carried him the few hundred yards to his shack. The sympathetic old Cuban had never seen a dog so mutilated but had seen and attended several men similarly butchered while a medic with the Fidelistas, when Castro came out of the Cuban hills in the revolution over thirty years ago. He also had a small cache of medical supplies covertly squirreled away for the proverbial rainy day; today sure looked like rain!

Mixing several morphine tablets in warm milk, Dom Pedro gently flowed the potent brew down the reluctant pup's throat, unsure of its safety but fully aware of what he must do if the game pup was to live. Within thirty minutes the pup's hollow eyed head drooped and his reaction to noxious stimuli were in slow motion. Quickly and efficiently the old man took one of Havana's finest handmade cigars, tied a short string to one end, moistened it thoroughly with saliva and inserted it fully into the sedated pup's rectum. The potent nicotine went to work and ten minutes later he cut away the infected testicles and cauterized the remaining distempered flesh with a kitchen knife heated on his tiny propane stove to a glowing, cherry red. Within minutes the bleeding abated and Dom Pedro retrieved his cigar from the four-legged humidor.

The old Cuban's thoughts bounced back to real time as he fussed over the impressive pit bulldog – but one fleeting thought coursed his old, life weary memory: Did he ever smoke that cigar?

• • •

Chapter FIVE

"So, we have a job. Have to go to work, huh? Does sound interesting, especially since I end up at this particular farm about the time its owner gets iced and everyone seems genuinely surprised – no ... body knows no ... thing! Poor old Clax was really shaken when the news broke and it seems if there was anything going on, why ... Clax O'Steen would know about it or at least have suspicions." Samson's voice was tinged with cynicism, the humor not lost on Skeets Kirby as he listened to his partner after filling him in on his conversation with the FBI man.

Bone weary after driving all day, Skeets opted to detail Sam before turning in, especially after kicking back with a double shot of his pal's favorite single malt Scotch; his reply mirrored somnolence. "You think Clax was surprised? Who got the call? Old man Larry's wife or Clax?"

"I don't know, Skeets. Claxton showed up at the apartment late that morning and said "Big Jaxe is dead" – he was one shook up puppy. I didn't sense anything wrong and you know how I can sense things. Clax was truly upset." Sam took a sip from the fragile stemmed glass holding Macallan with a drop of spring water – at room temperature. Savoring the age-enhanced flavor of the brooding liquid, Samson's eyes had a faraway look as he abridged his partner's reply.... "Guess I'm ready to go to work. Where do we start, Skeeterman?"

Heading for the couch, the tired man's reply trailed off with a yawn. "Where? Here. When? Tomorrow. Nighty-night."

"Okay, candy-ass, JY and I are going for a little stroll in the cool night air – see ya'." At the mention of his name, the lithe pit bull got up and fell in beside Sam.

Halfway down, JY aired a low, warning rumble and stared into the shadow splotched alleyway separating the stallion stalls. Samson was frozen in place as he shaded his eyes trying to pierce the dimness. The scent was human, definitely male, pre-pubescent and unfamiliar to Sam Duff. Sam knew every groom and attendant by sight and smell and knew the stallion barn was off limits to visitors after dark, so this person did not belong here.

Curiosity blended with suspicion as Sam moved to see what was going down as the interloper moved, covertly, staying in shadow and trying not to spook the stallions as the sporadic snort or kicked wall marked his passage. Sam cautioned JY to stay, slipped down the stairs into the inky shadows and easily scent trailed the intruder through the darkened barn, stopping only when his keen sense told him the quarry had stopped – by HighandMighty's stall. Barely breathing, Sam strained to hear through the background noise kicked up by the antsy grand stallion. Exhaling quietly, he heard a soft whoosh like a spurt of escaping air followed by horse sounds as HighandMighty tried to tear down his stall. The acrid redolence of a heated petroleum product tugged at Sam's nostrils as he moved to intercept the intruder.

The slight figure moving through the alleyway seemed more surprised than scared by the man materializing like a phantom from the darkness, challenging him to stop. The curly haired intruder's thin, blue veined arms terminated in bony fingers that seemed more suited to insect appendages than limbs of a twelve year old boy. Calmly, offering no resistance the boy spoke. "Hi mister, I'm Benito."

• • •

The north end of Andros Island, the largest jewel in the necklace of sub-tropical islands that comprise the Bahamas, lies just one hundred twenty miles east, southeast of Miami and boat travel there forces a crossing of the Tongue of the Ocean, a trough of the mighty Atlantic Ocean flowing to depths of six thousand feet and creating a panoramic ocean floor to rival any moonscape or Red Planet topography. Deep-sea creatures freely roam this inky deep and the unbelievable walls subjected to eons of abrasive seawater have been sculpted into a diver's paradise: Neptune's backyard!

The striking, white sand beach blending with the emerald colored water marking the seaside Nichols Town at the northern tip of Andros bore witness to peace and tropical paradise, while the poverty and innate crassness of the human condition bespoke of more than a serpent infesting this little corner of tropical perfection.

Everywhere was sand, scraggly weeds, environmentally challenged trees, and nestled in a small grove of mango trees amid this hardscrabble flora was a group of men, some excited, some somber but all narcotized by a small chicken-wire enclosed circle. In this sandy round of death two feathered gladiators were watching each other with the same high-tension focus of their audience. Wings askew and at the ready, neck feathers fluffed like plumage umbrellas, the fighting cocks circled warily, four unblinking eyes seeking weakness or opportunity. Vantages would be few and fleeting.

"Come on, mon. Don't let that little sparrow clip your pretty wings." Each word precisely spoken by the small black man as his close-set dark eyes darted about in their sockets like pinballs. Samuel was his name, his only name, and one of the feathered warriors belonged to him. Samuel was a Haitian, born and educated in Port Au Prince and had worked many years at the Albert Schweitzer hospital, leaving there to follow his passion for more sanguine endeavors concerning animals and chance.

Samuel spoke perfect English, fluent French and was said by his close associates to speak animal. He was staying at Nichols Town with a lady friend waiting for the thoroughbred racing season to open in Florida. It was at Tampa Bay Downs that Samuel met Clax O'Steen and started exercising O'Steen two year olds, and a short time later that mutual interest in feisty roosters and macho dogs fermented to friendship.

Samuel had recently refused Clax's offer to work full time at VentureQuest but continued to work for him at the track.

"Watch out for your chicken, Guinea, he's afixin' to qualify for a Colonel Sanders extra crispy special." Raul Pena's eyes were fixated on the battling birds and his subtle warning to Samuel was so soft that Samuel wasn't sure what his friend and erstwhile competitor had said.

"What did you say, mon?" At Samuel's query his opponent's cockbird flared its wings and spurred up the other bird's body, the razor gaffs tattooing Samuel's little rooster like a feathered sewing machine making buttonholes. Dust coated dots of blood rolled off the beleaguered cock's feathers like crimson BBs and his gory beak hung open like a trail weary hound-dog jaw - but in the blink of an eye, Samuel's veteran fighter sprang back and up, spurring with the speed and synchrony of a vaudeville tap-dancer and in a blur of motion a two inch steel gaff penetrated the opponent cock's left eye, killing it instantly.

"Son of a bitch! ….Son of a bitch!" Samuel had no trouble hearing Raul's laments.

• • •

"Skeets, I'm telling you the kid acted like an iceman. This is no ordinary run of the mill young man. And he did something to that stallion Clax likes so much, HighandMighty." Sam was talking to Skeets over breakfast, having decided not to awaken his tired partner after the barn episode. "Man, I could literally smell this kid's self-confidence – arrogance – and I know he fired some sort of weapon just before that stud went bananas.

I'm not sure what it was, but he didn't have it on his person when I caught him."

"Did you search him?" Skeets quiet demeanor reflected his rested condition even though Sam's night encounter did pique his interest. "You think he shot the horse? Air gun, maybe?"

"No, I got the security guard and he called HighandMighty's groom and we looked him over good. Nothing, nada ... yet I know that kid fired something. Maybe you're right about an air gun, but the security man went over him with a fine-toothed comb and came up zero. I even checked him again and couldn't smell anything suspicious and this curly haired little guy kept saying the right things and was polite, even cooperative. Seems he really was a guest of Big Jaxe's grandson and when Clax finally got there he took up for the kid and that was that."

"Okay, Samson, let's do a thorough background check on that young fellow and I'm going to get those FBI reports and then I'm going to drive down to Tampa – maybe today – and talk to the detective that started this FBI thing." Skeets threw down the last of his lukewarm coffee, stood up and stretched. "Why don't you get serious with Clax and this grandson of old man Larry. Start sniffing around for real. I think, old horse, that there's more going on than meets the eye." Skeets bent down and patted JY on the shoulder. I'll be back late, or maybe I'll stay over in Tampa - got a hot little number in Brandon I need to check out. Anyway, looks like we're in business."

• • •

The sunsets on Hoostra Island were nothing short of magnificent and Roderick Osler made a point of absorbing this glorious end of day panoramic panoply of expressive clouds, explosive color, and expansive sea whenever possible. This evening as he walked the path toward the main house, he paused and turned to the west to enjoy one more sunset. Dr. Burgaard could wait. Even though Quentin Burgaard, III, had expressed a desire for Osler to hurry, he knew the man did this from habit; the same praxis that commanded the scientist to work at his preternatural pace.

Osler didn't understand Burgaard but appreciated the man's genius, somewhat misguided but genius nonetheless. And Rod Osler's moral pathway wasn't exactly the yellow brick road, allowing a clear conscience in spite of the untenable bent of Burgaard's grisly ambition.

Rod gulped a deep draught of sunset cooled sea air as the first fluorescent red colors lit the western skyline, bouncing back from the underside of fluffy, cotton ball clouds to create a rich, royal purple hue like vanilla ice cream scoops setting in a bowl of blueberries. The panting dog snorts and audible footfalls interrupted his reverie and Quentin Burgaard, III, and Goar were almost to him before his placid brain registered their presence.

"Hey, Rod, thought I'd catch you here. Goar wanted to see the sunset so I figured we'd just mosey on this way and join up with you." The rotund, curly bearded face of QB-3 reflected pure joy as he surveyed the deepening, scarlet tinged western sky. "Gorgeous, isn't it!"

"Yea, Quentin. Almost makes a person believe in God." Osler's cryptic cynicism caught the scientist off guard but his nimble mind flipped and landed right side up – as always.

"God? You want God, Rod? I'll tell you about God. You are God – I am God. God is mankind, more accurately, mankind the collective." The scientist's calm countenance was flushed with this putative challenge to his concept and acumen of THE GOD. Saliva flecked his lips and curly moustache as his rising voice competed with the dying sunset.

"What has the biblical God done that man hasn't done? How about that, Roderick, old buddy. Part the Red sea? Shit, we can part seas, rivers, go over them, under them, you name it. Rise to the heavens? Fuck, we put men on the moon and soon we'll have empty beer cans on the planets. Raise the dead? Huh, Rod, we can make the Lazarus act look a high school magic show." QB-3 was shouting as he focused his massive intellect on the Holy Ghost and the God of Abraham. "What about those poor souls lined up at the Treblinka ovens, taking their clothes off so they can get a bath? You don't think they thought those gun toting guards and jack-booted SS officers weren't God? I bet those hollowed eyed bastards hauling the bloated carcasses of their friends and loved ones from those gas chambers knew the real God: Man. Mankind the collective! What about the CEO in his fifties who just sailed through four-way heart bypass surgery? Who's his God? Not some obscure Jewish carpenter begat from a virgin mother. It's the surgeon and his highly skilled team." Burgaard added hand gestures to his heated rhetoric and Osler could see the glow from his dilated pupils; 'more,' he thought, 'from inner zeal than reflected sunlight.' "Or ask the poor innocent slob who was found guilty of murder by a jury of his peers and ended up strapped in old Sparky at Starke ... ask him who God is, just before they light him up with six thousand volts of thunder juice - also made by man!"

Roderick Osler knew the focus and intensity his putative partner brought to the party and this one was definitely getting out of hand.

"Quentin, fuck off ... forget it. I don't give a toy dog turd about what you think about God or anything religious." Osler didn't know if he believed in THE GOD or not, only that he was uncomfortable with Biblical discussions, preferring to avoid his own theological beliefs. He was also uncomfortable with the lip-curling snarl on display by the drooling mastiff in reaction to his master's angry rising voice. Osler knew when Goar heated up he would attack anyone or anything, including QB-3.

"Anyway, Quentin, you're making that beast of yours rattle and I don't think he gives a double dip shit about God or mankind or whatever." Osler was relieved that Goar was sporting the head halter instead of the heavy choke chain that proved useless when the beefy dog wasn't in a compliant mood.

"Hell, Rod, you know you don't have to worry about old Goar dog. He likes you." The strident scientist lowered his voice to dulcet tones and the patronizing, comical reply struck Osler as funny ... really funny. He reacted with tension easing genuine laughter, defusing the latent hostility that had slipped into the discussion and as Osler's laughter competed with Burgaard's voice, the fuzzy faced genius began to laugh – the laugh of a basso from a dark opera. Goar whimpered.

Darkness settled on Hoostra Island like a setting hen as the trio made their way to the main house, both men maintaining a respected degree of silence after their conversation ending guffaws - but not for long. Quentin spoke first. "Rod, how are you coming with the new recruits? Any problems ... like with that last bunch?"

Osler paused to swat at a covey of mosquitoes circling his head like a mordacious halo. "No, and we've got one really good prospect for Myrmex Terminus. You should be getting him the next day or so." Even though the men had stepped up the pace, Osler cut the small talk. "Come on, Quentin, let's get the hell out of these goddam bloodsucking, needle-nosed buzzards that pass for mosquitoes." As they trotted toward the house, Roderick Osler caught himself feeling a twinge of pity for the insect beleaguered dog. He quickly repressed it.

● ● ●

At a distance the casual but smartly dressed middle-aged man appeared quite normal: Thick, faded looking brown hair combed straight back with bushy, somewhat darker, eyebrows. His was just short of prissy with board-flat pelvis carried slightly forward in apparent deference to humongous masculine endowment or perianal pruritis ... or both.

Closer inspection revealed a thin, gangly, dog bone of a man with ropy veins coursing every inch of visible skin, but not emaciated: Muscular thin, tan, as if fat didn't exist in his world.

The subtle bulge just below his zipper always appeared on the left side and at times seemed disproportionately large, depending on how tight his pants were. The seemingly out of place full lips completed the profile of the Director of Student Activities at Myrmon Academy. His credentials displayed at the Academy office were impeccable, that is, in regard to their physical appearance, not their credibility for they were forged, but nonetheless impressive. Except, of course, to Quentin Burgaard, III.

As the man approached the well dressed couple nervously pacing small circles in the lush, close cut, blue green Bermuda grass, his usual defensive attitude gave way to a cheery, convivial façade as he greeted Ronnie's parents. He knew why they were here and he knew how to handle the problem – non-problem, really – business as usual.

'Hi, Ronnie's dad … and mom! I'm Harrie Smithcors. We met when Ronnie settled in for the summer and I want to tell you what a fine young man master Ronnie is …"

"Well, uuh, Mrs. Van Cleef and I are very upset …" The nattily attired graying tycoon, master of the polished oak boardroom was no match for the glib Myrmon headmaster.

"Now, Sir … and Madam, Ronnie is fine and I assure you the source of his displeasure has been promptly and properly chastised and disciplined; in fact, the obstreperous lad has been expelled. It was totally his fault. Master Ron was an innocent bystander and Myrmon Academy simply will not brook such behavior." As he talked, Harrie led the way up the path to the public recreation room where the doctored photos of Ronnie Van Cleef at play occupied a very prominent position. Harrie Smithcors was in somewhat of a hurry as the patronized pair followed a few steps behind – anxious to get to his afternoon class. He considered the Myrmex Terminus group to be his greatest accomplishment as well as his signal challenge. And he hated being tardy or missing a session.

With a "Listen, mom and dad, your priceless young lad is on the verge of becoming a man and we at Myrmon Academy - and I speak for every faculty and staff member – want you to know that we hold this credo as a sacred pledge. Ron is in good hands." Harrie turned to the door as he saw the 'okay, I'm satisfied' grins creep up the faces of the placated pair allowing him license to leave. "Here's my personal card. Call me anytime you wish, day or night." With that, Harrie Smithcors, Director of Student Activities, was out the door.

• • •

"Sit down, Rod and listen just a goddam minute." The impatient scientist had banished Goar to a small but well ventilated glass walled cubicle at one end of the room. The confinement was equipped with water source and food service, which for the sullen bull mastiff consisted entirely of muscle meat sprinkled throughout with offal and visceral organs; decidedly more gourmand that gourmet. The huge, recalcitrant dog was only fed three times a week resulting in a constant, edgy hunger that made him even more volatile.

"Notice anything about Goar?" Burgaard's sweat from the sunset episode had dried and though he absentmindedly scratched a few itchy mosquito bites his demeanor seemed calm as a cut cat given his earlier tirade about God, and his trained fingers were blurs as he played the computer keyboard ... while talking. The peculiar humming from the computer offered only token competition to his voice.

"No ...Yes! The son of a bitch has food and hasn't chowed down like the garbage disposal he is. What's the matter, Quentin, your only son sick?" Osler's cutting reply was merely touché for him in the constant verbal battle of one-upmanship avidly played by the two hard-core egos. The barely amused scientist laughed. Barely.

"Okay chief, come here and watch this ... on the screen."

Stepping behind the desk, Osler greeted the impressive screen display of a canine body in such detail as to defy description. At the touch of a key the image darted around the screen, changing in dimension and view faster than he could comprehend.

"I've stopped the big guy from eating by overriding his olfactory and gastric secretion stimuli centers of his brainstem. I also lowered his pituitary output of thyroid stimulating hormone slowing his metabolism, so even though he's hungry his body will not respond to the urge."

Burgaard's eyes danced with excitement at the enormity and success of the demonstration. "Now watch this, Myrmon Academy headmaster and tell how this grabs you ... hell, I'll tell you what

I'm going to make that ornery bastard do – I'm going to make him drool. Buckets of it!" That said the gleeful QB 3 attacked the keyboard like a truant schoolboy in a video game arcade.

Roderick Osler watched with opened mouth amazement as the mastiff stood and began turning in the cubicle as if the floor was hot. On the second turn the fixated man witnessed great, ropy strings of saliva flowing from the ragged flews of the consternated animal. "Goddam, Quentin, how in the fuck did … do you do that?" The headmaster's face went slack as his benumbed brain tried to comprehend the magnitude of what he was seeing. Still the good Dr. Cube pressed on.

"Now watch, Rod. You'll appreciate this. I'm going to make him act like Raul when he has a hangover." Nimble fingers danced lightly over the keyboard as highlighted anatomical and medical terms flashed on and off like Christmas tree lights as the screen display depicted the canine olfactory–adrenal–hepatic-renal organs in various sections. The screen icon touched the 'renal' display and QB III depressed the enter key.

Goar jumped as if stuck by a hot poker, simultaneously emitting a subdued, pathetic whimper that quickly metamorphosed into a low warning growl, complete with lip curl. The stimulated dog now seemed unsteady on his feet and started walking in small circles, licking his nose and lips compulsively. Staggering to the self-filling water reservoir, the confused beast began to lap the water as if he had just crossed the Sahara desert.

"Hey, Rod. Open the door and see if Mr. Goar will come to you – or after you!" Burgaard's laugh caused the hair on Osler's neck to stand. He knew he had no chance to distract the ravenous dog and glared at QB-3 as he played the compliant keyboard.

By now the bull mastiff appeared bloated from the massive water intake and even the scientist was showing concern as he released the torpid dog from its electronic Circe. The befuddled Goar staggered to a corner and vomited several gallons of water before collapsing.

Rod Osler had never seen any thing like this. He was mesmerized! Totally. Goar's bloodshot, little pig eyes stared, unblinking, at his tormentors.

"What about those little green apples, Roderick, old boy. Ever see anything like that?" QB-3 turned off the computer as he spoke and walked to the glass wall drawing Osler with him. Osler didn't reply. His gaze was still fixed on the mastiff's abused body as the steamy dog breath slowly fogged the glass giving the dog an indistinct, ethereal appearance. "Now I'll have to restrict the old boy's water for a week. You up to that?"

Still entranced, the Myrmon headmaster made no effort to acknowledge the request and his very subtle side-to-side headshake seemed more a dismissal of his awe than a reply to Burgaard. Rod Osler wouldn't touch the flushed, overwrought beast with a ten foot pole, much less monitor his water meter!

• • •

Chapter SIX

Cruzo Dominguiz sat passively in the small classroom as the instructor pointed to the various topics flashing across the king-sized video screen. This was his fifth day in Myrmex Terminus and interest in his five classmates was minimal; camaraderie was not a priority. No boy sat next to another by design, but paying attention was stringently mandated.

Mendacity was not tolerated concerning classroom work or interaction with the Myrmex staff, but on a personal level deception was the order of the day and was fundamentally supported by the handpicked Myrmex Terminus staff in their frequent one on one encounters with their psycho-warped students.

No matter how strict the Myrmex Terminus program, the disposable Havana street urchin knew he had it made. He had clean clothes and food and shelter, commodities he used to fight and even kill for in the cluttered streets and back alleys of Cuba's largest city. Cruzo Dominguiz really did have it made.

Unlike the other myrmidons in training young Cruzo knew his parents. His mother was an underage street prostitute fancied by a young Cuban army officer. He took her to wife and when Cruzo was born was sent to Africa on military assignment, leaving his 14 years old wife and baby to play house in the slums of Havana. Returning on leave when he could, he found his child and young wife had turned into strangers. The baby Cruzo was left unattended by his child-like mother and in the three years before the young officer returned home, the boy Cruzo was running the streets like a two legged alley cat, intimidating and controlling the less aggressive urchins until his parents could no longer deal with his insolence and burgeoning male ego.

Stunted by lifestyle, warped by lack of moral guidance and parental discipline, the freewheeling Cruzo Dominguez became the King of the street urchins.

At six, he quit going home and was not missed.

● ● ●

Quentin Burgaard, III, went to extremes to recruit his Myrmon staff and in the process of starting Myrmex Terminus scaled new heights in the selection process to obtain qualified personnel with enough skeletons in their closets to allow him absolute control. Plus, the pay was good.

The idea to hire behaviorists instead of psychologists came to him as he was researching animal physiology with behavior relating to neuro-hormonal and neuro-chemical control mechanisms. He realized early that psychologists differed radically in their views over the nature-nurture concept of mental growth and self discipline amid the social confusion that is western civilization, while behaviorists were more tuned to genetic influences and basic innate traits in explaining and relating to proximate or learned behavior. It was easy for QB-3 to handpick a few behaviorists with serious enough police records to disqualify them from legitimate employment in their chosen field, or any field for that matter.

All he had to do was describe his planned operation, their potential involvement and watch them swoon from the incense emanating from the bundles of green shoved under their noses. Done deal!

Such was the hiring of Donna Ileana Villareal, the only distaff instructor at Myrmon Academy. American schooled and trained in the behavioral sciences with a masters degree in juvenile social development, the hot blooded Brazilian, Donna Eye, as QB-3 called her had stood trial in Sao Paulo for murdering and mutilating her younger sister by gouging out her eyes after surprising young Maria in bed with the current favorite of Donna Eye's erstwhile lovers. Of course she also did in the errant stud and redid his circumcision, starting at the navel – after gouging out his eyes ... or before. Who knows?

Arrested and put on trial, the fiery, flamboyant behaviorist played the part of a cuckolded machismo and would expect acquittal in any Brazilian court on similar charges. With her attorney using the murder of her sister plus the mutilations as proof of her severe and untenable emotional distress, all caused by the hapless Romeo's careless flaunting of his ill advised, if not illicit, sexual congress with the defendant's own sister plus the shrill textured support from every woman's group in the world, Donna Eye was acquitted.

She met Quentin Burgaard, III, at a party in Havana when he was negotiating with the Castro faction for the political and financial blessings needed to start Myrmon Academy; they were eminently successful.

Donna Ileana Villareal was intelligent and articulate, fluent in English, Portuguese, Spanish and horny man-speak. QB- 3 hired her on the spot.

Donna Eye hated Harrie Smithcors. Donna's official position at Myrmon Academy was Director of Social Development and Recreational Supervisor; her real job was taking the empathy deficient boys that filtered into Myrmex Terminus and teaching them the difference, as well as the benefit, of willful obedience over respect as methods of social and financial advancement.

Donna Ileana, along with her new mentor, Quentin Burgaard, III, whom she affectionately called Dr. Cube, wanted the Myrmidon to respect nothing or no one in the pursuit of their goals; just be charmingly obedient in their quest for success. Successful outcomes justified any means. Dr. Cube called the Myrmon graduates Myrmidon in deference to the ancient Greek term for 'henchman.' And they were.

And Donna was an efficient, dedicated teacher being borderline schizoid herself and had conquered her anhedonic tendencies by learning to gain pleasure by mimicking pleasure. She quickly learned the response of normal, empathetic people to pleasant situations and stimuli and acted accordingly. Even sex.

The voluptuous Brazilian learned early the putative pleasures of heterosexual couplings and could put an eager and aggressive hot-blood through his paces with all the right moves, moans and groans suggesting the Queen of orgasms without really feeling anything. This limbic brain defect allowed her to play the black widow spider to her partners in copulation on more than one occasion without remorse, regret, or hesitation.

Though socially deficient, Donna Eye did have a hint of genuine emotional affection for Dr. Cube, recognizing in him a likeness – a totally cerebral, dominant though warped, sociopath; a genius. A real turn on.

Her sexual appetite was instantly whetted and almost as quickly consummated as QB-3 never turned from sex, especially when offered by such a tempestuous beauty. QB-3 was to sex what a bowling ball was to a tenpin. The torrid relationship Donna Eye had with her boss was the closest she ever came to real love – her one brush with life.

Donna Eye hated Harrie Smithcors.

• • •

Sam had been gone no more than three hours when he arrived at the stallion barn and expectantly bounded up the stairs to take JY out to exercise. He was always amused at the stoic beast's repressed joy at his arrival, and on occasion the muscular dog would bound, stiff legged, around the room like a spastic, albeit frisky, colt.

Skeets was due back later and Sam wanted to be briefed on whatever information the Skeeterman had gleaned from his Tampa visit and he and JY were yet to exercise. He was upbeat and in a hurry when strange man-scent on the stairway stifled his bounce and softened his footfall as his suspicion light came on. Silently opening the door, a chary Samson locked eyes with the JunkYard Dog, knew then the room held no surprises and silently entered, quickly closing the door. Clax O'Steen's fresh scent intermingled with that of the stranger as Sam cautiously scanned the room for signs of mischief, even as he acknowledged JY's hip wagging greeting.

"Had company, huh? "Bout an hour ago, I'd say." At the sound of Sam's voice, the languid pit bull got up, stretched and walked lazily toward Sam. "Wonder who Clax's friend is? I've not run into him before – for sure. And why did he bring him here.... Oh well, big guy, let's get going." Sam's mind was working buttonholes as he jogged through the stallion barn to access the miles of cypress mulched pathways that coursed, unobstructed, throughout the sparkling, emerald green VentureQuest property like cracks in a green mirror, hardly noticing the stiff legged, jaunty gait of his canine partner as the laconic dog easily kept pace.

Turning the corner at the back of the barn, Sam thought he heard voices against the breeze and coming from the small, antiseptic breeding room. With the wind currents against him he couldn't be sure but he surmised that Clax and his strange visitor were in there talking. Still, he wondered why O'Steen and the mystery man had visited his small apartment. Oh well …

"You were right about that dog, Clax. He sure is a specimen, even with the one eye." Roderick Osler kicked back on one of two shiny, all metal folding chairs in the confined tile floored cubicle, casually surveying the hodgepodge of sparkling stainless steel receptacles and instruments in the glass fronted cabinets displaying their rubber stoppled vials standing in rows like potent little soldiers. Only the bulky autoclave with its bank vault-like door ajar seemed out of place in the over organized cubicle.

"I told you, Rod, he's the finest pit bull you ever saw and probably the smartest." O'Steen's knurly forearms were crossed over his chest as he relaxed in the other chair. "I've tried and tried to get my pal to let me stud that beast but he's so goddam gun-shy about dog fights he won't give me the time of day. And I've got the perfect bitch for that canine Rooster Cogburn!"

"Shit, Claxton, lease the son of a bitch... pay for him then breed him to any one you want." Osler's tanned face took on a quizzical look as Clax interrupted him.

"Sure, man ... Rod, you don't have the foggiest notion of Sam's attachment to that dog. Shit, he hardly lets him out of his sight. Lease, my ass!" Clax's laughter was forced and clipped.

"Better yet, Claxton, let's see if we can get him to the fights coming up and roll him with something solid. See what he's made of - for real." Osler's amicable smile had turned down a few notches and his hooded gaze sent a chill down O'Steen's spine. "All I got is your word. For all I know the bastard may turn away from a real dog." The Myrmon headmaster's mocking tone definitely veiled a challenge.

"Hah, your ass, Rod. The JunkYard dog wouldn't turn away from the dog from hell, much less any mutt you put in front of him." Clax's tone was fading from levity to aggravation and his conversational banter rolled into confrontational argument. "Aw shit, Rod, let's go get a cold one and talk horses or something ..."

"Fine, Clax." Roderick Osler's eyes were slits in his forehead as he reached into his briefcase and produced a small, notebook sized object. His tone was throaty, his words clipped. "Let's do just that. In fact, I have wanted to talk horse with you since I got here. Especially about stud horses ... a HighandMighty stud horse.

"What about HighandMighty! What about him?" Clax's explosive response was protective, almost defensive as he sensed the sea change in his friend's demeanor and knew something was wrong – very wrong!

"Well, Mr. O'Steen, lets just say that some interests I represent have noticed your big stud and now that you've got me turned on to your buddy's dog, I think a little demonstration is in order. By the way, Claxton, where is the big horse about now?" The words dripped from Osler's mouth like ice water as he coolly flipped the top of the clipboard looking object revealing a compressed computer keyboard.

"Fuck you, Rod, what in the shit is wrong with you? What's that you're fooling with … some kind of computer?"

"Clax man, calm down. Where's the big horse now? Everything is going to be all right." Osler's tone was lighter, almost mocking as he walked through the breeding room door and headed for the massive double doors opening into the stallion paddocks.

"There he is, Rod. Over there by the walkway." Clax's words sounded gagged up as he pointed to the magnificent stallion grazing calmly at one end of the lush two-acre enclosure. Rod Osler was up to something – but what?

"Isn't that your friend and his dog?" As he spoke the ominous man pointed the compact computer at the placid horse as a jogging man accompanied by a dog silently moved down the pathway on the far side of HighandMighty's paddock; a scene from a silent movie. "Well, my friend, let's see what mister JunkYard is made of."

Osler's cold tone sent a chill down O'Steen's spine and as he fingered the small keyboard, Clax's furrowed brow began to sweat. His head began to pound as he realized that something was way out of kilter and that he was going to be powerless to stop it – hell, he had not the faintest idea what was going down.

With a savage snort, HighandMighty sun-fished ten feet into the air, hit the ground bucking and kicking with his fine fox ears pinned tight to his skull and grass filled mouth agape like a horse from hell.

With a barely suppressed chuckle, Osler pushed another key on the tiny keyboard and as if by magic the agitated stallion laid down twenty feet of parallel skid marks in the soft turf, the envy of any reining cow-horse, rolled back on his hocks and headed straight for the far side of the well kept paddock – and two innocent figures doggedly trotting up the pathway totally unaware of the immediate arrival of twelve hundred pounds of disaster. Delivery…. C.O.D!

Claxton O'Steen's lips tingled and went as slack as an overworked anus while his unbelieving brain tried to convince his eyes that they were misinterpreting reality.

HighandMighty hit the fence like an Olympic hurdler, taking the electric wire off with the top-rail without missing a stride. The splintered boards echoed the only notice Sam and JY were to have before the delusional stallion was on them.

Sensing the oncoming horse, Samson and JunkYard gave way instinctively as the careening beast reached them, trapping them between the fences demarcating the narrow pathways. HighandMighty struck Sam as he rolled against the fence in a tight, protective curl. Missing with his savage jaws, the maniacal beast caught the prostrate man with the full force of his driving forelegs and propelled him along the fence like a fleshy medicine ball, simultaneously striking the reacting pit bulldog as he turned to face the equine avalanche, and sent him into the fence with the force of a cannon-shot.

Clax O'Steen stood as if transfixed by Medusa's writhing visage until the princely stallion crashed the fence. Shouting at the top of his lungs, the thoroughly confused trainer sprinted toward the carnage as he hollered for his grooms and at HighandMighty with the same breath; Roderick Osler.... Forgotten.

Deftly, Rod Osler punched the computer keyboard as he calmly walked toward the breached stallion paddock to get a better look. What he saw caused the silky tongued manipulator to gasp and stop in his tracks. HighandMighty was on his powerful hind quarters poised over the prostrated Sam Duff, striking blindly with his flailing forelegs – there being no place for the besieged man to go – when a burnished red blur climbed up the pitching stallion's back with the ease of a monkey going up a tree trunk. Vice-grip jaws clamped his neck just behind the poll. H&M went totally berserk, squealing and shaking his head like some huge vibrator. Sam was totally forgotten. Two jumps down the lane the dog-caught horse suddenly ducked his head and with deadly intent tried to scrape the locked-on pit bulldog off, using his forelegs like bone hard spatulas.

The first blows, unavoidable, would have disabled a lesser animal but JY absorbed them and gave up his hold as the squealing stallion went to his knees as if praying. In a flash the game dog landed on his feet and caught HighandMighty by the nose – a full mouth-full – and locked on.

Samson staggered to his feet, unable to help his pal.

Clax was just getting to the break in the fence.

Rod Osler was putting the small computer back into his pocket while slowly shaking his head as the scene played out.

Whatever demons had possessed the agitated stallion now deserted him, being exorcised by the crunching pain that was his nose. Twice he feebly tried to strike the hanging dog, but striking with his fore feet necessitated raising his head that also raised the dog's body and resulted in extra punishment as the solid pit bulldog's weight exerted its toll on the stud's already tortured nose.

Sweating, shivering, eyes bulging with fear and glowing like highway reflectors, the mighty horse stood immobilized by the canine lip-twitch!

Claxton O'Steen nodded at Sam as he put his belt around the beaten horse's neck and helped Sam take the one eyed JunkYard off its nose while exhorting Charlie, the out of breath stallion barn groom, to call the veterinarian. Rod Osler was not mentioned.

After quietly retrieving his briefcase, no one remembered him driving off – still shaking his head.

• • •

"Skeets, I tell you something's going on here … at VentureQuest. This horse incident today wasn't just another day at the office." Sam's voice had slowly been rising as he recounted the details of HighandMighty's unprovoked attack, and this unnatural falsetto caught Skeets attention.

"Okay.... Okay, I believe you. Glad you and the mutt didn't get hurt worse. I guess those bruises are no fun but you toughs will get over them quick enough." Skeets had driven up about two hours after the incident and Sam was just finishing showering after having JY examined by the veterinarian called to attend the stallion's mangled nose.

"Funny thing, though, Skeets. Clax flat out lied about who he was with. Said it was just a drummer and they only talked for a few minutes in the barn. I know the guy was here for hours and I know Clax took him to my room – but why? Not a hair was out of place in the apartment, and JY wasn't bothered. I couldn't very well jack him up about me knowing he was in the apartment but he sure was clammy about the guy".... Samson paused as if thinking of something else. "And the guy was with Clax when HighandMighty flipped over the edge but he was no-show at the scene and Clax never mentioned being with him prior. And I stopped by the breeding shed room on the way back to HighandMighty's stall and Clax and the guy's scent were all over. They were both there ... definitely." Again the bruised Samson Duff paused as a far away look sneaked into his eyes, unbidden but unavoidable, as his mind flashed back to the horrific storm in the Everglades when he and JY were separated and the gallant pit bull savagely injured.

The fixed, mydriatic stare caught Skeets attention as quickly as his pal's conversational tailspin. Skeets sensed that Sam was up-set but had no way of relating to the big guy's feeling of dread since Kirby's emotional core was basically bulletproof. "What is it, Samson. What's wrong? You look like you've just seen a ghost or some shit like that." Getting up, Charles 'Skeets' Kirby took a step toward the entranced man.

"Wh ... What - oh shit, Skeets ... I just flashed back to the Bloodtooth-Everglades thing but goddammit, I've got this nagging feeling that something's going to happen to JunkYard. Can't shake it ..." Sam's gaze returned to earth as the unperturbed Skeets turned and headed for the cabinet.

"Lets have a little snort," Skeets chortled as he reached for the bottle of single malt Scotch. "And talk about something else."

"Like what, Skeeterman?" Sam took the proffered amber liquid and held it up so the reflected light rays could do their crazy little dance in its fierce, albeit friendly, wetness. He took a sip. Long and slow.

"Like what we've been hired to do, old hoss – remember? Like what I found out in Tampa – remember?" Skeets chuckled as he took a slow, tongue-washing sip of the Macallan.

• • •

Roderick Osler was tired. He had travelled by car from Ocala to Miami and then, without rest, hopped on the Myrmon thirty six footer and boated straight to Burgaard's lab on Hoostra Island, arriving just past midnight. Dr. Cube wasn't to be denied when he wanted to talk. That meant right now!

"So, Rodman – what happened? Did our Claxton get the message?" Quentin Burgaard, III, leaned back in the oversized swivel chair as he posed the question.

Even as he mouthed the words to reply, the travel weary Osler picked up on the low, rumbling growl emanating from behind QB-3's desk, an ominous threatening vibration that seemed to rise from the very bowels of the sleek mastiff.

"Quiet, asshole. You know the Rodman, so shut uppa you face!" Mockingly, QB-3 reached down and slapped the hyper-muscled thigh of Goar, provoking a final mutilated lip-curling snarl followed by a noticeable exhalation – then quiet.

"Why'd you bring him? I thought ..." Osler's words were cut off as the Machiavellian scientist interrupted him.

"What about O'Steen and the horse, Roderick? Did you pull it off?" Burgaard's insistence bordered on command.

"I think so, Quentin. At least the demo was sure impressive. You should have seen that stupid horse when I hit the 'go' key. Son of a bitch! Went totally bananas. But I've not been able to get back to O'Steen – not enough time and he's hard to get on the phone. You called too soon. I needed another day - two - at the least."

"For what, Rod? To check out that goddam pit bulldog of O'Steen's friend? You had plenty of time to do what I wanted, but you had to fuck around, you and your dog fights!"

"Listen, dammit, Quentin. I did exactly as you said and as fast as humanly possible. So don't give me any bull-crap about fighting dog shit." Osler's tanned visage was squeezed to full choke as he shot back at the combative scientist.

How the fuck did Dr. Cube know about Clax's friend and his dog? Osler's mind was cranking a mile a minute as he struggled to maintain his mental balance in the face of Burgaard's off the wall accusation. "I'll get to O'Steen as soon as it's daylight. He'll do what we want. He loves that frigging horse. He'd sell his mama's ass to save that stallion. One phone call, that's all it'll take – no problemo." Osler's voice had recovered from the initial shock of QB-3's unexpected query and his ego was smoldering. How dare that warped son of a bitch criticize me for fighting dogs. Dogs that were bred to fight, bred to be tough, to face each other without flinching or turning away. To die if need be.

"I need a drink, Quentin – you?" Osler's directive coincided with his short journey to the small, self-contained bar that held the stash of spiritus frumenti so necessary for Roderick Osler's daily well being.

"Yeah, Rod, Jack on the rocks." Burgaard's reply was status quo with Rod Osler who knew what Dr. Cube wanted to drink and when he wanted it. He poured the drinks slowly to allow his courage to catch up with his mouth. As much as he despised the whacko scientist, he feared him and though he had many goals in life, serving as hors d'oeuvres for an eighteen foot hammerhead shark was not one of them!

He also knew Dr. Cube's condescending attitude toward pit bulldogs and dog fighting. Quentin Burgaard, III, thought the finely tuned, sleek pit bulldogs were way overrated and that his Goar could clean their clocks. He had, on occasion, dropped unfortunate young pit bulldogs in with the hulking mastiff and Goar made short work of them; overpowering the game but inexperienced pups like a bulldozer in a bumper car concession.

Rod knew that Goar had never faced a mature, battle tested male pit bulldog; in his opinion, the gamest beast on earth pound for pound. But he had seen Goar in action and knew the physical strength and toughness of the one hundred eighty pound mastiff; knew how Burgaard conditioned and tormented the aggressive animal giving him an edge not found in any other fighting dog that Osler was aware of – even the most scarred veteran.

He shuddered at the thought of a contest between a significant pit bulldog and the brutish Goar. There would be no way for human hands to break such combatants once they did their tango.

There was no doubt in Osler's mind that the mastiff was a force to be reckoned with and certainly the only dog he had ever seen that truly threatened the image of invincibility he thought copyrighted by the sleek pit bulldog.

A mischievous impulse coursed the Myrmon Academy headmaster's rebounding mind as he envisioned Dr. Cube's ferocious beast facing a dog like the Havana street dog or even Clax O'Steen's friend's – what's his name – Sam - dog. He was still mulling over the one eyed dog's fierce, efficient handling of the enraged stallion. Unbelievable! Now what would Goar do with an opponent like that? One thing for sure - it would be one hell of a dogfight!

"Hey Rod, we going to have a little snort tonight ... or not?" Burgaard's steel shot words pierced the fog filled balloon that was Roderick Osler's mind like darts, causing him to turn with a noticeable jerk, spilling whisky as he did.

"Hey, man, I'm pooped." Rod proffered the Jack Daniels and sat down as he took a hefty mouthful of his vodka and orange juice. As Dr. Cube took the glass, He heard Goar-dog rumbling like a slumbering volcano.

• • •

Chapter SEVEN

Harrie Smithcors was unhappy. He had just been informed that Donna Ileana Villareal would be instituting a new recreational schedule for the next quarter. He had been so informed by interoffice memo over the headmaster's signature – period. No discussion, no reason, no nothing!

It was bad enough that Harrie had to share classroom space with the tempestuous Brazilian but to be superseded by her for a full quarter just wasn't to be tolerated. Student recreation was his primary duty, not to be subverted, as his interaction with the boys was serious business to him.

Harrie especially did not want to leave young Toby, the newest and youngest recruit to be shanghaied to Burgaard's academy by the third world flesh peddlers. Harrie did not know which country vomited out the poor seven year old but the ghostly white skin highlighted by bushy hair the color of polished onyx caused the Myrmon Academy Recreational Director's heart to beat faster. This kid was drop dead gorgeous.

Harrie had taken the forty-six pound child as soon as he arrived and was in the process of restoring the cachectic youngster to reasonable health. Toby muttered in an Arabic dialect but verbal communication was not a necessary part of Smithcors' equation. He could and would teach the child English as well as the required Spanish – in due course.

Donna Eye didn't care a wit about Toby, and the more care Harrie bestowed on him the more Donna Eye groused, which prompted Harrie to even greater heights in his salvage attempts concerning the wormy waif.

Harrie Smithcors hated Donna Eye.

• • •

Raul Pena was pacing like a caged bear. He was not a man of initiative and his last words with his boss, Roderick Osler, were heavy on his mind. Like most still breathing Myrmon Academy employees, Raul knew better than to disobey or not carry out orders. Whatever contempt or cynicism he harbored toward the muy loco, bushy faced gringo known as Dr. Cube and his Myrmidon staff stopped way short of mutiny.

"Humberto. Señor Rod wants that dirty looking Havana dog. He wants him for the fights next month in Miami. But how do we do this?" Raul's voice was low pitched and pleading.

"He will be hard to fool with a second time. This I know, Raul. The old man, Dom Pedro, he watches these dog like a hawk. A person stealing these dog will have to be very, very careful" Humberto's reply did little to allay his cousin's apprehension.

"Humberto, I'm going to call Samuel." A trace of a smile teased the worried face of Raul Pena.

• • •

"There they are!" the deeply tanned, barrel-chested man shouted as he leaned into the top-rail of the swaying tower and grabbed the seven foot spinning rod resting in the rocket launcher like a kid grabs a pencil. As if in one motion, the big man tossed the change purse size crab into the middle of the boil made by the dozen or so tarpon roiling lazily in the lime green water just off the beach on the west side of Big Gasparilla Island. Galvanized by the shout, the other three men ran to the starboard side of the teal green, twenty four foot custom Morgan inboard where the deeply tanned, white haired one pointed knowingly at the coppery fish gliding like shadows beside and in front of the idling boat.

Johnny Dugan set the hook and handed the screaming reel and rod to the short, round-faced man standing next to the silver haired Big Johnny, Johnny Dugan's father and referred to as BJ

The one hundred thirty plus pound fish came to the surface with a crashing leap and took line like the straining spinning reel was in free-spool. Up the beach the pressing tarpon went, trying to drag its mettlesome linear burden and keep up with the rest of the pod.

"Better go after it, son." BJ's words, though quietly uttered were duly noted as the Podzilla turned and followed the obstreperous fish, allowing the short man to gain a few dozen yards of line. Only ten minutes into the contest yet the human combatant was drenched in perspiration and his rod holding left arm felt like arm wrestling King Kong would be sweet relief. Two hundred yards in front of the boat the gaping face of the struggling tarpon broke the surface and threw huge gouts of salt spray as it shook its head like a fox terrier worrying a rat.

"Want a belt? Your arm's going to get awful sore before you get that hoss to the barn." Johnny's words of encouragement ran off the stout man's head like water down a slide as he tried to pump and reel against the stubborn force still stripping off yards of the twenty-five pound test line. The old lighthouse located halfway down the island and across the road from the Eagle's Nest was just off Podzilla's starboard side as the powerful fish pulled them relentlessly north trying to keep up with its buddies.

"Hey, Johnny." BJ cupped his hands over his mouth and squinted into the glaring sun as he pointed his face at his son. "Be careful. Those rocks are just north of the lighthouse, about where that old gal is headed. It's only eight or nine foot deep ..."

As Big Johnny spoke, the hyper-flexed rod straightened with a barely audible 'swoosh' as the silver scaled force found the rocks, severed the line and was gone quicker than memory loss.

"Goddam, Johnny, that heifer broke off!" BJ's statement of the obvious did little to assuage the pleading look on the short man's face as he handed the now straight rod to Johnny, blurting out, "Let's find some more of them - damn, that was fun!"

Johnny Dugan throttled down as his dad pointed to the commotion in the water several hundred yards to the north and Podzilla surged forward, her three hundred fifty horses gurgling like contented babies. Chasing tarpon to Johnny Dugan was like bloodsucking to a mosquito – in the genes. He had kicked around for years, much to the dismay of Big Johnny but when he finally got serious about fishing, the forty years old man found a foothold in the wall of life and became a fishing guide guru.

Johnny had guided around Charlotte Harbor and Boca Grande for going on five years, having moved from the lower east coast where he had fished a little and bummed around a lot until he landed in the Bahamas and settled down to some serious fishing.

His father was an architect, a perfectionist and a student of motorcars, women, sailing and boats in general. The slender, white-haired ladies man with the prominent nose had built the Podzilla from the deck up – singlehandedly. It took Big Johnny Dugan a year to finish, arguably, the finest tarpon fishing vessel plying the waters of west central Florida.

"Look at that!" The short man's cry ricocheted off the gray bronze, three foot dorsal fin protruding from the frothing surface stirred up by a covey of anxious tarpon. Suddenly, a tarpon jumped from the foam and fell back only to be buffeted like a soccer ball in short grass. The ominous fin trailed by only a few feet as the frantic fish tried to sound.

"Goddam ... Goddam ..." Johnny, from the tower, was muttering like a stiffed whore. "It's a shark – big hammerhead – it's

Hitler!" Every hammerhead in Boca Grande pass and the adjacent waters was called 'Hitler' for the past fifty years. As he spoke, Podzilla eased up to the commotion and any one of the three could have reached over and stroked a patch of hide on the eighteen foot <u>Sphyrna mokarran.</u>

Working the bewildered tarpon like a cat with a lint ball, 'Hitler' slapped and batted the frantic fish with his grotesque snout, keeping her on the surface thereby frustrating her efforts to seek refuge in the lime green depths. There would be no sanctuary this day.

It only took several, very short minutes before the coppery fish was barely able to move, stunned, and being positioned by the merciless predator like a snake caught mouse. Pushing the tarpon's head forward, 'Hitler's' final approach was from the rear. As the goggle-eyed men looked on, the huge shark belied its size with a display of agility usually awarded smaller creatures and pushed the catatonic fish into its serrated maw, tail first, until only the head and gill plates remained.

With the force and ease of a trash compactor, 'Hitler' severed the scaly body, giving freedom to gouts of blood that slowly widened in the gorgeous green water as the tarpon's lifeless head sank into the refuge it had been denied.

The swirls created by the departing shark quickly flattened with only a slowly enlarging, smoke-like stain a token to the dramatic encounter.

"Look, Johnny, I see more tarpon - north." Even as he pointed and shouted, the short man shivered.

● ● ●

The soothing Macallan marched down Kirby's throat introducing its pleasant burn to crevices and cul de sacs heretofore snubbed by the more pedestrian liquids following the same path. Skeets coughed.

"Okay, Skeets, hows about this Benito kid. Anything turn up on him?" Sam was standing by the table drumming his fingers as he contemplated his Scotch and his partner.

"Big fat zero, pal. Fingerprints not on record and no one ever heard of him before he showed up with Gherrie Larry. All we know is that he supposedly attended the summer academy.... What's its name ... Myrmon? Same one Big Jaxe's grandson attends and was staying at VentureQuest and was in Orlando with Gherrie and Big Jaxe when Jaxe bought the farm." Skeets paused and savored another sip of the bottled lava, gingerly swishing it around his mouth as if building up courage to gulp it down. "And," Skeets continued, "I checked with the Tampa detective and he reviewed the homicide report, called this Myrmon Academy, said he spoke to one Roderick Osler, head-master, and that no Benito Lopes – or any kid named Benito was, or had been, registered at Myrmon Academy ... thank you please!"

"Well, Skeets, old buddy, I know there's more to that kid than meets the eye." Sam slid into the recliner next to JunkYard and ran his fingertips across the rounded profile of the placid dog's head. "So, while you were gone I thought I would look up young master Benito and have a private chit-chat – mano y mano – without Clax or anyone else around to screw it up and guess what, old pal ..."

"He's gone. Outta Dodge." Skeets laughed as he interrupted the quizzical Samson.

"How the fuck did you know? But you're right on the money. No one, not Gherrie, his grandmother, Claxton or any fucking body knows when or where he went. I even tried to follow his scent trail around the farm but no luck." Sam's surprise at Skeets' re-mark was reflected in the blank look settling over his face as he again asked Skeets, how he knew.

Laughing, the Skeeterman strung out his reply. "Just ... a hunch!"

• • •

The short, swarthy Cuban in full camouflage fatigues, sporting sunglasses, was just leaving Quentin Burgaard's office on the Myrmon Academy grounds as Rod Osler rounded the corner by the short stairwell that led up from the ground floor. Commandante Jorge Solar grunted acknowledgement of recognition as his snappy, well-armed, three man entourage swept past the stony faced Myrmon headmaster. Rod Osler stopped short of the office door and as the last man disappeared around the corner flipped his finger in the familiar salute of disrespect, while words too quiet to hear slipped between clenched teeth. "Up yours, you Cuban commie bastards!"

As bent as his moral centerboard was, Rod Osler hated communism and communists and Quentin Burgaard, III's dealing with the Castro regime was a dump-truck load of gall for the spurious headmaster to swallow. If there was no honor among thieves, there was opinion and Rod had a very strong one concerning communists.

The good Dr. Cube, of course, thought it amusing and rubbed this raw nerve in Osler's psyche every chance he got. To QB-3 communism was just another avenue of opportunity; a veritable interstate!

"Come on in, Rod. What took you so goddam long? I wanted you here when Soler-ass was detailing the latest hit list." Burgaard's get right down to business style always grated on the older man but of late it was getting too much to bear.

"Shit, Quentin, you know I don't give a fuck about the latest Cuban ex-patriot scratch-off lottery. I came," Osler lied, "as fast as I could. Who's on it this time?" Osler's query was offered with some concession to the financial benefit of the situation and his hackles slowly settled into place. He well knew where the money for Myrmon Academy originated – Cuba.

"Just a few motor-mouthed guys from Little Havana in Miami. Usual run of the mill, self styled Jose Marti types. Who we got to send - how about Benito? He's through with the Jackson Larry thing. Or, maybe Jacques? Hell, who knows, maybe one of the new Myrmex Terminus class is ready." Burgaard's blather tailed off, as Osler interrupted him.

"Glad you mentioned Bennie. We need to talk about him. I think the Larry snuffola is drawing a little heat. I had a call from Florida law enforcement about him and when I was at VentureQuest, Clax O'Steen mentioned Benito and how he may have been involved in something to do with the horses. And Harrie told me that someone called while I was gone asking about Benito. Said he was a friend and wanted to know how to get in touch with him. Harrie pressed him for a name or phone number but the guy said he'd call back. So, Harrie had the call traced, and lo and behold it came from VentureQuest farm. And the only person there is O'Steen's friend. Apparently this friend is some kind of snoop or just nosy – this Sam Duff fella." Osler's tone was subdued and business like as he detailed QB-3 on the possibilities concerning Benito Lopes. He also knew how the good Dr. Cube would react.

"So, someone is interested in young Mr. Lopes. Can't have that." Burgaard's reply sported an acid edge. "Too bad we couldn't get him out before the gendarmes swarmed. Had to play that hand out - not like Jacques. He split before any investigation and got back here like he never left."

Rod's "So?" was more agreement than query.

"So, we're going to have a little picnic and get-together for young master Benito – sort of a going away celebration." Dr. Cube's voice again the basso of a dark opera. "Rod, be so kind as to get Donna on the phone."

• • •

Bennie liked boats and boat rides. From his perch in the bow, the spider-legged, blue veined fourteen year old let the insistent sea breeze bounce off his face as the Myrmon Academy cruiser headed out from Hoostra Island for the Salt Cays and a picnic outing. He had been on many outings during his five years at Myrmon, so his increasing awareness of himself, plus his recently acquired realization of lifestyle differences did little to dampen his spirits or arouse suspicion.

Even the sight of Harrie Smithcors cleaning out Benito's room, randomly throwing all the boy's earthly possessions into plastic bags probably would have been of only curious concern to the anomalistic young man. The sight of these bags being tossed into the incinerator may have gotten a rise from the emotionally stale boy, but for sure he would harbor no suspicion and if told that one hour after boarding the cruiser, no evidence of Benito Lopes being at Myrmon Academy existed, he would smile and say. "Oh yes, I'm Benito."

The only life Benito remembered started with his arrival on Hoostra Island in a group of five urchins taken off the streets of Brazil. His life prior to that was a vague blur of basic survival and raw instincts: Of garbage, cold alleys, fights, assassination attempts by government exterminators. Cursing and running. Always running. The first bath of his life occurred on the day after arriving at Myrmon Academy.

Young Bennie never knew his mother, in fact, did not understand what a mother was. He came to understand, through some unfocused intuitive assimilation, that a mother could only be female – a woman – and they were to be respected and in some instances, revered, to the point of worship. He really never understood this.

He also never equated sex with motherhood or specifically with females. Bennie had masturbated as long as he could remember, either alone or with other street urchins, male and female. It was as natural and relief evoking as a bowel movement or a thirst slaking draught of cold water. He was given to intercourse at the age of eight, again with male and female partners, whomever was available. So Donna Eye's seductions of Benito Lopes was not of the fifth dimension to him; merely physical gratification that he accepted as a well fed puppy accepts its next meal – and he still masturbated every day.

Donna Ileana Villareal's classes were designed to heighten the innate iniquitous instincts of the malleable young men and she went about her daily rounds with more than a little enthusiasm.

Any student that displayed a developing empathy was quickly given a failing grade and termination at Myrmon Academy was serious – very serious!

Young Bennie's emotional well was so shallow that no water of empathy sprang forth when certain time-honored moral codes were transgressed as in premeditated murder. The emotionally bland youngster, should the occasion arise, could pump eight or nine .22 caliber bullets into Donna Eye's nectarous body without remorse; before or after sex would make no difference – ditto Harrie Smithcors.

He did, however, have respect for Roderick Osler and Quentin Burgaard, III. Benito understood authority - as power - and the Myrmon Academy headmaster and his boss represented the ultimate power in Bennie's universe. This power lay in what these Gods could give rather than in what they could take – certainly not his life for Benito Lopes had no understanding of death, including what was happening to the five humans he had so casually assassinated. Their pain was certainly not his pain and his lifestyle precluded the possibility of any future contact, so as far as he was concerned their demise by his hand meant nothing.

Armando anchored the boat to the beach and silently motioned the passengers off while he unloaded the picnic supplies. Comments by the young men and Donna Ileana were met by a blank look and unintelligible grunt. The north side of the big Cay had the only decent beach of the entire chain of forbidden rock. Eons of wind and water working in concert had filled the lagoon-like cul de sac and the surrounding moonscape with enough sand and organic debris that grass could grow and this five acre area was like a shimmering grassy jewel in a landscape where trespass was limited to those with tough footgear - or latent masochistic tendencies.

Armando had been up early transporting the recreational gear to the secluded beach and setting up the volleyball nets, the tents and tables plus the other playthings standard for a Myrmon outing.

Raul Pena usually helped but he was gone and Armando had to make do alone; this did little to mollify the bandy legged Brazilian's dour mien.

This was a rare intermingling of Myrmon Academy tyros including the Myrmex Terminus cadre whose level of training was sufficiently advanced to allow such melding. Benito Lopes was soon caught up in the frenzy of activity when the pent up energy in the hard-wired young men vented and they turned the gin clear waters to froth.

• • •

The red ball of sun was letting itself down in the cloudless western sky when the white, twenty five foot Mako glided to the beach and a stout, round-shouldered man in a silk brief, more suited to a male model, jumped out and effortlessly carried an anchor through the knee deep water to the beach and secured the boat. Salt spray coated his curly beard as he marched through the calm water to the well-balanced craft. He was alone except for a large, black masked dog standing at the bow of the gently bobbing Mako. He was muzzled, with an unsecured leash snapped to his thick leather collar.

"Come on Goar-shit, hit the water… it's show time!" The somnolent water exploded as one hundred eighty pounds of mean dog meat awoke it, soaking the gleeful Dr. Cube as he struggled to clear his vision while groping blindly for the twelve feet of nylon leash.

Goar surged toward the beach with machine-like effort in spite of his laughing, choking, curly faced anchor.

As soon as the Mako appeared, Armando made Donna Eye notice and started rounding up the stuffed, played out young men. Bud York showed up and the three chaperones quickly packed the perishables and had some of the boys wading to the cruiser as Dr. Cube and Goar rambled up the beach.

A baleful stillness pervaded the activities as the once boisterous boys prepared to leave.

No one spoke. Movement was mechanical. Benito Lopes was not among them.

Quentin Burgaard, III, had control of the surging dog-beast as he waded through the surf and hit the packed beach sand. Trotting with Goar in front, he headed for Donna Eye who had separated from the group and met the dripping scientist well out of earshot.

Conversation was brief and garbled. Donna held a black plastic object resembling a wafer–sized T.V. remote, and pointing it away from the beach pushed a key resulting in a red flicker at the top of the tiny remote. Pocketing the object, Donna Eye walked to the beach and splashed to the departing boat. From the beach Armando waved, halfheartedly, as the loaded cabin cruiser got under way.

Benito Lopes was confused. He never drank alcoholic beverages and had no way to know he was drunk. Bud York had taken Bennie to the small rock building on the far side of the grassy area away from the beach, and from a cooler hand-fed the eager Myrmidon pineapple juice laced with one hundred fifty proof, five star Haitian rum.

Bennie didn't remember anything, especially time. He had staggered to the only door in the small room over an hour ago and could not open it. Head throbbing like a hammer hit thumb, the slightly built boy had prostrated himself on the cane recliner, knowing only that it must be late afternoon as he could see dim light through the one tiny window.

The starkness of the metallic clicking sound focused his besotted attention on the door, as the loud mechanical click seemed to emanate from that direction. Crawling to the sound he brushed against the door and it opened – easily and silently. Relieved by this freedom, Bennie crawled outside onto the beggarly grass, purposefully willed himself upright and headed toward the sea like a crapulous lemming.

Clad only in a bathing suit, Bennie had no idea of what was happening - or had happened. He only knew that the sun was low and he needed to get to the beach.

The unsteady boy didn't notice the slobbery dog until Goar was on him. The snarly growl was totally beyond comprehension as the mastiff grabbed the shocked man-child by the shoulder, pulled him down and began shaking and tearing deeper into the one hundred fifteen pound body with the sureness and synchrony of his own savage heart beat. Reflexive and feebly the stricken boy struck the beast with his free arm only to have the entranced Goar grab the flailing appendage in merciless jaws and break the bones of Benito's forearm like stale pizza crust.

Benito's eyes were bulging with widely dilated pupils. Unseeing. His nervous system had shut down and even as the Goar-beast worried the tortured flesh like so much gory taffy, the boy felt no pain.

The cold arms of Thanatos reached to the pitiful little throwaway urchin and as the life force abandoned his mangled remains, the only mother this God forsaken child could ever know closed her bony arms around him.... Death!

The feel of muscular contractions peculiar to hemorrhaging flesh sent the mastiff into renewed frenzy. Seizing the curly headed skull in his blood slathered maw, Goar stood with the lifeless remnant of what had been Benito Lopes and shook as if to gain the attention of two men on the beach putting a hatchet and saw into a cooler containing several black plastic bags.

• • •

Chapter EIGHT

"Good job! Much trouble? Is he okay?" Questions tumbled from Rod Osler's mouth like broken teeth. He had arrived in Nichols Town on Andros Island an hour ago and his first sight of the muscular Havana dog sent chills down his backbone. "My God, what a beast!" Walking around the reinforced wire cage, the Myrmon headmaster took in every perfect angle of the placid pit bulldog.

For his part, Dirty Dog lay in a corner of the cage with his massive head resting on extended forelegs, eyes locked on the movement of the three men. The effect of the tranquilizer was abating and the passive canine did not realize he was captive.

Raul Pena suppressed his grin as he surveyed the prize. "Was not a problem, Señor Rod. We, Samuel and I, along with my cousin, Humberto, did this thing without a hitch. This impressive animal is totally unhurt, is one hundred percent okay." Slyly averting Osler's gaze, the less than humble Cuban machismo threw a hooded wink in the direction of Samuel. "No problemo, Señor Rod."

"Okay, Raul, I want you to keep him here – if it's okay with Samuel – until the Miami rumbles. I'd better not keep him at Myrmon ... yet. And see if you can get on his good side while you're at it." As callous as Roderick Osler was he could not resist the lure of this particular pit bulldog. "And keep him tranquilized as long as you think necessary. Can't have him breaking teeth on this gorilla cage trying to chew his way back to Havana." Noticing the dog's eyes lock on his face, Osler whistled sharply, noting the sudden forward shift of the scarred, uncropped ears: Recognition ... a start.

"Also, Raul, you might see if any of those bitches of mine are in heat. This guy could be just the one to punch their ticket – might make him feel more at home if he had a little snussy to keep him occupied".... Osler's voice trailed off abruptly as Samuel interrupted.

"Hey, Mr. Osler, mon. Do you not know that this fine specimen of a fighting dog is an 'it'? Did you not know this?" Samuel turned his quizzical expression from Roderick Osler to Raul Pena. It was the Haitian who had gotten the acepromazine tranquilizer for Raul to use but had no part in the abduction of Dirty Dog. It was only when the tranquil animal arrived at his girlfriend's place that the astute Samuel discovered the missing jewels.

Rod Osler exploded. "What the fuck! You mean this magnificent son of a bitch is a gelding? A goddam no nuts eunuch?" Raul Pena stepped back as his agitated boss shoved his red face into the grimace of the embarrassed Cuban like a Marine Drill Sergeant introducing himself to a jarhead.

...."Ahh, Señor Rod ... I never knew, I swear. Humberto never told me ... Humberto, he never knew or he would have told me ..." Totally flustered, Raul turned, pleadingly, toward the smirking Haitian but Samuel had nothing to offer.

...."Okay, okay. You're sure of this, Samuel?" Osler's tone calmed as he turned toward the Haitian but winced when he saw the affirmative nod. "Alright, then let's go get a cold one. This son of a bitch doesn't bite with his cahonies - noway." Turning as he spoke, the disappointed pit dog fancier headed for the house with:

"And I might just have another job for you dog-napping experts. Come on"

• • •

Dom Pedro looked through the ratty screen door for the umpteenth time but no Dirty Dog materialized on the sandy board porch. It was three days since the old man had seen the maverick pit bulldog and he was beginning to worry. One or two days without his shadowy canine friend, he expected, but not three days. A thunderstorm had blown in from the south and as the tropical deluge vented its energy, old Dom Pedro wondered if his buddy had found adequate shelter. Not that the impressive animal would melt.

By the fifth day Dom Pedro knew something was wrong – seriously wrong. He had, for the past several days, searched the area he knew the dog to frequent. He knew that the neutered dog was not driven to estrous bitches, thereby avoiding the bloody fights that ensued among the pack of intact males; the kind of fighting that was life threatening, even to one so formidable as the Havana stray.

On the seventh day the weary old Cuban hollered at one of the street urchins common to the area. Dom Pedro was aware of the dog's penchant for avoiding humans and knew that none of these homeless could have harmed the man shy pit bulldog unless, by chance, a gun was involved. Not likely, he mused, as he approached the ragged street-child. The only guns in Cuba belonged to Fidel Castro and his toadies.

Old Dom harbored a boatload of sympathy for these street waifs but the reality of interacting with them made him defensive. These child-men were formidable survivors as aptly demonstrated by their look-you-in-the-eye-and-not-blink attitude about life as they lived it.

They did not lie or tell the truth, saying only what was prudent and necessary for a next meal or survival. Truth and consequences belonged on the radio or in the world outside their garbage littered streets. In their stark universe, words were letters you strung together to aid in survival.

The lanky, towheaded youth approached the old Cuban with a diffidence born not of shyness or humility, but of novelty, for the urchin well knew of old Dom Pedro; just the old eremite never allowed a relationship to develop, ignoring the juvenile beggars and avoiding them when possible. Now, being asked to approach by the old man, seemed investiture to the tattered boy and with bowed head he answered Dom Pedro's queries, all while nervously fidgeting with an ugly scar that ran the length of his right forearm.

"Do you play here often?" Dom Pedro asked, well knowing that it was not play that kept the urchin here.

"Yes, Señor, I do." Dom Pedro had to strain to hear the boy's quiet reply.

"And what is your name, my young friend?" The soft smile that played on the old Cuban's face was real as he sought to put the youngster at ease. "Julio, Señor." At the sound of his name the boy traced an imaginary line in the sand with his bare toe. Clearly, speaking his name caused him concern.

"Aahh, Julio. Julio what? What is your surname … your family name? My name is Dom Pedro."

"Julio, old sir. It is the name I have. May I go now? The boy's reply mirrored a nervousness that confused Dom Pedro. This child of the street was actually showing respect to the old man – something he thought not possible. He was unprepared for this display of consideration by what he thought was a delinquent juvenile beyond the pale of esteem; even the pale of redemption.

"Ah, Julio, I only wish to ask a question of you. Do you know the dirty looking bulldog that frequents these pathways? The one that is quiet and makes you say 'ahhh' and hold your breath when he comes by. Do you know of this animal?"

"Yes, Dom Pedro, I know this dog very well. This cut I have here." Holding out his scarred arm, the gaunt eyed lad continued. "Is when my friend, Cruzo, and I tried to cut this dog when he was a small, little puppy. Yes, I know him well. I am afraid of him. He is not friendly."

Dom Pedro's eyes narrowed to weathered slits as his mind processed what he was hearing.

"Ah, Julio. Tell me the story of this thing you and Cruzo did to this Dirty Dog." Old Dom tried to disguise his interest in what the grimy street urchin was saying but he knew he couldn't. Casually, he dug into his lint filled pockets, hoping that he had not eaten all the candy he usually carried on these outings.

"Here, I have some candy to share with you. It is very good candy … very sweet. You will like it, I think. Here." Dom could see the lights come on in the smirchy recesses of the urchin's privation warped mind. Without hesitation the boy grabbed the proffered bribe and quickly guided the sugary blob between his chapped lips. There was no thank you.

Slowly, almost painfully, Julio told the fascinated old Cuban his story of the blotched castration. Dom Pedro did not interrupt but grinned several times and choked back a laugh when the saga of Cruzo losing two fingers was told.

"And what happened to your friend Mr. Cruzo?" The question tiptoed from Dom's lips like a sore-footed cat crossing a gravel road.

"Señor, Cruzo was taken by those that take us. Cruzo is dead these past years." The boy's eyes were downcast and the old man could not maintain eye contact. Julio was now distraught and Dom Pedro felt the urchin wanted to run or hide; would flee if not distracted.

"About the dog, Julio …" Dom Pedro quickly interjected, and just as quickly the nervous waif fired back.

"He is gone. Taken. The men who did this were the same as the ones who did it before. The Dirty Dog is gone and I am not afraid no more." These last words erupted from Julio's throat like orgasmic fluid as the grimy backstreet nomad turned and disappeared down the darkening alley.

"Wait … wait …" The old Cuban's plaintive plea dissipated in the warm humid air like puppy breath. He was stunned – both by the unexpected flavor of the conversation and by the finality of Julio's dictum concerning the fate of his beloved Dirty Dog.

Turning for home, Dom Pedro could not stop the flow of tears that silently washed his honest old face, a watery testament not only to his great loss but also for the unfortunate throwaway children that ended up in the streets and alleys of his little part of the world.

● ● ●

Clax O'Steen sifted through the breeding charts like a blind man playing solitaire. The confining business office seemed stifling as the perplexed farm manager tried to lose his troubled thoughts in the thready hum of the overtaxed window air-conditioning unit. Usually he liked this aspect of his work since he stood to make a fair piece of change from the stallion shares he owned, not to mention his two mares he hoped to get in foal.

But today he was troubled. The phone call he had with Rod Osler two hours earlier weighed on his mind like a concrete sombrero. How in God's name did Claxton Shamus O'Steen end up in bed with a snake-oil salesman like Rod Osler – or better yet, how or why did Clax let this man in bed with him?

He really did not know the Myrmon headmaster all that well, having met him only a few years ago after seeing him at various dog or cock fights and sharing veiled laughs or grimaces, depending on how well their particular combatants fared. Clax had never talked thoroughbred horse with the deeply tanned and obvious savoir-faire pundit of fighting dogs and cocks, so the episode with HighandMighty chipped away at his mind like an icepick trying to cleave an iceberg.

Cold sweat speckled his brow as he tried to fathom the meaning, if not the method, of Rod Osler's part in making the big stud go bonkers and try to kill Sam and JY. And what about that weird, skinny kid, Benito, whom Sam caught that night in the stallion barn? Clax had later tried to question the youngster after calming Samson and downplaying the incident but all he got from the vapid youth was name, rank and serial number. Then the little shit up and evaporated … and all he was left with was the questions that Sam kept asking – stupid, little things – in an effort to pry, covertly. It almost made him think that his buddy, somehow, knew he had taken Osler to see JunkYard. Impossible! At that thought, Claxton Shamus O'Steen laughed and pushed the pile of plastic coated breeding records to one side. Why in the world would Sam Duff be interested in these doings when he was only visiting Clax for rest and recuperation? Strange …

Though Sam and Clax were friends since high school, their paths had not crossed in eight or ten years, and it was only a chance meeting in Gainesville that renewed this friendship and resulted in Sam and JY getting invited to VentureQuest. Even with Sam's obscure, possibly ominous background, Clax could put no motive other than R and R. as reason for their visit.

But, he thought, most of this was small potatoes compared to the gist of his recent phone conversation with Roderick Osler.

• • •

'I'll be back late tomorrow night so exercise the mutt at least once. His food is in the fridge in two zip-locks, so, no problemo. See you later. Sam.'

Skeets reread the short note and chuckled as he retrieved the jagged piece of white paper taped to the refrigerator door and continued his quest for a cold one so he could plop down in front of the T.V. and crash.

The Skeeterman had overheard the telephone conversation his buddy had the day before and knew it had to be Elise. He also knew she had relatives in Gainesville and two plus two still equaled four so 'God bless them,' he thought, as he settled on the over-stuffed couch.

Skeets Kirby understood the powerful pull of a superheated man-woman thing, but after the fires of passion have cooled, what do you do with the smoldering ashes of commitment? Skeets didn't have a clue! Chuckling, the bemused man lifted the sweating long-neck to the dog shadow lying against the far wall. "Here's to you, you hardheaded son of a bitch. You and I have the same attitude about our women – we can only be in love for as long as our dicks are hard … I'll drink to that!"

At the sound of Skeets' raised voice, the placid JunkYard got up and ambled to the refrigerator, stopped a few inches from the door and nonchalantly sniffed as if trying to decide if its contents were suitable for canine consumption.

"Hey, big guy, ain't time to eat and I know you know the difference between dog pussy and fridge door so go on back and lie down or come watch T.V. with me." Amused by his levity, Skeets clicked his teeth in cadence to the shuffling gait of the humorless pit bulldog as he backtracked to his resting place and with an audible sigh eased his body down; his head resting on his forepaws, his steely eye bored into Kirby like a transparent laser beam.

Inwardly, Kirby hated the dog and felt the beast mirrored these feelings. He could not understand Samson's deep regard, almost spiritual, for the dog, though he knew full well the animal's capabilities and unshakeable loyalty to Sam. 'Oh well,' he thought, 'some things are better left to confusion and if the pit bulldog made his pal happy, then he was happy, too - he guessed.'

But then there was the itty-bitty problem of taking care of the recalcitrant beast, even minimal care. Samson could walk the pit bulldog off leash, even run with him and never raise a hair, but Skeets had to walk the dog on leash because he ignored anything the frustrated man told him. And, as man-fearless as the sociopathic Skeeterman was, he was afraid of this dog. Skeets' fear was that he and the goddam dog would get into it and he would have to kill him and that, he knew, would precipitate a deadly showdown between him and his best – maybe only – friend; Samson Hercules Duff was as formidable a man as JunkYard was a dog.

The ringing phone jerked Skeets' wandering thoughts back to prime time as he snatched the instrument to his ear and unconsciously muttered "Kirby."

"Hey, Skeets … this is Clax. Sam there?"

"Nope. I just got in and found a note ordering me to take care of the dog and ... sayonara. Guess he didn't bother to tell you he'd be gone a day or two, huh?"

Skeets relaxed tone eased the tension coursing through the agitated horseman and he felt his sweat-beaded brow begin to cool. Clax knew Sam was gone – what he didn't know was that Kirby would be there to take care of the Dog. He had figured that Sam would ask him to care for JY and everything would be okay, but now he had to figure a way to factor the formidable Skeeterman out of the equation - at least for a few hours.

"Hey, guy." Clax continued. "What are you doing this evening? Hows about a cold one down at the Stockman? I've been meaning to get to you about some things, but shit, you're either going or coming. How about I meet you there about eightish ..."

"Aw, hell, Claxton. I just settled in and popped a top not five minutes ago." Skeets' cord-like voice held just enough threads of hesitation to cause Clax's cooling brow to heat up again.

"Come on, Man. For old times sake. Besides, I got some info you need to hear ...' bout that little shit kid, Bennie, that Samson caught snooping in the stallion barn."

"What info? Who from?"

"Whoa, pardner. Too involved to go over the wires. Meet me. I've got to check out a few mares down at Reddick but I'll make the Stockman by eight – eight-thirty. See ya." With sufficient pause to belie hanging up on his slightly piqued friend, but not enough to allow a reply, the harried Irishman eased the phone into its cradle, took a deep breath and exhaled like a surfacing whale.

"No ..." The finality of the metallic click as the line went dead frustrated the Skeeterman as he mechanically cradled the silent instrument. What could that screwy Irishman know that would be of any possible interest to him? With a puzzled irritation, Skeets' mind flashed back to his last meeting with the F.B.I. contact. They had established that all the connected killings had been done with .22 caliber short rifle ammo. Also, smooth bore barrels – no rifling marks were found. 'Unheard of' was the FBI man's comment ... totally off the wall. Maybe there was a possible connection to the elusive Myrmon Academy. Skeets had been told there was reason to believe that a student from the Academy had been a houseguest of the Smithson children at the time of Rick Smithson's assassination; however no proof could be found save the word of distraught siblings and the maid. Not one thread of solid evidence could be produced to confirm, or deny, the presence of a guest. All FBI calls to Myrmon Academy came up blank. No one there had heard of Rick Smithson or his children. All of this information swooshed through Kirby's mind like a dirt devil in a sandy paddock. He hadn't had a chance to discuss this with Sam but would as soon as the dallying lothario returned to roost.

Meanwhile, he had to deal with the irrepressible Claxton O'Steen. For whatever reason, he knew he was bonded to meet him at the Stockman restaurant.

• • •

The small frame house was confining but comfortable as the three men sprawled around a bare, worn wooden table. The room served as a kitchen, dining area, game room and on many occasions a spare bedroom – all eighty square feet of it. It belonged to Samuel and it took about an hour by boat to get to Nichols Town once you reached the small basin where the creek emptied into the Gulf. Samuel's house was about a mile up the creek, navigable only by a shallow draft boat. Very isolated. To the north and east lay thick woods with myriad tidal creeks and naturally camouflaged blue holes. Very foreboding!

Samuel had made a trail from the basin to the house so that he could use a small vehicle when he had supplies to bring or the creek acted up and isolated him. Otherwise the small house was inaccessible unless you knew the way.

Facing the sandy backyard was a large opening framed by a moth-eaten, plastic screen panel allowing air and bug circulation, and providing a clear view of the sturdy cage confining the Havana pit bulldog. Empty beer cans festooned the table top like overripe fruit fallen on hard ground.

"Samuel, I want you to help Raul with this job. I don't want any screw-ups 'cause this will have to be done with some precision." Rod Osler paused as he sucked at the rapidly warming can of Budweiser, the cool beads of condensation trickling down his wrist totally unnoticed. Osler continued. "I've arranged transportation for you guys and when you get this son of a bitch, go right to Doctor Cordrerro's kennels and you can unload that mother and get back here A ... S.A.P." Again the Myrmon headmaster paused ... "no fuck-ups!"

"Ahh, Mr. Osler, mon ... "Samuel's interjection was cut off as the hard-wired Myrmon headmaster continued: "And I especially do not want anyone hurt. Not that I give a mouse fuck but we can't afford to suck in the big boys and the chances are slim to none that they'd give a popcorn fart about a missing dog." Getting up from the spindly chair, the white-haired conspirator stood in front of the porous screen panel and stared, hypnotically, at the quiet mass of dog flesh lying hulk-like in the shaded cage. "And Raul. Listen up. You listen to Clax O'Steen. That short fused mother is on a fairly long chain but its wrapped around his curly hairs, so he'll cooperate ... but if he tells you the time isn't right, you goddam better listen!"

"Hey, mon." Samuel interrupted and this time wouldn't be denied. Osler snapped his head around as the dapper Haitian went on. "What about the good Doctor Burgaard? Do we report to him, too, mon, or no?"

Osler thought he detected a touch of sarcasm in the high pitched, proper voice of the querulous Samuel but wanted to avoid confrontation if possible, so his reply was clipped, short and aimed right between the Blackman's dancing dark eyes.

"This is none of Professor Burgaard's business. He doesn't understand fighting dogs and I don't give a fish flop if he ever does." Osler sensed that the beer was starting to stir the conversation and dutifully lowered his rising voice to more normal tones.

"So, Samuel, man, just you don't worry about the good Doctor. I'll pay you and Raul for this, myself." Rod Osler turned his intimidating gaze on Raul as he turned away from the grinning Samuel. "Raul knows – we'll all make money from this. Mucho dinero."

The look of pleasurable anticipation on Raul Pena's swarthy face was real.

• • •

Elise Jones depressed the button on the answering machine and stared into space as the mellifluous voice of George Martinez sought her ears like mellow cigar smoke seeks nostrils. This was the third time this week and she knew she would have to answer as he was seriously courting her.

Her Aunt Cecile's cottage was on the north shore of Orange Lake just outside of Ocala and very secluded. Though George Martinez was only an hour's drive away, Elise knew it unlikely that he would visit unannounced. She also knew that his overgrown ego was not predictable and that even the thought of rejection could morph into a self control problem with him.

What to do? Her recovery from the Everglades ordeal had been uneventful save for her newfound affection for all things dog, especially the pit bulldog. Her piqued interest in the mysterious Sam Duff had resulted in a relationship that the pretty nurse had not been able to disguise – or control – and fleeing Centra County seemed to be the only sensible recourse; she needed time.

Aunt Cecile was a dedicated old maid, world-class equestrienne, independently wealthy via old money and opinionated on all subjects ... especially affairs of the heart. Elise had unlimited use of the cottage and had no trouble finding work as a private duty nurse, relegating her previous hectic hospital routines to the 'don't recall bin' of her memory. She saw no reason to change her situation and stirring the embers of previous relationship with George Martinez just didn't compute.

Her new work made her a moving target and precluded any prolonged or close association with the young, beelike males attracted by the nectar of her particular beauty. She could call in for her assignment, pick up the needed supplies and perform her duties with little, or no, face to face contact save with the patient and family members.

The most difficult part of her recovery was trying to rationalize and accept the brutal demise of the Cajun boy and Can Martin. Many times she awoke in the wee hours of the morning, confused and bathed in cold sweat, wondering for just the blink of an eye where she was. Return to sleep was then impossible. She vividly recalled the rescue when Skeets Kirby and his team arrived just hours after Joe Billie's death and how, despite her pleas, she was hustled into a swamp buggy and taken to a hospital in Miami without a word to Sam or any information on JY's condition. Elise had disliked the taciturn Skeets Kirby from day one and his abruptness during the rescue did little to change her mind. Whatever good he accomplished by this robotic competency was totally neutralized, in Elise's mind, by his unemotional mannerisms.

The slap of the back porch screen door shattered her reverie and she turned as Aunt Cecile strode through the small archway into the kitchen where Elise sat by the telephone.

"What's up, gal?" Cecile shot the question at her niece. "You got any calls this afternoon that can't wait?"

"No, why." The curious Elise replied.

"I've just bought a new hunter-jumper I want you to see and now's a good time … get your coat and come on."

With that, Aunt Cecile turned, marched back out the door and headed for her pick-up truck, the introspective niece in tow.

The chili pepper red Ford F-350 dual wheel pick-up eased down the dirt road leading from the cottage to the two-lane blacktop road just over a mile away. Aunt Cecile's irrepressible demeanor had given way to a more somber mood.

"What is it, Honey? I know something's wrong and I'd like to help if you let me." Cecile's words caught Elise by surprise as she truly thought her Aunt had bought into her tale of abduction, captivity and horror at the hands of Joe Billie Bloodtooth.

The rough ride along the dirt road made Elise uncomfortable and her Aunt's query irritated her. "No, Aunt Cecile, I'm okay … just need more time to put that Everglades stuff behind me. I'm fine … really."

A nervous quiet filled the pick-up's cab as it came up a little hill and turned sharply onto the hard-road, barely missing a half-grown armadillo. Elise believed that Cecile couldn't know of Sam's visit last week as she had been to a hunter-jumper puissance event in Tampa for three days, having been one of the sponsors. Elise didn't plan to hide her nascent relationship with her savior but really had not had time to fully comprehend it or its main character – one Samson Hercules Duff. He was unlike any other man the young nurse had ever been around or knew of. His behavior and certain abilities were incomprehensible to her. Her attraction to this man scared as much as it amazed and energized her. His unsolicited acknowledgment of her femaleness and mood swings was absolutely uncanny. He seemed to know her better than she knew herself. Elise knew that until or unless something changed in the relationship, she would, could, book no other man.

Her Aunt's quiet "Elise, darlin'," rippled the calm water of her thoughts. "I don't want to be pushy but you must know I check the phone messages at the cottage. I have heard the messages from George and they imply that you aren't answering him. What's going on, Sweetheart? I thought you loved him."

"I thought so, too, Aunt Cecile … but now, I just don't know." Elise's reply was only buying time as she knew Cecile Masters wasn't going to bury this juicy bone. Cecile's family had founded the Masters Paint Co. in Alachua County and grew it into the largest paint manufacturer in the State of Florida. They also owned the obligatory horse farm in the Ocala area and young Mistress Cecile, an only child, was raised on parental doting and blue-blooded horseflesh.

Cecile Masters was very attractive but could not decide on a suitable mate so she became an accomplished equestrienne, a playgirl, and lived her life as she wished. She was reasonable, though frivolous at times, but overall a very decent person.

Elise wondered if her Aunt did know of Samson's visit last week. With her, nothing was safe to assume.

"Honey, if you have questions about your feelings for George, you should definitely get answers before you get back on that horse." Cecile turned off the hard road onto a lane lined with crepe myrtle as far as she could see. The pensive niece was so distracted by her thoughts that she failed to notice the picturesque sign over the entranceway. Of course, Elise Jones had no reason to have the word 'VentureQuest' occupying space in her cerebral archives. "Do whatever you have to, Sweetie, just don't wait until you are backed into a corner." Cecile seemed to focus on the drive lane as she spoke. "If there is someone else in your life, tell George up front and avoid more heartache. Life happens ... at least write a letter and put him on notice."

Aunt Cecile's sage advice ended abruptly as she pulled up in front of a large, well kept barn. Elise groaned inwardly and closed her eyes. Her Aunt did know about Sam ... she must. Her surge of self-pity was abruptly cut short.

"Come on, young lady. I'm going to show you a horse that can jump over the moon." Cecile slammed the truck door and turned to face the barn entrance as she waited for her niece to exit the pick-up. Seeing movement in the barn, Cecile shouted. "Charlie, wait up. I've brought my niece to see that Warmblood-Percheron cross that thinks he is a grasshopper!" HighandMighty's personal groom turned toward the truck as he visibly acknowledged her presence.

• • •

Goar let out an audible sigh as he located the sweet spot and flopped his massive body down with a burp-like grunt in homage to his full belly. This was food day for the canine beast, an occasion that came three or four times a week and never at the same time, unless by coincidence. The mastiff never knew when he was to be fed, but over the many months of this Spartan routine the huge dog had picked up on certain signs that dictated food. He knew when Armando put on his white rubber boots and went for the blue wheelbarrow that food would soon follow. QB-3's Brazilian go-fer would dump the load of bloody meat and offal, open the gate and get the hell out of Dodge – Armando Montedinegre wanted no part of the massive beast at dinnertime.

"Hey, Armando … you seen Osler?" Armando stopped the wheelbarrow and turned into the glaring sun, shading his eyes to make out the beefy outline of Quentin Burgaard, III.

"No, Señor Doctor. He has not been seen by me since two days ago. Maybe Señor Raul has seen him. I do not know …"

Burgaard interrupted, his voice rising slightly. "No, Raul is off to Andros on some stupid dog business and Osler was supposed to be back from Ocala by now. If you run into him today, tell him to call me ASAP!"

"Yes, yes, Señor Doctor." Armando's reply tapered off as he saw the backside of his retreating boss-man.

Burgaard stepped it up a notch as he paced back to his lab, the midday sweat dripping from his face. He was agitated. Rod Osler had not checked in and he was worried. Ever the perfectionist, he needed – demanded – punctuality.

• • •

Skeets Kirby returned to Sam's loft around midnight - tired, bored and beer quiet. Losing Clax O'Steen had been tougher than losing your shadow on a sunny day. The cot in Sam's room was getting softer with each slogging step up the short stairway leading to the loft's door. He was some tired and he bet JY needed relief, too, but for a different reason. Thinking that he could never sneak up on the canny pit bulldog, and unwilling to do evidence based testing to prove it, Skeets started whistling and stiffened his footfall as he keyed the door. Briskly opening the door, Kirby greeted JY as he flipped the light-switch and headed for the couch while cautiously scanning the room for any sign of change. He saw none … nothing. Not even JunkYard!

• • •

Rod Osler sipped the warming beer as he listened to the end of Raul Pena's story of the kidnapping of the old Cuban, Dom Pedro. They were finishing lunch at a native eating-house in Nichols Town and were the only patrons in the creative little café.

"It was pretty easy, Señor Rod. Humberto just tell the old man that he would take him to where Dirty Dog was and he could see him and the old guy almost cry, Humberto said, and he jumped into the auto and was no more trouble for Sanchez, my cousin … but he did not want to get on the boat so maybe they ruffled him some, eh? Anyway, Señor Rod, he is safely with the dog and we will see them shortly."

Roderick Osler stood, drained his beer, fished a wad from his pocket and dropped 50 bucks on the brightly decorated oilskin covering the table. It had been a hectic week for him and he had to wrap it up quickly or risk the ire of one Quentin Burgaard, III – a grossly underrated unpleasantness! In fact, he was going to call Dr. Cube as soon as he finished this business with Dom Pedro and the Havana dog.

"Come on Raul, finish your brew and let's split. I can't sit here all day!" Osler's voice tailed off as he stared out the glassless, screen-less opening that passed for a window, fixing his stare on the green golf cart awaiting them.

The Havana dog hadn't eaten in a week and Rod Osler was at his wits end trying to entice him. Nothing he or his savvy cohorts came up with was working. It was Raul's cousin who suggested getting the old Cuban to tend the dog and get him to eat; also, Myrmon Academy needed a new recruit since Benito Lopes was no longer 98.6 degrees. Osler had heard, via Raul, via his cousin,

Humberto, who got it from Sanchez, about a potential Myrmon candidate roaming the area the Dirty Dog frequented. The wiry, animal-like urchin was thought to be around 12 to 13 years old with a large scar on his forearm and said to know one of the current Myrmon trainees – three-fingered Cruzo Dominguez.

Raul turned the golf cart around and headed inland as Osler questioned him. "Think both of them are there by now?"

"Sí, yes. Humberto said so and he is very proud. They will be there." Raul ran the silent vehicle as fast as it would go.

"Good. I want to meet this Dom Pedro, get the throwaway kid on the boat to Hoostra and help Umberto and Sanchez get things ready for another guest before I head out for Miami ... and a real dog ... I mean a REAL dog!"

• • •

Sam was stunned ... this had to be a macabre joke even as he realized that the man on the other end of the phone line was not capable of any such machination.

"You're sure he's not wandering around the stable checking out the horses ...?"

"No way, Samson. I've searched the grounds and there is absolutely no sign of him, nor has any of the help seen him. Clax didn't come back last night so I haven't talked to him but he was with me the entire evening." Skeets hesitated as he tried to prod his beer-fogged memory of that night.

"Skeets, shut the apartment up and don't let anyone in or near the entrance door. I'm on my way." Sam's tone booked no reply as Skeets Kirby listened to the phone disconnect buzz ... terminus!

Claxton O'Steen was seriously conflicted. It was nearing noon as he sat on the edge of the rumpled bed in the Ocala motel. His head throbbed from the prior evening excesses but he had detained Kirby long enough for Rod Osler's stupid plan to be carried out. How successfully he didn't know, but he did know that his story about the putative disappearance of Sam's pit bulldog had better be watertight! He had known Sam Duff since the third grade and they had been best friends. Clax had been very athletic at that age and it was a gimme that he and young Samson would be friends. As the early years passed, Clax's athletic prowess seemed to plateau while Sam's abilities caught a second wind as he developed the remarkable self-discipline that would define his life and further separate him from ordinary talent.

The remarkable young Duff learned from the old German, Carlos Otto, the most difficult lesson in life – that of delayed gratification. In doing this he learned the value of patience and that no matter how long anything took, its reward was just as sweet next week, next month or next year as it would seem to be in the next minute. Mastering this degree of self-discipline was the PhD of self-control and the hallmark of a true warrior. No one in Samson Duff's peer group had achieved that level of karma in their quest for self-discipline.

The warrior dog achieves that high plane of moral turpitude through his ignorance of any reward for doing what comes naturally and any recompense for heroic action was judged on its own merits and never thought of as payment or reward ... serendipity? No pit bulldog ever engaged in mortal combat with the idea of self-gratification - timely or delayed. What they do is what they do ... period!

Clax and Sam remained friends through their college days and after graduation both went into Law Enforcement. It didn't take long for Clax O'Steen to run aground in the shallow water of FBI Academy discipline ... seriously strict. Finally graduating, Clax decided that Law Enforcement as a career wasn't for him and resigned; he had to be doing something involving horseflesh, preferably live horseflesh; Clax went into the Thoroughbred horse business and Sam Duff stayed with Law Enforcement. As their careers unfolded and they experienced the trials and tribulations of life, their personal contact shriveled.

● ● ●

Chapter NINE

The Cessna seaplane was about 60 miles from Nichols Town on the Northern tip of Andros Island in the Bahamas chain of islands. Its southeast heading was into a slight headwind but the weather was on its best behavior and it was a beautiful day. Five thousand feet below, the becalmed Gulf of Mexico sparkled and glinted like a massive jewel, with only an occasional whitecap or surface breaching creature to enhance the sparkle.

The two men in the front seats were quiet. The pilot did not speak good English and Roderick Osler in the passenger seat was not in a talkative mood. The only baggage was a portable dog kennel filling the space behind the front seats. Intermittent radio static pierced the tomblike silence of the cockpit, the only competition for the appreciated drone of the journeyman engine. The sleek, jet-black muzzled face of JunkYard raised and slowly turned until his vision eye could see forward, allowing a partial view of the businesslike pilot. JY remembered Osler's scent as the man who visited Sam's apartment while Sam was gone. There was no spoor of the men who had taken him from Sam's loft apartment. He had never seen Raul and Samuel before they cleverly lured him into the portable dog kennel just outside the loft entrance door and expertly darted him with an immobilizing drug. Their voices were instantly categorized in JY's memory bank but their scents, the gold standard of canine identification, were chiseled into this memory storage, never to be forgotten ... not always a good thing.

Rod Osler was thinking about what a sweet deal they had with the Cuban government allowing the small aircraft of the Cordrerro kennel to fly freely in Cuban airspace. Don Cordrerro, a Castro acolyte, was embedded in the anti-Castro movement in Miami and also did contract work for Myrmidon. It was the good Dr. Cordrerro who was setting the stage for the Clayton assassination and to fly the Myrmidon killers to Miami. All undocumented. Getting the JunkYard dog to Andros Island was a huge coup for the Myrmon headmaster and he owed the erstwhile veterinarian. Turning to face his captive, Roderick Osler stared into the eye of the warrior dog and winced inwardly ... what a prize!

Silently, the cautious pit bulldog lowered his head and relaxed. He sensed no danger and the throaty hum of the engine was all but hypnotic. He slept.

● ● ●

Armando Montedinegre grouched to himself as he snapped 12 feet of nylon leash onto the head halter of Goar. As the huge mastiff matured, he decided that this bandy-legged Brazilian who fed him wasn't all bad and he didn't have to rip him up. He now tolerated Armando with some limitations, though Armando was not exactly sure of his limits and didn't see the need to test them. He knew that Burgaard, III, often let the impressive dog run off leash in the sand and surf of the private, isolated beach of Hoostra Island.

Hoostra Island was totally owned by QB-3 and was kept as isolated and secure as if a secret military base. The beautiful beaches were posted with officious looking signs warning putative visitors away, under guise of dangerous radiation research underwritten by an even more official sounding government backed agency with a very impressive seal – all very fictitious but, to date, unchallenged in any of its three languages. So, the beleaguered Armando pursued his uneasy chore with eyes on the beast and no thought of other human presence save the punctual security patrol.

Goar loved the beach, chasing and digging for the myriad beach crabs, attacking the breaking waves while trying to bite their frothy crests. This image, when seen from off shore, was totally natural and gave observers a warm feeling while reinforcing preconceived notions of being licked in the face while trying to hold a cuddly puppy, portending a lifetime of love.

Sixto Gul was just 15 years old and the ancient pirogue with the five horsepower outboard, hewn from a tree trunk from God knows where, was his prized and only possession. Hoostra Island was almost ten miles from the young man's resident isle and he pursued the Bahamian marine life with a passion; crabbing, fishing, diving or lobstering every waking hour. He knew no other way given his chanced outcome in the lottery called life. On the water he could exit and enter the quirky pirogue like a shadow and his prowess at what he did was such that his largesse was responsible for the well being of three families as well as his own. Sixto knew of Hoostra Island and its reputation for having one of the most beautiful reefs, off its Eastern shore, in the entire Bahamas. These reefs were seafood heaven to Sixto Gul, and all that was required was transportation and time for him to shop – free – at seafood central. Nearing his fifteenth birthday, he felt more confident in venturing further from his home-place and given the right weather knew that Hoostra Island was reachable.

Such was this day and Sixto had beached the crusty pirogue, and aided by mask and snorkel was busy collecting a share of the many lobster inhabiting the air clear water just off the beach. He had grounded the craft at the base of a no trespass sign and tied a line to it that connected to his keep sack soaking in the surf … Sixto Gul could not read.

On a low ridge above the eastern beach, Armando was having a hard time with Goar. The head halter was custom made with a noseband encircling the massive muzzle and terminating about six inches below his chin in a stainless steel ring, just smaller than the nose ring used by bull handlers. The twelve foot nylon leash with a breaking strength of 1200 pounds ended in a stainless steel snap used by horse trainers on the lead shanks designed for fractious Thoroughbreds. All in all, a formidable piece of equipment.

Goar was trying to pull loose but the cleverly designed head halter would cause his mouth to shut when he pulled backward. When released, he could open his mouth to its normal capacity, but let him pull and the tightening noseband clamped his jaws shut with unquestionable authority. Armando was trying to calm the agitated mastiff, looking only at the head-thrashing beast as he totally trusted the enforced solitude of Hoostra Island. Armando Montedinegre did not see Sixto Gul as he waded to the beach to put his lobsters in the keep sack. Goar-Mastiff saw Sixto Gul. Goar-Mastiff went nuts!

Armando realized he was losing the tug of war with the worked-up dog and wondered what had caused it. With each jerk the powerhouse beast moved the squat man two or three feet. Desperately, Armando ran towards the writhing mastiff and slipped the leash hand-loop over a blackened tree stump protruding from the volcanic ground like a misplaced appendage. Now firmly anchored, the tortured leash and snap felt the full weight of the bulky Goar and the snap popped like an over-tightened guitar string, freeing the 180 pound behemoth. Stunned, Armando's eyes followed the dog as he streaked for the beach with a low growl the only witness to his sighting of Sixto Gul.

Sixto saw the commotion on the low ridge as he was transferring two lobsters from his stringer to the keep sack. Unable to comprehend the scene, he knelt in the warm surf and shaded his eyes with his hand as he watched the man and dog unceremoniously part ways. 'What a large dog', he thought. 'He is bigger than the guy ... guess he'll have a hard time getting him back.' His thoughts tailed off as he realized the huge dog was running straight toward him like a runaway freight train. Innate self-preservation kicked in and the 115-pound boy headed for the deeper water – just as the hard-wired beast hit the surf. Three powerful surges and the slavering mastiff struck Sixto's back, biting at his head as the bewildered young man folded into the agitated surf. He neither heard nor saw the screaming Brazilian as he reached the beach, arms flailing helplessly as tears streamed down his sun-wrinkled face.

The clever head halter, absent any leash counter-pull did little to hamper Goar's biting ability and he dispatched young Sixto Gul with ever increasing efficiency. Spinning like a Tasmanian Devil, lipless snarl unmistakable as to intent, Goar-Mastiff warned the erstwhile benefactor away.

The mortified Brazilian sank to the wet sand and openly sobbed, unable to fully grasp the reality of what was happening. He dismissed any hope of help since the security patrol would know of his presence with the dog and not patrol. He also knew that until the agitated mastiff calmed down it would not tolerate interference and if Quentin Burgaard, III, found out, Armando Montedinegre was shark food ... period!

Slowly, Armando's rattled psyche settled and rational thoughts appeared in his brain like tiny points of light as he viewed the macabre seascape. The tide was incoming and the windless day drove no waves to move the mangled remains of Sixto Gul to the beach, so Goar left his gory prize to the deepening water and trotted up the beach, stopping at every protuberance to piss.

Armando, trance-like, wended his way to the nearest maintenance shed among the many that dotted the Isle. He knew the drill and he knew his life depended on the total erasure of this unfortunate screw-up. Securing a pick and shovel, he quickly identified a secluded area off the beach and feverishly dug a hole as deep as the recalcitrant ground would allow. Returning to the grisly scene, now almost pristine due to the water's cleansing powers, he emptied the youth's keep sack and retrieved the remains, butchering whatever was necessary to fit the sack. Unrecognizable pieces of flesh were ignored and left to the sea. The sack was buried and the topsoil carefully returned to its previous condition. The outboard motor and gas can were deep-sixed, the pirogue overturned and axed to float off like some scabby piece of driftwood. Armando Montidinegre, with Goar, had erased Sixto Gul ... he never existed.

• • •

Samson Duff's ingrained self-control was sorely tested as he paced the room of the loft at VentureQuest Farms. He had gone over the premises with the thoroughness of a vacuum cleaner. Skeets Kirby paced with him, listening more than talking as his friend vented his frustration.

"Skeets, I've been over every inch, all the way to the main gate. There are only two scents new to me and both are at the door and in the parking space in front of the barn. JY never went down those stairs. He was taken from the doorway in a carrier of some sort, put into a vehicle and driven off the farm. My guy is not on this farm." Sam's words resulted in a low whistle from Kirby as he marveled at his pal's faculty.

"I hate to ask, Sam, but dead or alive?" Skeets' voice lowered to a whisper as he vented the crucial question.

Sam never blinked. "No sign or scent that would even imply a fight, much less any fatal encounter. You checked the help ... no one saw any strange vehicle or anything unusual. I'm convinced he's alive because no one would want him dead and I don't think this is a shakedown or retaliatory action for any of my transgressions. Whoever took JunkYard wanted him and we're dealing with some very capable bad-asses."

"So," Skeets replied. "We just have to connect the dots and we get the picture?" The deductive question caused Sam to pause and his expression changed from a mask of consternation to one of determination. "Right on, old buddy. You have a point. All this weird shit that's been happening these past few months may have a common denominator and if put in perspective may find us my purloined pooch and clear the boards about what's going on at VentureQuest. Let's go sit our asses down, pour a couple fingers of Macallan and line up these dots." Sam headed for the liquor cabinet.

• • •

Quentin Burgaard, III, was more than a little worried. He had strong feelings of misfortune and his structured existence seemed to be a little disjointed ... small things, but troublesome, nonetheless.

The Cuban Connection had contracted a hit on one John Andrew Clayton, aka JAC Clayton, a Miami conservative and potential gubernatorial candidate married to the daughter of a rabid anti-Castroite; she also fanatically anti-Castro. This could be, by far, Myrmon Terminus' most auspicious contract assassination and if successful could guarantee continued Cuban largesse. No small thing to the good Dr. Cube.

He was also concerned about Goar. The rapidly maturing mastiff had taken on an aura of dominance that surprised even him – the man most responsible for it. Armando could barely deal with the dog-beast other than feed him, and Quentin was aware of a dramatic sea change in the bandy legged Brazilian's attitude toward himself. What had, or was, happening?

Burgaard, III, had noticed the change in Goar when he walked him. Subtle changes in the mastiff's responses to the Brillo-faced scientist now begged for interpretation. One such incidence occurred when Goar wanted to dig up a crab while on leash and QB-3 wanted to get back to the lab. It was all he could do to get the beast distracted enough to get him headed home. The low, throaty growl emanating from the disgruntled dog's throat lasted way too long for the scientist's comfort. QB-3 usually packed a gun. He made a mental note to never walk the Quixotic mastiff without one.

Dr. Burgaard's research was going good. The only real problem, as yet unsolved, was how to transmit the computer directives to the target recipient without a direct line, and how to insure the correct target received the message and not every one else with an implanted receiver. The attempts with several of his Myrmidon, in Florida and New York State, had been iffy, though successful. The latest attempt with the crazy Thoroughbred stallion and the one-eyed pit bulldog was better, but Rod Osler's computer control was unable to maintain its hold on the stallion.

His newest and most promising was a version of the emerging field of microchipping. Borrowing from this technology,

QB-3 developed a tissue neutral microscopic dart embedded with a singular number and terminating in an indestructible hair-like filament. Placed in the skin by a pneumatic dart gun, the receiver caused the recipient no discomfort and looked exactly like a hair. Once placed, the target person or animal was at the will of one Quentin Burgaard, III, and his computer – unless out of range.

• • •

Called the Sleeping Giant by the locals, Andros Island is the largest in the Bahamas Chain of Islands, and by most standards the most forbidding. Thick stands of pine and hardwood trees, palm trees of various types, bushy, shrub sized trees and thick and thorny vegetation of all description cover most of the Northern end. Within the confines of this miniature jungle are found various mangrove lined tidal creeks, cracks, blue holes and blowholes, all of which are cut from, covered by, or running through the unfriendly volcanic soil that is Andros Island. Roads are few and mostly unpaved. Most inhabitants reside along its unique, breathtakingly beautiful Eastern shore. An Andros Island harbor is merely a deep enough pock mark along its beach edge that some hardy souls managed to access via landside. A dock is ghost-like bare pilings extending out from shore resembling a seascape painted by a budding artist. Any planking is optional. While fresh water is in abundance, the Sleeping Giant is not user friendly.

The Cessna seaplane bobbed lazily in the rippling water off Nichols Town at the Northern tip of Andros Island. The three men in the wide beamed, flat-bottomed skiff lifted the dog kennel and its patch-eyed occupant from the plane and carefully placed it in the skiff. Raul Pena broke the silence. "Quite a dog, eh, Samuel. Too bad he only has one eye."

The grinning Samuel laughed. "Señor Raul, one eye, two eye … no eye. I do not think this is the guy you want to catch!" His laughter carried over the clear water like a skipping stone.

JY moved not an inch as he adjusted to the movement of the skiff. The only hint of recognition of Raul and Samuel was a squinting of his eye. The boat followed the beach south and east through a channel in the shallow flats, arriving an hour later at a tiny secluded beach, tying up next to a white Mako. Efficiently transferring their burden to a golf cart, the two men silently wove their way westward until they reached Samuel's little house.

Raul broke the silence. "Let's put this patch-eyed SOB in the cage next to the Havana dog. See what they think of each other." Chuckling as he finished talking, Raul stepped from the golf cart and headed for the house, Samuel a step behind. Inside were a local, hired by Samuel, Dom Pedro, sitting against the far wall and a small boy highlighted by a stark white straitjacket embracing him like a scared monkey. The boy was sullen and red-faced but showed no sign of abuse. Roderick Osler sat on a tired looking sofa across from the boy.

Dom Pedro and the local had been in animated conversation as only Cubans can. Samuel interrupted them. "Okay, mon, you may go ..." simultaneously handing him two fifties. "Thank you, mon, and always remember that Samuel is a man of his word." As he delivered this parting advice, he dramatically ran his extended index finger across his throat in a slashing motion. Rod Osler chuckled. The local fisherman well knew that the jovial Samuel was not referring to his promised payment for this job, but a repayment if ever deemed necessary ... retributive. He quickly evaporated in the thick brush surrounding the house.

"Ah, Señor Dom Pedro. I see that you are settling in quite nicely. I trust your wants have been seen to." Raul had come to like the quiet old Cuban in the few hours since their initial meeting. And, he felt no malice from the old man, as well, since he held none himself. He also knew that Dom Pedro was no fool and that his reunion with Dirty Dog was based on conditions that he had yet to discover. The old Cuban was merely playing the hand that had been dealt and knew that he soon would know what the game was ... bet on it!

Raul continued. "Señor, we have brought you another guest to keep company with the other dog. But, I think you had better not let them get too cozy ... may spoil our little party."

Osler interrupted. "See, Señor Dom. I told you this was all about dogs, not you. Again, I apologize for our crudeness in your transportation to our humble facilities but you must know that we wish you no harm. We ... I ... only want this magnificent dog to eat and settle down for a while. As I said, I will pay you well for your time. I just need your word that you won't try to leave without my permission. Again, Sir, I mean you no harm."

The old Cuban's eyes appeared as wrinkled slits in his weathered skin as he nodded slowly in recognition of Osler's mission statement. Of his reason for being on Andros Island and in this house, he did not doubt the Myrmon headmaster's words. Of his dispensation of largesse after his goals were achieved, the old Cuban's skepticism meter pegged out. Unless he and his Dirty Dog could find a way to escape, they would never see Havana again. Terminus!

"Okay, Raul, let's go. We're taking this kid to Hoostra and get on the right side of one Quentin Burgaard, III. Samuel, do what you have to but don't let anything happen to those mutts ... we're out'a here."

• • •

Chapter TEN

The smooth Macallan single malt was calming to Samson as he relaxed and thought about their situation. Skeets had filled him in on the FBI's problem and plan, so he knew that any effort to find JY would have to be in concert with their quest to stop the Cuban-American assassination in Miami.

"How about it, Samson, you think old Clax is connected? Your dots lining up in that direction?" Skeets' question caused Sam to sit up and swirl the amber liquid like a miner panning gold. Unable to avert his gaze from the mellow swirl, Sam, in a low monotone replied. "Don't know for sure, Skeets, but I can't help believing that there is a connection … way too much frigging coincidence for my taste. Clax's story just doesn't fit. For Christ's sake, Skeeter, this is a top-notch thoroughbred farm and breeding operation. Nothing … goes unnoticed. Everybody here, including the fucking chickens, are on high alert for anything unusual – so how does a boy just up and disappear along with seventy pounds of cantankerous dog meat and nobody's seen shit? Not adding up for me … you?"

"Nope. And I didn't tell you the kicker." Skeets proceeded to fill him in on Clax's comical attempt at getting Skeets to the local pub the night JY was taken. And how much bullshit the important information about Benito Lopes turned out to be.

"Hmmm ... sounds like my old high school buddy may have a dog in this hunt." Sam sipped the Scotch as he processed this tidbit from the Skeeterman. "Now that all this shit is hitting the fan, I suspect Clax and the unknown man who visited the loft was, maybe, not just sightseeing. How about it Skeets ... just a tad suspicious to you?"

Skeets Kirby's cynical reply: "Sure is. That curly haired SOB's been just a mite too friendly for my taste. Ass-kissing ... with you, too, I think."

"Right on." Came Sam's reply. "I think we need to have a little sit-down with Clax and see if we can't clear up some of this mess. Much as he loves this farm, especially that HighandMighty stud, we shouldn't have any trouble getting him to open up ... cheers." Sam aimed the crystal Scotch glass at his buddy and drained it.

●   ●   ●

Roderick Osler's hurried trip from Andros Island to Hoostra and the Myrmon Academy dock had been quick and quiet. The trussed boy, Julio, was sullen and mute: Raul seemed introspective: Rod Osler was rehearsing and refining his version of the past few days. Dr. Cube was no man's fool!

Arriving unannounced and probably unexpected, the anxious man was surprised to see Armando at the dock, as if he expected them. Sharpening the focus on the 7x50's, Osler saw the bandy-legged man pick up the dock phone and speak briefly into its receiver. Still looking, he commented to Raul. "Looks like the good doctor knows we're here ... Armando just took care of that little chore."

"Why you think Armando is here?" Raul seemed to be asking himself that question and did not appear to hear Osler's "Damn if I know." reply.

The Myrmon headmaster adroitly sidled up to the dock and Raul tossed the bowline to Armando. "Raul, take the kid to Smithcors ... get Armando to help. I need to get to the lab, ASAP. I'll call you later."

• • •

Unannounced, Sam and Skeets approached Clax O'Steen's office in the breeding barn at 8:00 PM, casually walking across the grassy entranceway as if on a sightseeing tour. They did not want O'Steen to raise his antennae as they both liked him and did not want to harm him. Both knew that Clax O'Steen would crumble when faced with dire, but very plausible, consequences to his horse farm, while personal threats would be viewed as a long awaited chance to justify his considerable machismo ... and could only end in his death. They knew he went to the barn office around 7 PM and stayed until whenever, depending on the season and number of outside mares being feted at VentureQuest.

As Sam approached the door, he froze and motioned for Skeets to stop. "Something's not right here, I smell it ..." As he spoke, he was trying the doorknob and finding it locked, crashed the door like an estrous driven bighorn ram ... all in the blink of an eye.

Clax O'Steen was sitting in his office chair slumped over his paper strewn desk, arms splayed in front as if to break a fall. Blood oozed from multiple blackish dots peppering the back of his neck and head. Clax O'Steen was dead. Terminus.

• • •

Quentin Burgaard, III, looked up as his Myrmon headmaster strode through the office door and glanced around for an empty chair. Goar rumbled like a gassy stomach as Osler moved several books to the floor and sat down.

"How's it going, Mr. Osler?" QB-3's voice was like an ice bath to the recalcitrant man. Burgaard never addressed Osler formally.

"Fine, Quentin. Got the new recruit and everything went off without a hitch ..."

".... I mean about those goddam bulldogs of yours ... that you're fucking everything up with." The reddened face belied the quiet monotone of Quentin Burgaard's voice.

"Now, Quentin, wait a minute. I haven't done anything but attend to business." Osler's voice lowered an octave and became stronger as he shifted into defensive overdrive. "Getting those dogs to Nichols Town didn't take any of my time. Plus, I had to pick up the Havana throw away anyway, and you know we need him ..."

"Yeah, Mr. Osler, we do and I'll remind you why. This latest petition from the Cuban connection calls for the erasure, with prejudice, not only of John Andrew Clayton but also his wife and father-in-law!" The scientist's florid countenance had noticeably flushed as he spat out the Cuban dictates. Burgaard now focused on the papers in his beefy hands, raising his voice slightly as he spoke. "Look Rod, the Castros' not only want Clayton iced but also his wife and her father. I tried to convince their camo generals that this was not a good idea. We've never done anything that would really piss off the authorities but if we do this, I guarantee we'll be numero uno on every law enforcement agency 'kill' list from D.C. to Hong Kong!" Pausing, the scientist looked up and saw the grimace on Rod Osler's face. "Rod, we can't not do this ... we're toast if we fuck up. And I need you to be one hundred percent committed and this doggy bullshit needs to be taken off the stove! Comprende?" Burgaard had lowered the papers and was purposefully maintaining eye contact as he continued. "And I have a few news items that may be of some interest to you." As he spoke, he leaned over the desk and handed a packet of papers to the mute headmaster. "You need to review this dossier and see just what kind of shit bucket you've decided to stir. I'd like you to go over these data ASAP and get back here so we can come up with a workable plan. I've alerted the necessary Myrmidon staff and we're in recent contact with our Miami people, so all I need is to sit down with you and fine tune the logistics - for either our apotheosis or our Armageddon, Roderick, old pal, so do your homework and lets get back tomorrow afternoon ... if you need time to go to Clax O'Steen's funeral, we can probably afford that. Just let me know."

At these last words, Quentin Burgaard stepped to the private door behind his desk and exited as the blood slowly drained from the headmaster's face.

Rod Osler was stunned but realized instantly that his friend was dead and that Quentin Burgaard, III, had ordered the assassination ... but why? Trying to process this dagger thrust of information caused the perplexed headmaster to delay his response, and as his brain settled he jumped to the door QB-3 had exited but found it locked. As he worried the doorknob, a throaty growl emanated from the far side of the room and Goar stood for the first time.

"Fuck, fuck, fuck!" Osler turned and left the room, not stopping until he was alone in his apartment, sweat dripping from his face and a glass with vodka over ice dancing in his shaky hand.

Three vodkas later, Rod Osler sat at the polished oak dining table with the packet contents spread over its glossy surface.

Three more vodkas and three hours later the intense headmaster knew everything any investigative reporter or nosey neighbor knew about one Samson Hercules Duff, a one-eyed pitbull called JunkYard, and a nebulous human force named Charles Kirby – Skeets, to his few friends; of Elise Jones, Dr. George Martinez and the one and only, Joe Billie Bloodtooth.

Osler's sweaty shirt was clinging to him and the vodka had mostly numbed his senses as he staggered to the sofa and stretched out. Thoughts swirled around his mind in bits and pieces, none of it making much sense. Cataclysm! He realized that it was no wonder the pit bulldog handled the crazed stallion like he did. Why did Clax not tell him about Sam Duff and this dog ... maybe he didn't know? Now, Sam Duff and Skeets Kirby – how to handle them? The swirling bits and pieces in his vodka fogged mind continue to settle out and did nothing to ease his apprehension. He wondered if his impetuous boss even realized the significance of the relationship between Duff and his dog and that Sam Duff would find his canine buddy or die trying. The enormity of his dognapping mischief struck the befuddled Myrmon headmaster like a well-aimed wrecking ball. Holding his sweaty head in his quivering hands, Rod Osler could only moan. "What the fuck am I going to do?" Sleepiness and stupor met in the middle and the contrite fighting dog fancier fell into a brain numbing drunken slumber.

● ● ●

Sam helped the Skeeterman move Clax's arms from the desktop without disturbing the papers. Both intuitively realized that this was the work of the same outfit that had killed Big Jaxe and Rick Smithcors ... but Claxton O'Steen? Why?

"Skeets, if we're to find my pooch and do this Bahamas thing for the Bureau, I think this is where we should start. Somehow I feel a connection, what with old Clax getting iced for no reason ... just too much intrigue for it to be only coincidental. What you think, Skeeterman?" Sam spoke as he carefully avoided the papers on the cluttered desktop.

"Right on, Samson. But let's be careful 'cause if we call the locals now, we're screwed. It's going to take a while to go through this mess ... we don't have a clue what we're looking for." Skeets had locked the door and was closing the window blinds as he answered. Methodically, he searched the dead man's clothing for personal effects. Taking a wallet-sized booklet from a shirt pocket, the Skeeterman carefully leafed through it.

Samson was gingerly sifting through the skewed papers. Due to the method of assassination, there were only a few areas of blood, mostly from wound seepage, leaving the papers virtually blood free. The focused man quickly found Clax's scratchpad and several unattached note-sized scraps with what looked to be Clax's scribbling, hurriedly written and unorganized. Skeets requisitioned empty envelopes and the two men filled them with any paper discerned to be non-horse related.

"Let's get the hell out of Dodge, Skeeterman." Sam's order caught the sardonic operative as he was dialing the phone on the desk.

"No way Jose! We need to call the locals and act like we just stumbled on this by accident ... we can't purge this scene of our prints, so, let's not tempt the devil. Hide the envelopes and let's get this little drama put to bed." As he spoke, Skeets opened the blinds and opened the damaged door. "Sam, take the papers to your loft and see if you can find Charlie. I'll wait for the gendarmes ... hurry back ... ta-ta."

• • •

The sun was well past the horizon on its daily trek to the heavens when Roderick Osler arose from the sofa. Wormy eyed and cotton-mouthed, the perplexed Myrmidon headmaster headed for the kitchen sink. The ringing phone was ignored as Osler splashed the cold water over his face and swished its wetness around his fried oral cavity. Still, the ringing persisted. Wiping his face, the harried man turned toward the phone as his three brains settled on being one and he realized the noise had a source.

"Hello? Who? Samuel? What the hell's wrong? Why you calling me?" Osler's head was throbbing like a hammer-hit thumb.

"Mon, I call you. You said to call you if anything go wrong. Mon, everything go wrong ..."

Osler cut the nervous man off. "What the fuck do you mean ... what could go wrong?" Rod's head seemed ready to explode.

"Hey, Mr. Osler, mon, the old Cuban and the two bulldogs ... gone, vamoosed!" Samuel's singsong voice grated in the hungover man's ears.

"What the fuck you mean? Spit it out you Haitian asshole!" Foggy mind or no, Osler recognized the dire implication of

Samuel's delayed response. "Samuel, I'm sorry. Didn't mean to say that. Drank too much last night and Dr. Burgaard has given me hell over the frigging dogs …"

"Okay, Mr. Rod, okay. Señor Dom and both dogs gone when I get back from the store early this morning. Gone about two hours and no sign of them when I get back. No one helped them. They went east and best I can tell, the two big guys were not leashed – were following the old Cuban." Samuel's voice was rising like steam from a boiling kettle.

"Slow down, Samuel. You know well as me that those two dogs – especially those two …" Osler's rising voice spit the words into the mouthpiece like poison darts. "Are not going to get along, uncontrolled, in a goddam football stadium, much less follow an old Cuban fart into the fucking wilds of Andros Island! Fuck, man, what are you trying to tell me?" Osler's sobering voice had risen to screech level as he paused for a breath. "If they got together and tore each other to shreds, maybe killed the old Cuban … just lay it on me! I'm a grown sum bitch. Don't feed me bullshit like that, asshole – just tell me what the fuck happened!" Roderick Osler was screaming at the phone receiver.

Samuel could taste the fear in the Myrmon headmaster's voice. He also could taste the acrid flavor of retribution if he didn't resolve this situation – ASAP! "No mon, no. It's true. They go off together. No way to track them in the bushes. They done gone, Señor Rod, they done gone!"

"Samuel, you find those dogs … whatever it takes. I can't get away now, so you have to find those pitbulls! You call me back in two days and you better have good news – period. Bye!" Roderick Osler slammed the receiver down.

The few minutes that Samuel held the phone after his boss' explosive hang-up seemed a lifetime. The savvy Haitian was no fool and his mind cranked out possible scenarios like a popcorn machine on steroids; none to his liking. The stern-faced Samuel had no fear of the Myrmon headmaster, considering him a wannabe machismo who lived Mittyesque in the world of dog-fighting, cockfighting and whatever shadowy intrigue he could align with. Samuel never had reason to believe that Rod Osler carried a handgun. Guns in the Bahamas were practically non-existent and even so, were only usable one time, after which the authorities would be all over the perpetrator. The only gun carriers were the professional assassins and they were eggshell wary. Dr. Bugaard, though, was definitely from a different litter … a truly dangerous man!

Samuel well knew that even though he was indentured to Rod Osler, it was the Myrmidon founder who had the final say – and that it could, indeed, be final … bang, bang, bang! For the perplexed Haitian, that fact alone took fleeing off the table. He would have to find the old Cuban and his pair of unlikely escorts – if they were still alive, and get them back to Roderick Osler in one piece.

Dom Pedro and his warrior dogs were a very unlikely trio and Samuel knew that word of their presence on North Andros would spread like spilled gasoline. He had many friends in Nichols Town, and Coakley Town at Fresh Creek further South, plus some located in isolated communities along the entire Eastern shoreline of the island. Two-three days, he should be able to hear of their whereabouts, information that could prove to be life insurance if passed on to the proper person. Samuel had a good idea of who that person may be.

Absentmindedly, the introspective Haitian placed the phone in its cradle and headed for the door.

• • •

The old Cuban winced as another thorn-studded branch whipped his face and ear. His tortuous passage with the pit bulls through the unfriendly terrain of Andros Island was beyond nerve wracking. Always orderly, the anxious man's brain began to relive the past few hours.

When the garrulous Samuel had mentioned that they needed supplies and that he was going for some early in the morning, the wizened old man knew it had to be then or never. He had studied the demeanor of the two dogs as they lay with only two wire panels between them. He had noticed that Sucio Perro covertly averted the gaze of the one-eyed dog lying just six feet from him … but no other reaction – not even a lip curl.

The one-eyed dog, still groggy, had sniffed the wire panel nearest the other dog and unsteadily raised his leg and pissed on it. Walking in a tight circle, he plopped down facing Dirty Dog. Again Dom Pedro noticed no sign of aggression …very strange?

What was going on? The old Cuban had no idea who the impressive one-eyed pitbull was, but intuitively recognized him as something special. The visible scars on his magnificent head and left shoulder did not come from dog fighting and his demeanor, in concert with that of Sucio Perro totally confused him. He suspected that the stoic one-eyed dog was some man's special pet and may be leash broke and trained. But even such a magnificent specimen of his breed would still be subject to its stringent genetic demands – the cardinal one being … not dog friendly!

As he stared at the unlikely pair, he began to pick out certain characteristics that seemed to defy the breed rationale concerning such an impromptu meeting between two males of this caliber. Though ten pounds heavier, the Havana dog's head and general conformation seemed to mimic that of the one-eyed dog. As he stared, Dom Pedro was surprised to see the bigger dog get up and walk to the cage panel where JY had urinated. JY seemed to pay no attention. Sniffing the wet wire, Sucio Perro raised his leg and squirted a few drops of urine, walked the few feet to the other side of the cage, partially lifted one hind leg and emptied his bladder on the ground. The old Cuban shook his head as his thoughts sought a rational explanation for this behavior. Nothing in his experience could explain this behavior and he could not remember any tales, often recounted by his old dog-fighting cronies, about anything remotely close to this. It just should not be happening.

JunkYard sized up Dom Pedro and found nothing that threatened him. The decaying scents of Rod Osler and Raul were no longer prime and the air currents brought him no hint of familiarity. His life experience had hammered home the value of patience and until threatened, he was content to wait. The strange dog seemed to pose no threat and for some reason he felt a strange comfort with the bigger pit bulldog.

Slowly becoming more animated, JY searched his cage for a way out. Finding none and eliciting no response from the dirty looking dog or the old man, the steadfast JunkYard lay down.

"One way to tell ..." Dom Pedro's thoughts gave way to voice as he prepared their food. He had fed the Havana dog many times and knew what he liked so he made the same mixture for the new dog. Placing the food bowl in the cage of the Havana dog, the old man took the other and quietly placed it in the cage with JY. As he closed the door he remarked to the sleek JunkYard. "I'm going to call you the Seeing Eye because I think you see more with your one eye than other dogs see with their two. I think you really see my friend, Sucio Perro ... I think ..." Losing his train of thought, Dom Pedro saw that the bigger dog had stopped eating when he put the food bowl in with Seeing Eye. "Hmmm ... what is wrong big dog? Do you taste something bad?" Glancing, he saw the new dog eat cautiously while Dirty Dog stood quietly.

Finished, the one-eyed dog went back to his resting place and lay down. The Havana dog slowly, cautiously, finished his food. The old Cuban scratched his head ...

His reverie vanished as another barbed wire branch cut his neck in this botanical version of Dante's Inferno. His reflex move to remove the offending vine from his neck caused him to jerk the short rope looped around the neck of the dog he called Seeing Eye. The dog stopped and stood quietly as the old man freed himself. "Ahh ... pretty man. You are smarter than I credit you for." The rope loop hung loosely around JY's thewy neck and Dom Pedro realized what a remarkable beast this one-eyed dog was. "Come, let us go on. We need to get to the east shoreline. I have a friend there." Dom Pedro spoke in a low, soothing monotone as he tried to psych himself for the daunting journey.

The old man's friend dated from the Castro revolution when he had spent considerable time on Andros Island, especially the North end. He only hoped his friend was still alive and of sound mind.

The Havana dog followed like a tethered pack mule since his Cuban savior was the only connection he had to his home ground, and the strange dog portended no threat to either of them … he knew.

• • •

Samson and Skeets were going through the miscellaneous papers and scraps scavenged from their dead friend's desk. So far, nothing of interest had emerged. They knew of the Myrmon Academy in the Bahamas that supposedly spawned the fragile-looking killer child, Benito. Skeets' FBI orders were to check the place out for whatever could be found.

"Hey Samson, look at this." Skeets was thumbing through the pocket–sized booklet taken from Clax's shirt pocket. Two days prior to JY's disappearance Clax had inked in the words, 'Cordrerro' and 'Miami'. "This name mean anything to you?"

"Nope. Strange name, if it is a name. Miami? Clax does horse business all over the goddam state … probably an owner trying to book a mare to old HighandMighty."

Three hours later both men were slumped in their chairs. "Damn, Skeets, nothing! You would think there would be at least one or two suspicious jottings, or letters, or something. I know O'Steen was methodical 'cause his horse records are impeccable. He writes everything down … wait a minute. Clax tried his best to get me to go to Miami for some dogfights. He begged me to take JY or let him take him. Now I remember …" Sam looked as if he had just chewed on a hot electrical cord.

"Okay, what now?" Skeets also seemed more animated as even the prospect of covert action stimulated his hard drive. I'm going to assume that 'Cordrerro' is a name and has some connection to Miami. I'm going back to O'Steen's office and look for any client from the Miami area or anyone named Cordrerro. If I draw a blank I'm heading to Miami. Got to get after that mutt of mine …

you?" Sam's stated plan narrowed his partner's choices and Skeets reply mirrored this. "Guess that leaves the Bahamas for me. Can't keep Bob Long and his disciples on hold forever. You head for Miami, or wherever, and I'll be off to sunny Nassau come morning's glorious light."

Both men headed for the liquor cabinet.

• • •

Quentin Bugaard, III, fidgeted as his fingertips danced over the computer keyboard. He was seriously put out by Rod Osler's activities over the past several weeks and hoped he could resolve this thorny issue since he needed Osler and the rest of his eclectic staff to function smoothly if he was to continue his work on computer enhancement to modify animal neuro-physiology and thereby alter their behavior - to his ends. He had made several improvements in the past months but he needed to step up to human subjects since dogs and horses were simply not cognitive and did not allow him to test his sophisticated improvements. He had devised an ingenious method by which to implant the hair-like microchip into the targeted subject: A pencil sized pneumatic 'gun' powered by a unique CO_2 reservoir that was accurate, reliable and silent as a shadow. The recipient merely felt a minor bug bite and no human eye could identify the hair-like filament.

QB-3 chuckled as he recounted his microchip implantation of Harrie Smithcors, Armando Montedinegre, and yes, by God, Roderick Osler! 'If only these computer programs would show more consistency.' He thought. 'Oh well … give me another year …'

His overloaded skull vented these thoughts like a burst air hose as a chagrined Roderick Osler sidled through the half-opened door.

• • •

Samson had been on the road for two hours when he passed through the toll booth signaling the West end of Alligator Alley, and now every mile – every inch – evoked memories of his torment in this watery wildness. He had departed the loft apartment at VentureQuest at daylight while Skeets was prepping for his Bahamas sortie. Urgency beat in his chest like a second heart. The thought of not finding JY in Miami, or at least a credible clue, just could not be entertained by the hard-wired Samson Duff.

As these thoughts swirled, the enigmatic man glanced to the east, trance-like, and did not see the 'Watch for Panthers' sign as he sped by. He grimaced as he clenched the steering wheel of the rental SUV in anticipation of the darkening cumulus clouds gathering over alligator alley. He had scoured the Miami-Dade County phone books and came up with several Cordrerros. One, however, seemed to stand out - Cordrerro Kennels. He had noted that there was no advertisement for this kennel in the adjoining Yellow Pages and this heightened his interest in this particular Cordrerro. Also, the map showed a location well to the West of Miami in an isolated area on the eastern edge of the Everglades. The storm driven rain struck the SUV like a giant hand slap. Samson leaned forward as he adjusted the wiper blades to top speed, automatically backing down from eighty mph to a more manageable fifty mph.

The memories of his fight with Joe Billie Bloodtooth, evoked by this drive across alligator alley, collided with his malignant consternation as to the whereabouts of his beloved JunkYard. The forced concentration dictated by the restricted visibility and his impotence in prioritizing his thoughts caused him to clench the steering wheel like it was Joe Billie's throat ... and he was sweating.

• • •

Skeets Kirby's voice was almost jovial as he relaxed on the sofa in the VentureQuest apartment. Sam had just left for Miami and the Skeeterman was on the phone with his old friend, Big

Johnny Dugan. "So, Big John, you and junior still fishing the Bahamas?"

"Some, Skeets." The mellow voice of the senior Dugan never seemed to vary. "Junior does most of it. I'm just too long in the tooth to cross the big water and, hell, I sure don't need to catch another fish ... why you asking?" Big Johnny's antennae always went up when Skeets Kirby called.

He had met Skeets and Samson many years ago when he was chartering tarpon fishing along the West Central Gulf coast and had become good friends, although it had been a while since Big Johnny had talked to either man. He was well aware of the Bloodtooth fiasco, having read the media accounts, plus having the Centra County game warden, Roscoe James, as his ex-wife's brother.

"How's Sam doing ... and that hardwired dog of his?" Dugan didn't allow for an answer. "What's up with the Bahamas?"

"Ever hear of Hoostra Isle ... and Sam and the mutt are fine, thank you." Skeets knew he didn't need any conversational foreplay with the straight-shooting Johnny Dugan and he didn't want to have to explain about the JY incident.

"Good to hear that ... there are plenty of little cays in that bunch of islands that I never heard of ...why?" Big Johnny's tone seemed just a tad curious.

"I need to go there, on the Q-T, and soon. I want you and Junior to take me ... how about it?" Kirby's voice carried a subdued sense of urgency that Dugan was not used to hearing – no small talk here. "I'll charter you guys for two weeks fishing in the Bahamas and around Cay Sal ... everything on the up and up. How 'bout it?" The Skeeterman's sense of urgency now morphed into a hint of pleading as he recited his request.

"Look, guy. Let me talk this over with Junior and Dave Rosen. Dave runs a dive charter out of West Palm Beach with a sister charter at Nichols Town and knows those islands better than the natives. I'll find out about this Hoostra Isle and if you behave, we might just give it a shot. I think Junior would enjoy a little ... let us say ... adventure? I'll get back to you tomorrow evening."

Skeets Kirby smiled as he recradled the phone. He dearly loved bullshit–free conversations!

• • •

The three unlikely vagabonds had been maintaining a slightly north of east direction as best old Dom Pedro could navigate. The wind, in spite of the frequent gusts, was generally steady from the southwest and mostly at the backs of the determined travelers. Twice the thorn-whipped Cuban had to skirt a blue hole, greatly adding to their misery in this arboreal nightmare. The sun had travelled over their heads more than three hours ago and the weary old man was almost happy when the one-eyed dog stopped and curiously sniffed the air. This caused Dom Pedro to mildly chastise him. "What is wrong, Sir Mister Seeing Eye? Do you smell something? I trust it is a good smell as you don't look worried and your quiet friend does not even seem to notice!" As he spoke he turned his gaze to the Havana dog who stood silently in the dense shadows. A sudden gust of wind carried a freshness that even the old Cuban noticed. JY's quiet demeanor changed and he began to search the evocative air currents as if trying to locate something. Sucio Perro moved closer to Dom Pedro and also began testing the crosswinds, though his eye was still quiet; JY's cold, one-eyed stare was now only a few degrees short of ice.

Something wafting along on those crosscurrents portended no good to the battle-scarred pit bulldog and neither Dom Pedro nor his tag-a-long Dirty Dog seemed aware of it.

"Come along, muchachos. Vamanos. We have to go far before we can stop. The ones who are after us will not rest and they know this leafy hell as we do not!" The wily Cuban knew they were headed in the right direction but had no idea how far it was to the coast. He needed to get to his destination by dark, if possible, as a night in the wilds of Andros Island was all but unthinkable.

He had noticed the change in attitude of Seeing Eye, and again mildly rebuked him. "Come along wise one … there are no dragons here for you to fight, only big, lazy lizards that climb trees. They would be no contest for you two big boys!" Turning to go, Dom Pedro tugged lightly on the rope since JY seemed to hesitate. "Come, come. We have to go and I do not wish to lose you. Someone special must be looking for you and I do not wish him to be disappointed … or you. Probably you are sniffing out the Chickcharnie, but he would not hurt one such as you. He only makes a man's head twist around, and only in dreams. Come, come!"

The reluctant JY moved toward the clucking man as he turned and headed south to skirt the blue hole. The determined Cuban did not notice the altered, now tentative, gait of the wary pit bulldog. The Havana dog, trailing a few yards behind, noticed: The one-eyed dog's tenseness and change of body language: The stiff tail with the hair risen along his back and the rhythmic anal contractions. The entire aura of the strange Seeing Eye was silently shouting danger and Dirty Dog's destiny demanded response, and as if on cue, his hair stood and his lip curl suddenly birthed sound, more rumble than growl, as the tension in the green hell thickened like simmering stew.

• • •

Samson turned at the Cordrerro Kennel entrance sign and drove to within a few hundred yards of the main building before he pulled off the road. He had chosen the early morning hour to visit and wanted to get a feel for the layout before he drove in. It was truly isolated, and to the west were the Everglades with no visible roadways; the ever-present drainage canal - dark, deep and foreboding - was the only other unobstructed pathway in the area. He noticed a small grass landing strip just south of the last kennel outbuilding and what seemed to be a small hangar at the far end of it. A few small, single engine planes were tethered to the ground, scattered around the off side of the hangar - all in all, a very inauspicious place.

He was reaching for his binoculars when he saw the white, four-wheel drive utility vehicle pull alongside and the white-shirted man get out. Large, black letters on each door proclaimed 'SECURITY' and the man was at the rental vehicle's door as its window was going down. His right hand was casually resting on the .45 caliber handgun hugging his hip.

"Good morning, sir. Having car trouble this beautiful morning?" The man spoke with an almost Irish lilt and his ruddy complexion seemed to confirm it.

"No sir. Car's okay and I'm fine. I'm visiting the kennel for the first time and I wanted to get some papers together before I got there. I didn't realize that I was doing anything wrong ... Sam spoke very deliberately as he tried to get a feel for the security guard and the strong dog smell emanating from the white vehicle.

"Nothing wrong sir. This property belongs to the kennel, once you turn off the road onto this driveway. We have to keep it clear, what with all the expensive dogs we kennel here. Can't take a chance on something happening." The man's voice had suddenly acquired an edge and Sam did not want to precipitate an altercation at this stage of his inquiry. An inner voice whispered 'cool it Samson!'

"Thanks for the info. I'll just be on my way. You think the office is open yet?" Sam's voice was almost mellow.

"Sure and there's someone there. Go right on up ...have a good day." With a military pivot, the pleasant guard turned toward his vehicle giving Samson a chance to view the two large, black heads showing through the rear window.

'Mmm. Rottweilers ... both males and they didn't make a peep.' Sam thought as his hope went up a few notches. 'This place is being watched like a prison, not some dog-boarding place. Got to check this out. Sure wouldn't want those two black boys on my ass, and I'd bet the mortgage they're both trained to kill.' Pulling back onto the blacktop, he headed for the kennel office.

Skeets glassed the deserted shoreline of Hoostra Island with the eye of a pirate. He was looking for anything to help him in his planned foray to find out just what was going on in that mysterious place – supposedly a den of baby-faced assassins. He had benefited from the FBI's satellite layout of the buildings but had no idea of the security logistics or alarm systems. Junior Dugan kept the gurgling engine at trolling speed and the calm water barely interfered with his use of the binoculars. He noted the myriad warning and 'keep-off' signs as well as the occasional Spartan looking outbuilding, standing in stark contrast to the low growing greenery.

Skeets well knew that some type of security patrol was in force, but he saw no sign of any moving object during the two-hour looksee. He really needed that info and turned to Dugan the younger. "Hey, Junior. What's the chance of anchoring offshore in the morning and having a little daylong picnic ... maybe with some bottom fishing thrown in. Maybe just off the beach closest to the main buildings and that dock. Maybe far enough they won't notice, but my 7x50's will still be adequate. Doable?" The Skeeterman thought that if he had at least 12 hours he could monitor their security patrol and work around it when the time came. How he wished his buddy were here. With his sense of smell, they could avoid almost any type of security ... but ...

"No problemo, Señor Skeets. We'll pack a lunch and see if the old man won't go with us. He loves bottoms ... even if you only get to fish them!" Just as Junior finished his reply, the port rod bent to the water and the tortured reel screamed as yards of line peeled off. Skeets grabbed for the rod but couldn't free it from the rod-holder, causing the younger Dugan to slam the throttles into neutral and put his 240 pound bulk into lifting the bent rod and handing it to the grinning Skeets Kirby. Fight on!

• • •

The three men swooped in from behind the harried travelers with no more sound than the swish of bending branches. Both dogs were aware of danger but had to await its arrival. Old Dom Pedro only guessed and was caught totally unaware. The leader, Samuel, quickly knocked the old Cuban to the ground while the other two turned their attention to the dogs. The second man was the hired hand that had stayed with the dogs at the house. The third man was a stranger. All three carried dog catch sticks and had rope nooses affixed to their belts. None carried a gun.

JY reacted instantly and pulled free of the old man's rope leash before Samuel could knock him down. Jumping sideways, the savvy pit bulldog caught the second man by the hands as he tried to noose his head and instantly had him on the ground squalling like a banshee. The third man had managed to get his rope noose over the Havana dog's neck and tripped over the dense underbrush as he did so. The unspeakable pain that shot through his body when Dirty Dog clamped onto his thigh caused him to pass out.

The hyped up Samuel could only react to this rapidly deteriorating situation and began beating JY with his catch stick. The hand-caught man's screams made the dog bite harder, a fact known to the Haitian as he begged the man to be quiet even as he moronically thrashed the one-eyed dog and caused him to bite even harder. "Shut up man, shut the hell up!"

JY endured the wild thrashing as a boar hog puts up with a fly. He was not into this battle. The men involved were nothing to him and had really done him no harm. He instinctively didn't like them but this was not his fight. He wanted to find Samson Duff and had no desire to be sidetracked. With no sound, the determined pit bulldog loosed his grip and vanished before the agitated Samuel knew that his thrashing was now being administered to the dog-freed man who vigorously renewed his squalling. JY had smelled the seabreeze for some time prior to the attack and instinctively headed east.

The confused Haitian squirreled over to the man caught by the Havana dog and tried to slip the catch stick over the dog's front leg but couldn't. The man was groaning and seemed to be trying to push the clamped-on pit bulldog off of his leg. Samuel looked around and saw the hand-caught man sitting in the bushes with both hands in his lap like a school kid who just had his knuckles rapped by the teacher's ruler. Tears streamed down his face. Suddenly, the thigh caught man let out a scream, causing Samuel to whirl around just as Sucio Perro disappeared in the thick underbrush.

Dom Pedro, shaken by the sudden assault but unhurt, had watched the gory scenario play out and marveled at the fact of both dogs giving up their holds to run off in the bush. He well knew that neither of the two had 'run off', but had decided that this was not their fight and left. The old man chuckled as he recalled the Seeing Eye's unworldly reaction to the attack and his effortless skill in grabbing the man's hands like a canine handcuff. He had never seen or imagined such an episode, but now that he had, any doubt about the Seeing Eye's pedigree or ability was removed. Rolling onto his knees, the wizened old Cuban reached for a limb to aid his effort to stand. As he rose up he caught a glint of color in the overwhelming green montage surrounding him and reached out to retrieve the red eye patch worn by the magnificent one-eyed pit bulldog.

'Ah yes, my dog-friend. I will keep this as a souvenir of our adventure and maybe to convince a special searcher that you are really alive. Good fortune to you and to your newfound friend, who, I am sure, is following you at this very moment. I …' His thoughts were disrupted as Samuel pulled him to his feet and stood glaring like a frustrated breeding bull. He did not notice the old man slip the red scrap into his pant pocket.

Samuel Reyes was seriously conflicted. He had truly believed that he could capture the pit bulls with the help of his friends' as they knew every inch of the island between the house and the eastern shore. They also knew dogs, or so they thought, but these dogs were human-like in their actions and reactions. Both compadres were now neutralized and it was only the luck of a few inches that the femoral artery had not been severed in the stricken man's leg. The Haitian remembered his last phone conversation with Rod Osler and he knew he had to make the one-eyed dog disappear or risk the wrath of his boss … and probably that of one Quentin Burgaard, III. A wrath, he knew, would not be repeated. The only way that could happen would be for the dog to be killed and never found. He knew of several assassins on the island and one or more could probably be persuaded to locate and shoot the dog on sight, for pittance, or just for the practice. In any event, that was the only feasible option left for him and he needed to act immediately. The old Cuban may be of some benefit, especially if he had to bargain with Dr. Burgaard, and the house was well stocked. Gathering his dog-bitten companions, Samuel started for the house.

• • •

Samson had to persist in his discussion with the kennel manager but he finally persuaded her to let him talk to Don Cordrerro, the owner, and a very difficult person to get to. It was only when he mentioned his interest in pit bulldogs and hinted at a putative interest in 'rolling' the young dogs that the single-minded kennel manager finally called in her boss.

Don Cordrerro was fortyish, slim and well dressed. Likeable … and wary!

Samson went through the obligatory banalities of introduction and after some interesting dog breed discussion, got to the nitty gritty of his visit.

"I'm interested in a place to board a few 'highly trained' dogs when I have business in South Florida. I am new to this area but I like it and I will need this service on a continuing basis. My good friend, Clax O'Steen, from Ocala, gave me your name and highly recommended your kennel." Samson studied every mannerism of the dapper Cordrerro as he presented his request.

"Interesting, Mr. Duff, but the name 'O'Steen' doesn't jump out at me. Perhaps he knows of my kennel through a friend, or possibly left a pet here and is basing his recommendation on that experience, as I can assure you we go to great lengths to ensure every dog's safety and comfort … whatever the owner wishes." Donald Cordrerro's eyes narrowed just slightly as he answered Samson's query. He betrayed no stilted or pretentious attitude and seemed quite benign in his dismissal of Claxton O'Steen. "Perhaps you would like to tour the kennel and see how we operate here at Cordrerro kennels. I am certain that we can meet your standards and that your puppies will be right at home. My manager will be glad to give you a tour and if you have any areas of concern, I will be happy to address them." Standing and extending his hand to Sam, Don Cordrerro directed his office manager, Paula Alverez, to give the prospective customer a guided tour. The handshake was firm and final.

"What's behind the main kennel?" Sam's question seemed to distract the dark-haired Paula Alvarez and she dismissed it with a headshake. "Is that an airstrip?"

"Why yes, Mr. Duff, it is. Dr. Cordrerro flies his own plane and some of our high-end customers use it on occasion, but it is really not an official part of the kennel and I cannot take you there ..."

"Samson interrupted her. "Doctor Cordrerro?"

"Oh, I didn't realize you were unaware of that. I thought that you knew about him. He has a Veterinary degree from an offshore veterinary school but never got his Florida state license. He is very respected in the veterinary community and in the 10 years I've been here, has never had a complaint filed against him." The soft look in her dark eyes spoke of more than respect from Paula Alverez.

Sam knew that he would have to have a closer look at the little airport. The kennel tour had given him nothing as to his beloved JunkYard. He had detected no spoor that could relate to JY. He had carefully checked out every cage and run he walked by and came up blank. He shuddered at the thought of not finding any trace of his beloved pit bulldog. The airport was last on his list and he had been warned. It would not be easy, but tonight he would find out if JY had passed this way.

• • •

Chapter ELEVEN

Harrie Smithcors was worried. He had just left a meeting with Dr. Burgaard and Donna Eye to finalize plans for the Miami operation. He had detected no change in either QB-3 or the haughty Donna Ileana and the modus operandi had not changed. What caused the worry was the fact of Roderick Osler's absence. He was a key player in all of the previous murder by Myrmidons and had, in fact, been the prime mover and shaker in the implementation of those sorties, and rarely did Dr. Burgaard involve himself in the mundane blow by blow as the assassinations played out. Harrie had always readied the Myrmex Terminus candidate most suitable and best prepared for the job at hand. Rod Osler had always provided the background and necessary target information that allowed the innocuous incursion of the Myrmidon and the uncanny extraction of the assassins once their mission was accomplished. Dr. Burgaard had made no mention of this or any specific plan other than to get the young killers ready to go. Donna Ileana could care less, he knew, and, he was well aware of the tempestuous Brazilian's lust for her boss.

Harrie Smithcors was not burdened by any high value social amenities such as conscience, moral character, or sympathy. His only societal mantra was self-preservation … his! As much as he would like to discuss the meeting with his cohort, he knew that the provocative redhead was way beyond his influence and whatever he did would have to be solo.

Harrie Smithcors hated Donna Eye!

• • •

JunkYard was almost to the beach before he became aware of his follower. The Havana dog had caught up with him more than a half mile from the beach but had lagged about a hundred yards behind until JY trotted out of the thickets and into the patchy grass paralleling the water.

The wind was in his face so he didn't sense the other dog until he turned back to the bushes to avoid his exposure on the beach. He wanted no human contact and if he were to be cornered, he did not want an ocean blocking half his escape route. Upon seeing the big Sucio Perro, JY stiffened his gait, gave him the eye and slowly approached. When he was within twenty feet, the Havana dog simply sat down on his chest and placed his massive head on his outstretched paws. JY recognized the big fellow but had completely ignored him during their captivity. Cautiously, JunkYard circled and came into Sucio Perro's scent. He had never smelled a scent like this but it provoked no animus on his part. Slowly sniffing the big dog's rear, JY sensed that this encounter was stirring long forgotten memories and that the passivity being displayed by the recumbent dog was somehow related to him. This dog posed no threat to the one-eyed dog. The half-raised hackles along the back of the Havana dog relaxed as he hopped up and followed the mahogany hued dog north, staying just inside the bushes.

Eula Mae had just finished the dishes from the luncheon regulars at her little house-restaurant back off the beach on the outskirts of Nichols Town. The doors and windows were open but sweat ran down her once shapely face like condensation down the side of a cold can of Budweiser. No breeze today. Her seven year old grandson, Che Che, played outside under the scraggly mango trees she had planted many years ago and half-assed cared for until she finally gave up and let nature take its course. The trees never seemed happy in their Bahamian home but did grow and provide delicious fruit, and shade of a sort, so little Che Che's play area revolved around these trees. Many local events also took advantage of the hard won shade, such as the cock fights held regular in Nichols Town by the local hard-cases – all her friends, save a few imported spectators, participants, and on occasion, suckers. Sometimes she served lunch to well dressed men, strangers to her, who nonetheless acted as if they knew her ... they always left a huge tip. Oh, well ...

Breaking away from the heat driven daydream, Eula Mae glanced towards the trees to see if she could see her grandson over the scrubby bushes interspersed among the weeds. Not spotting his head or any movement, she instinctively reached for the seasoned oak staff standing sentry-like behind the kitchen door. Eula Mae was never very far from her big stick. She never knew when a stray dog, or a pack of them, was going to pay her little house of smells a visit. A single stray mutt was not much of a threat ... more of a nuisance, but in a pack the dynamic changed and she had a real problem, especially when tiny Che Che was out playing and she was distracted by her cooking. Though the diligent woman bore the scars of her myriad encounters with the dog packs, they sported way more busted heads and teeth than she did bite marks. Eula Mae didn't swing the big stick just to get a hit - she swung for the fence!

"Che Che. Where you be at?" Her strong voice carried way beyond the mangos, and hearing no reply started up the path that led through the scruffy weeds and grass towards the beach. She had only gone a few hundred yards when the running grandchild burst into view and upon seeing his grandmother began shouting and waving his hands.

"Mimi ... Mimi go back! Go back!" The frightened boy skidded to a stop as his grandmother stood her ground and grabbed his hand.

"What is the matter with you, child? The Chickcharnie done come to get you? Stop your squirming and tell me what's wrong …"

"Dog fight Mimi. Big dog fight! Two big bad dogs killing all the little ones! Lets go home … let's go right now!" Che Che was trying to pull Eula Mae back along the path but the ample woman held fast and strained to see in the direction her grandson had come from.

"I got my stick and I want to see what big bad dogs you talking about. Theys no dogs that can kill off a whole dog pack. I think you funnin' me. I don't hear a thing. Let's go … if I have to pull you, I will." Eula Mae started to drag the slight boy and he quickly relented and started following her. It wasn't long before the querulous matron heard the low growls and high pitched whimpering of dog interaction gone sour.

Even the stolid Eula Mae Gittings wasn't quite ready for the scene that greeted her as she rounded the small clump of scrubby bushes. Directly in her line of sight was the most ferocious looking dog she had ever seen. Sucio Perro had a huge German shepherd by the throat and when he fixed his emotionless stare on the jittery woman she almost fainted. Twenty yards to her left was a magnificent dark red dog locked onto a smaller, more muscular bulldog type, and Eula Mae swore she only saw one eye on that beast. Several nondescript mutts were scattered about, one was barking and several were whimpering as if in pain.

"Run, boy! Get to the house! Go!" Eula Mae's frantic voice spurred the scrawny kid into a sand-kicking scramble for the sanctuary of the little house. Turning just enough to see him evaporate into the weeds, she tightened her grip on the stick and squared her body with the Havana dog holding the dead German shepherd. As she caught the direct stare of the dirty looking beast, she felt a little unsteady and a feeling of dread crept up her body like a fast rising tide. The enormity of seeing the biggest, meanest dog on Andros Island stuck in the jaws of God-knows–what hit her like a Joe Louis right cross. Lowering the raised oak staff, Eula Mae Gittings turned and headed for the house as fast as her spavined legs would allow. She wanted no part of whatever those beasts were and if they were dogs, she hoped they were just passing through.

The German shepherd belonged to the postmaster of Andros Island and he stayed in Nichols Town most of the year, allowing his dog to run loose. Being a rabid fisherman, the postmaster named the beast Bonefish, who quickly took over the stray dog population by killing its leader and slashing through all the pretenders until they decided enough was enough. Oversized and gifted with an aggressive temperament, it wasn't long before he had a run-in with Eula Mae over her delicious food. Even though the hassled woman got in a few licks with her staunch oak staff, the self-righteous beast destroyed her kitchen and left her with more than one scar to complement her collection memorializing previous stray dog encounters. When she complained to Bonefish's owner, the bemused postmaster chuckled as he replied. "Eula Mae, if that stupid dog does that again, I give you my express permission to kill him." And that was the end of that discussion. The put upon woman tried for several years to kill the devil-dog but soon learned that a bowl of food scraps out by the mango trees kept Mr. Bonefish placated enough that he no longer terrorized her kitchen.

Slowing to a shuffle, Eula Mae was hit with the enormity of what she had just witnessed. Those two dogs did not come from this island. Something was going on and she wanted to find out what. Relaxing as she neared the house, she smiled as she realized what a big favor the ferocious dogs had done for her ... wow! Treating Mr. Bonefish like a chew toy! Who would believe ...?

• • •

Samson parked as far down the little-used road skirting Cordrerro kennels as he could drive. He needed to get downwind of the little airstrip so he could approach into the wind and try to avoid the security guy and his two Rottweilers. He wanted to avoid any violence if he could, or at least be prepared for it. Two trained male

Rottweilers were not to be trifled with. He also firmly believed that if his JunkYard passed this way, this was the most likely place to pick up his scent and start on his trail. So far, nothing said or done in his interview with anyone at the kennel had the ring of truth, and Dr. Cordrerro was into a lot more than taking care of a few pampered poodles.

Grabbing his utility backpack and adjusting his belt to accommodate the 9mm Glock pistol and his Randall fighting knife, Sam slipped under the fence and into the shadows.

He was 50 yards from the hangar when he saw headlights coming through the light ground fog that had just settled in. The lights appeared bouncy causing the furtive man to believe they were attached to the 4WD vehicle of the security guard and he was off road. Where were the Rotties? No scent coming his way hinted of the beastly duo, but Samson knew that if they were in the vehicle he probably would not be able to smell them. Stopping with an unobstructed view of the office door at the front of the hangar, Sam pulled his compact binoculars from the pack and focused on the hangar. The vehicle stopped and the guard walked to the office door and went in. Cautiously, the curious man eased closer to the vehicle, being careful to keep the wind in his face. He had yet to scent the dogs but still couldn't be sure they were not in the 4WD. He thought that when the vehicle door was open, dog spoor would be released and he could confirm their presence. He much preferred them to be in the 4WD than running loose on the premises.

The security guard opened the office door after thirty minutes, reentered the vehicle and drove off in what appeared to be the same direction he came from. The querulous Samson still did not know where the two Rotties were. Easing through the dew wet grass brought him to the six foot high chain-link fence encircling the hangar except for the front. Risking the light, he carefully looked for any sign of an alarm wire or device. Finding none, he quietly snipped a wire and unwound it like an angular corkscrew, opening the fence enough to allow his breach.

Skirting the long side of the hangar, Sam eased along the wall hoping to find a quiet way inside. He wanted to approach the office from within instead of through the office door. He was very wary of this 'kennel' operation and didn't want to step into a trap. He realized he was dealing with a very sophisticated organization and they may have been as suspicious of him as he was of them ... give the devil his due. Or live to regret it.

The hangar wall and ground reeked with stale dog spoor but nothing suggested the presence of any canine. Nor did he scent any fresh human spoor. He couldn't be sure how many were in the office but nothing suggested more than one. He knew that an operation this small could be well managed by one person. He also had the idea that Dr. Cordrerro wasn't given to excesses. Reaching the back wall of the structure, Sam cautiously turned the corner and felt his way along. The moon had set about an hour ago and it was pitch dark at the back of the hangar as there were no lights, and the influence of the front lights did not carry over to the rear due to design.

Slowly feeling his way along the backside, Samson was surprised to see a square of dim light emitted from what looked to be a small opening at ground level. Dropping to his knees, he hurriedly reached the breach in the wall and found, to his amazement, a full sized doggie door. Stale dog and human odors wafted from the opening but nothing fresh. Gingerly, Sam pushed in on the rubberized swinging partition and sensed no threat. A furtive look around as his head pushed through the opening reaffirmed that no threat was in view. The hangar was all but empty and the dim light was mostly from a few lonely looking forty-watt bulbs dangling from the ceiling. At the far end was a soft glow delineating the hangar side office door and flanked by a window.

Two planes and a car were in the hangar. Both aircraft appeared to be the same: Cessna single engine with one equipped with pontoons. The other, exactly the same except equipped with standard landing wheels. The pontoon aircraft was closer to the front of the hangar, prompting Samson to check out the conventional version first. The door was unlocked and the anxious Samson quickly determined that this was just another Cessna. No suspicious smells emanated from the interior of the squeaky clean airplane. A glance toward the office confirmed the status quo as he silently closed the plane's door. The lump in his throat was growing along with a certain sadness he couldn't shake off. Samson Hercules Duff desperately needed a confirmation that his beloved JY had passed this way ... alive!

Parked next to the office door inside the hangar was a Chevy SUV, about 25 feet from the Cessna. Sam approached the Blazer cautiously and tried the driver-side door. It was unlocked and sensing no danger, slowly opened it and quickly depressed the dome light button, limiting its awakening to a blink.

He crinkled his nose at the montage of scents in the closed vehicle. The driver's side spoor was strange, most likely belonging to the man asleep in the office. Leaning toward the passenger side, Samson was taken aback by the strong spoor of the VentureQuest manager, Charlie Sharp. No mistake. The back seat held the smell of another stranger. The man who had visited Sam's loft with Clax O'Steen, uninvited, while he was gone and was there when the crazed stallion attacked him and JunkYard. Who was he? Sam's mind was running over with unanswered questions that didn't seem to have answers trailing behind.

Dog smell swirled as he climbed into the back seat and saw the silhouette of a wire dog kennel in the rear section. Leaning over the kennel, unmistakable spoor of JunkYard stuffed his nostrils. This was the vehicle used to take JY and these had to be the men responsible.

Risking a penlight, he searched the floor, seats, and kennel for signs of blood or hair or any odor suggesting injury or death. JY had definitely left the Chevy Blazer alive ... but where?

And what part did Charlie play in this?

Putting his Sherlock Holmes imitation on hold, the adrenalized Samson Duff slipped from the Blazer and moved as if a shadow to the passenger side of the pontoon Cessna.

The seaplane was only a few yards from the office door and Sam realized that he could not gain his doggie door exit very fast, so silence and caution became high priority. He ran his hand over the worn hilt of the Randall knife and grinned at the ease with which he grasped the weapon; the 9mm he knew ... was locked and loaded!

The door of the Cessna was more difficult to open and he pulled down on it as it slowly opened, hoping the downward force would stifle any squeaks or metal related noises. On the seat were objects usually found in the driver's seat of any frequently used vehicle. No doubt this was the go-to plane and the human odor suggested that only a few people had been in this aircraft ... and again recognized the scent of the man at VentureQuest, Clax's friend.

Sam did not want to chance any light and the back seat area was shadowed from the dimly reflected light so he ran his hand behind the seat and felt the edge of a metallic object that took up most of the area. Straining to get his head by the side of the seat, he was struck numb by the sudden realization that he smelled old spoor of his dog! No doubt! JY had been in this back area, and risking a hand dampened ray of light saw a wire dog kennel taking up most of the room behind the seats. This Cessna had taken his dog somewhere and the strange man had been along. Samson was determined to find out where. To this point, his pit bulldog was still alive ... Hope!

Sam didn't know the security routine and it was still several hours before daylight. The only thing he cared about was finding where his dog had been taken and he didn't plan a return visit. His antennae went up another notch as he headed for the office door. He sensed no threats as he inspected the door locking mechanism ... very simple with no visible alarm wire. Nothing indicated more than one person in the office and Sam had scented no fresh dog spoor. He had less than two hours before daylight and getting back to his vehicle would be a crapshoot, at best, as he had no looming landmark to guide him. Sam Duff needed to get it in gear. Jaime Jimenez had spent a restless night, falling into a deep sleep only after the moon had set. The security guard had brought him a message from Dr. Cordrerro to have the seaplane ready for tomorrow morning, but no details. This half-assed flying job was all the young, expatriated Panamanian could find but it was better than nothing. Being a banished communist resurgent was not a resume enhancement in America and the short-fused Latino lived off what-ifs. Nothing that went wrong in his life was his fault. He even questioned his decision to take the Florida job as opposed to the Alaska bush pilot position every time he broke a summer sweat or had to deal with a horde of the buzzard-big mosquitoes common to the Everglades. Noting it was 4:30 am, the sleepy pilot tucked the light blanket around his shoulders and was asleep in two minutes.

The production-line door exploded off its hinges as Samson Duff busted it down. Even as the sleepy Jaime Jimenez reacted, the black clad Duff was standing over him like a specter in a bad dream.

"What the hell … who the shit are you?" Jiminez's query came as he sat up on the side of the cot and reached for the night table.

"Don't do anything stupid, amigo. I shouldn't be here very long and with just a little cooperation you could be sleepy-pie before you realize this isn't a dream." Sam's voice gave no hint of his desperation. "I'm going to ask you a few questions and I want straight answers. Nothing personal or about you …"

"No speaka da English, Mr. Sandman." Jaime's hand had remained on the table and Sam noticed it easing toward the drawer side as he drove the Randall through the stunned man's hand and an inch deep in the solid tabletop.

"Okay Mr. Spanglish. Just speak into the top of the translator and it will convert everything you say into the King's English. Oh, are you right or left handed? We may have to re-adjust the translator if its 'hooked up' wrong. You know how sensitive these new-fangled gadgets are … and I'm not the Sandman. I'm the Arkansas toothpick fairy." As he chided the sulking pilot, he deftly opened the drawer and removed the .45 cal semi-automatic Taurus and stuffed it in his belt.

"Now that your tongue is on the same page, let's have a chat."

• • •

Quentin Burgaard, III had just got off the phone with Charlie Sharp at VentureQuest farms. Charlie had carried out the assassination of Clax O'Steen with the finesse to convince the authorities of a similarity between Clax's murder and that of Big Jaxe Larry and Rick Smithson. He had given the good Doctor valuable information about the two men staying at the farm and with the information gleaned from his other resources had put together a very unsettling scenario about a Charles Kirby and a Samson Duff – two very formidable foes. He knew it was only a matter of time before they came calling. He silently cursed his headmaster for getting mixed up in the stupid dognapping scheme that threatened to overshadow his entire operation. How could Rod Osler be so stupid? QB-3 knew the threat of Sam Duff as concerns finding his pit bulldog and he was doing everything he could to keep that action on Andros Island and away from Hoostra and Myrmidon Academy. He had tacitly suggested that Rod take time off to attend the funeral of his friend, O'Steen, hoping the headmaster would go to Andros and end up keeping Sam Duff from getting to Hoostra. He had notified all personnel at the Academy that new student enrollment was curtailed until further notice, and had personally briefed Harrie Smithcors and Donna Ileana Villareal on the threat posed by Kirby and Duff. The security patrols had been amped up and equipped with attack trained guard dogs.

As much as the embroiled scientist would like to postpone the Miami operation, he knew the Cuban connection would accept no excuses and even the brilliant Dr. Cube's goose was cookable.

He had hoped to gain control of the VentureQuest farm and thoroughbred operation once Big Jaxe and his heir were out of the picture but he had seriously misread the enigmatic Irishman, Claxton O'Steen. Burgaard knew his Myrmon Academy had an expiration date and his intuition was buzzing. Owning the horse farm would give him admittance to one of the most intriguing and lucrative sub-cultures in the world. With his research in electronic control of animals a proven success, his entry into this world would give him carte blanche to launder money on a scale not otherwise possible. This could expand his international reach way beyond the little island that was Cuba and give him the funds and time to continue his research. It was only a matter of time before he would be able to duplicate his control of animals with people. He knew the road he travelled with the Cuban government, while paved with gold, was very short. Eventually someone would have to pay for the senseless killings perpetrated by his Myrmidon and no way would it be the Cuban Government!

Charlie seemed eager to cooperate with him in his attempt to purchase VentureQuest farm. Shutting down the Academy would be no problem unless … Samson Duff and Charles Kirby were allowed to toss the proverbial monkey wrench into Quentin Burgaard, III's operation.

Unburdened by the constraints of morality or social grace, the scientist knew the only way he could succeed would be to eliminate Duff and Kirby, along with Duff's damned pit bulldog. It was two days since Armando had told him of the boat loitering off the west beach and he had ordered telephotos of the occupants. Charles Kirby was not difficult to identify and Burgaard didn't care who the others were since Sam Duff was not aboard. He knew he was probably somewhere in the Bahamas looking for his mutt and whether found or not, Myrmon Academy was in their sights. The other players were subject to his will by their own venality along with his rudimentary electronic control. One thing remained. Kill!

Samson Duff, Charles Kirby … and the dog!

Picking up the secured office phone and dialing as if in a trance, the becalmed scientist spoke in a subdued voice. "Armando, get Chino El-Taino. I need him in my office soon as you can …" QB-3 could almost feel the dread coursing through the squat body of the bandy-legged Brazilian as he slowly placed the phone back in its cradle.

Chino El-Taino was a name to be dreaded.

Chino El-Taino was a man to be feared.

• • •

"Mimi, deres two bad dogs eatin' all your food under the tree and just lay back in the bushes all day." Che Che's high-pitched voice broke the early morning quietness like a waterbug agitating the surface of a windless pond.

"What on earth are you talking about, child?" The generous cook still placed the leftovers under the mango tree even though she knew several of the strays to be dead or crippled. She had noticed that no stray had been to her door since the episode of Bonefish's untimely demise, but she paid little attention given her busy schedule ... she had wondered whatever became of those two fierce dogs.

"Mimi, dat one bad dog with only one eye, he lets me get close. He like me. Tink he let me give him food?" The little-boy innocence of his query caught his grandmother by surprise.

"Boy, you stay away from those dogs. They bad ... you not even half big as either one of them. Don't you let me catch you foolin' with those two!" Inwardly Eula Mae was getting used to the idea of having the bad dogs on her property. It ended any problem with stray dogs since no stray would come within a quarter mile of that mango tree. She also knew that those dogs were special and sooner or later someone would show up at her little restaurant asking about them. And, she didn't think it would be too long in coming. Feeding them kept them close and no one went there without Eula Mae Gittings' permission.

• • •

The air was crisp and dry on the south slope of the Sierra Maestra Mountains of southeast Cuba. The pole house had a large open porch and room underneath for a man to walk with unbowed head. The surrounding area showed signs of long-term habitation. The ground under the house and along the pathways was packed as hard as stone. Bunches of big green plantains littered one end of the porch. Barely visible and scattered around the big house were several smaller dwellings of similar design. A good-sized creek flowed sinuously down the mountainside within easy walking distance of the bigger house. The main part of the house seemed lightly built and fragile, but this structure had been in use for the past two hundred years. Several outbuildings were near the house and built on the same level.

A man wearing cut off pants and a sleeveless shirt skipped down the porch steps and headed for the first outbuilding. He wore hand-sewn pigskin moccasins and carried a hand-carved, highly decorated wood box and a piece of hand braided rawhide thong. His bare arms and calves looked overdeveloped and his step seemed not to quite touch the ground. At only six foot, the muscular man looked to be several inches shorter. A ten-inch blade Bowie knife hung innocently from a strong, colorful, pigskin belt. A thick bush of jet-black hair added to his height and highlighted his natural tanned skin. An impressive package!

Chino El-Taino opened the door to his kennel, turned, uttered a short, soft whistle and squatted on his haunches as a large, rangy looking bitch with a wolf-like head slunk to his shortened profile. Her tits were hanging like ripe fruit and her hollow flanks bore witness to the strain on her system from eight nursing pups. Her legs, while lanky, showed muscle and both rear legs sported dew-claws so long and developed they looked like extra toes. She carried medium length hair with ghostly spots visible throughout the mottled tan coat, depending on the angle of view. Once seen, not easily forgotten. An impressive bitch!

Chino and his relatives was the last bastion of the long extinct Taino Indians that frequented the Caribbean Islands for thousands of years before Columbus discovered Cuba in 1492 and the Spaniards conquered it a few years later. The indigenous peoples quickly succumbed to disease or were randomly killed so that within less than 100 years the Taino people were gone. The small group of Tainos living in the Sierra Maestra Mountains had been overlooked by mainstream civilization for hundreds of years and had resisted interracial marriage with few exceptions until the Cuban Revolution birthed by Fidel Castro made the Sierra Maestra Mountains so popular that a final dilution of Taino blood was inescapable. Chino's father was three-quarters Taino and his mother was half mulatto and half Taino. Both dead.

Chino's grandfather had started breeding the strange wolf-like dog to hunt the wild boar common to the mountains when the typical muscular bulldog type just did not satisfy him. He took the common yellow-brown, prick-eared yard dog found in homesteads throughout the islands and started using wolf-like dogs to breed his own version of a decent trail and catch dog in one package. His pups started showing promise after ten years and the rear dew-claws showed up about twenty years later along with a smattering of the ghost spots, especially in the bitches.

Common gossip had it that the old man used wolf at first and many generations later switched to an imported German shep-herd dog that had rear dewclaws.

Grandpa El-Taino out-crossed his bitches for most of his life and his line of dogs became locally famous. Local hunting lore had it that the only way a boar could escape the Taino dogs was to either disappear or sprout feathers and fly off the mountain. Chino's father carried on the breeding program, but in his fif-ty years he never out-crossed his bitches. His savvy line breeding and tough-love culling produced a rangy, wolf-like dog capable of trailing, baying up and if not stopped, killing any porker that ever rooted up a farmer's crop.

These dogs were sacred to Chino's family and the only way to get one was to be divinely favored by the senior El-Taino or steal one. There was no dollar value ever put on one. Every dog death was mourned and earned a religious burial in a special cemetery.

When Fidel Castro came out of the Sierra Maestra Mountains to start the revolution, he had visited most of the people in the area and knew the El-Taino family. He persuaded the elder to aid the cause and the aging hunter and his son supplied the rag-tag guerilla army with much needed fresh pork.

It was during this time young Chino discovered the full extent of his dogs' talents. Fidel came to his father and requested help finding a traitor that had betrayed him to the Batista regime and had escaped into the mountains. Castro had a good idea of the trail taken by the turncoat and Chino's father agreed to use his dogs in an attempt to track the man. Taking two of his best dogs, the elder El-Taino set out with his barely teenaged son and two of

Castro's guerillas. As the trail opened up to the dogs, they suddenly went into a different gear and pulled so vigorously that Chino could not hold on and one of them pulled loose. The other one went into such a rage that Chino's father had to let him go, leash and all. The El-Taino dogs were silent while trailing but the elder man knew the dogs were close to their prey. Urging his son and the two soldiers to hurry, he set out at a fast trot.

Coming to a large clearing on the mountain trail, Chino's father saw the wanted man trying to climb higher in a stubby tree. His feet and legs were tattered and blood ran freely down his body. One dog was jumping high enough to tear at his thighs while the other worried his kicking feet. He could not climb high enough to escape the leaping devil-dogs and was weakening fast. His rifle lay useless on the ground. Seeing the men, the besieged turncoat pleaded. "No mas … no mas …"

The elder El-Taino made a grab for the leashed dog but was quickly seized by one of the guerillas while the other deliberately shot the harried deserter in the shoulder causing him to fall. In minutes the screaming man was eviscerated and his throat torn out. The revolutionaries had their orders and returning a runaway traitor was not on the list.

Chino's father pulled his knife and lunged at the guerilla that shot the pleading man. The second soldier immediately felled the enraged man with his rifle butt and leveled the weapon at the stunned Chino. The enormity of the unexpected carnage was too much for the quiet mountain boy and he jumped into the thick underbrush and ran until he was exhausted.

Thinking his father dead, he hid in the dense mountainside until hunger forced him home. He found his father, head bandaged, acting as if nothing had happened. Nothing was ever mentioned about the incident and Chino's rare, mousey inquiry was always met with a shrug of the old man's shoulders and a sad, staring glance toward the sky. The dogs were in much more secure pens and from then on pig hunting became secondary to manhunting and the El-Taino dogs no longer pets. The young Chino became a part of this by default and soon became legend.

It was after his father passed that his mother told him about the coercive nature of their relationship with the Castros and how they had threatened to kill him, his family and all relatives and – the dogs.

Chino tied the nursing bitch to a post and duck-walked through the low-cut door into her spacious whelping box. Feeling around in the dim light he produced a dark-colored pup and carefully examined its rear feet. The pup was a male and its rear dewclaws were attached only by skin with no bony union to the rear leg. With quietness verging on reverence, the man slipped the small rawhide cord around the pup's neck and with practiced efficiency strangled him. He picked up each pup and found two, a dog and a bitch, with no rear dewclaws and strangled them. One pup with a funny shaped nose and mouth was also strangled. Each still-warm body was carefully placed in the ornate box along with the rawhide noose to await internment in the hallowed El-Taino dog cemetery.

Leaving with the box, Chino stooped, loosed the stoic mother-dog and wiped his tear-stained face with the top of his hand.

• • •

Rod Osler reached the little house on Andros Island just before dark and was in the cramped kitchen talking with Samuel. "So you couldn't find those mutts. I just can't believe those two pit bulldogs would ever get along together." Osler hesitated as he pulled on the can of cold beer.

"Oh, Señor Rod, these dogs more than get along together. They took out my men like they were trained. And they never touched the old man. I don't think he even had a lead on them … they ran free with him." The Haitian's words did little to salve the scorched ego of the Myrmon headmaster. He had returned to Andros under the guise of attending Clax O'Steen's funeral and though he suspected Dr. Burgaard knew where he was going, he really didn't care because Duff and the dog had to be eliminated and as long as the one-eyed pit bulldog was on the island, Sam Duff's appearance was guaranteed.

"Where do you think they went?" Osler asked the predictable question even as he knew Samuel's answer.

"To the east, Señor Rod, to the east; to the beach. They look for a way home. They know the way home. They will be found at the nearest point on the beach to their home. If we patrol the beach, we will find them." Samuel's voice went up a few octaves as he finished his folklorist prediction.

Rod Osler chuckled as he turned to the other chair in the kitchen and spoke to its occupant. "And you, old one. What do you think?"

Dom Pedro grinned as he answered the Myrmon headmaster. "You will not find Mr. Sucio Perro and the Seeing Eye unless they want to be found. The Seeing Eye belongs to someone … someone I think you may not want to meet." Still grinning, the old Cuban raised his bound hands and spoke directly to Rod Osler. "Mr. Osler. Sir: Please be so kind as to set me free. I can go nowhere and I have no desire to chance the bushes again. I have nothing to tell anyone and I only wish to be allowed to return to my home in Cuba."

An ominous look clouded the headmaster's features as he listened to the old man's plea. Truly, he meant nothing, and did not factor into this drama in any way but he knew the all-or-none philosophy of Dr. Quentin Burgaard. He brooked no loose ends … period! "Tell you what, Señor Dom Pedro. You tell me all you know about a Cuban named Chino El-Taino and if it seems to be true, I will see that you get back to Cuba in one piece and no one will be the wiser." Osler knew that El-Taino was on the way and that regardless of any guarantee, QB-3 would have the final say. He did want to find out more about the fabled Cuban mountain man and his feared ghost dogs.

Every one on the island seems to have heard of Chino El-Taino but no one knew anything of substance about the wraith-like mountain man, hunter and … assassin. Osler had never met the man but had been briefed on several manhunts that ended in assassinations and knew that he was the go-to guy when the Cuban connection had such a need. He also knew of the man's reputation for being dedicated to his dogs, wolf-like beasts that had a reputation as vaporous as their master.

"Ah ... Señor Osler. How will you know I tell the truth? Do you have some new meter with which you can test me? I feel that maybe you would not have the final say-so about my welfare and maybe the person who will does not share your opinion of my impending case of 'lockjaw.'" Smiling now, Dom Pedro again lifted his bound hands and chuckled as Samuel cut the rawhide straps.

"It will be with great pleasure that I tell you of this man you ask about. Your revelation of my only chance for salvation gives me a great hope." Relaxing, the old Cuban straightened his back and smiled at Rod Osler. "Mr. Osler, sir, would it be too much if I begged a cold beer from you?"

The Myrmon headmaster frowned as he reached into the cooler for another can of beer. He thought he detected a slight edge to the old man's query. "No problem Señor Dom, no problemo ... uno frio cuerveza."

Taking a long swig of the heady beverage, Dom Pedro turned and locked eyes with his 'savior.' "I knew Chino El-Taino's father very well and visited his home many times. We shared many common things such as our love of dogs and simple things like fishing and hunting. I was there when he first used his dogs for mantracking. Chino was only just coming to his teen years and I served Fidel Castro as a medical officer and I had access to medicines that I sometimes gave to the senior El-Taino to use ..."

"Not that kind of information old man. Tell me about his damn dogs and how he operates." Osler's interruption was pointed. "I've heard so much about his devil dogs - how they can't be seen or heard until it's too late ... all that bullshit."

"Not all bullshit, Señor Osler. El-Taino breeds these dogs like a religion. He took over when his father passed and he bred them not only for their hunting ability but also for their killing prowess. When the manhunting became a common call, he stopped pig hunting with friends and became very secretive about the dogs. He never sells one or gives one away." Dom Pedro took another sip of the beer.

"The dogs, old man. The dogs!" Samuel had been listening and didn't give a rat's ass about Chino El-Taino's early life. He had heard so much about the Cuban devil dogs that he sometimes thought them a fairy tale.

"The dogs are identical." Dom Pedro voice mellowed as he continued. "Chino wanted a certain kind of dog and he dedicated his life to develop it. If you see one El-Taino dog, you've seen every El-Taino dog. They are all male. Chino never hunts the bitches although he culls them severely. They all have brownish color with ghost spots throughout. No one can describe an El-Taino dog. They make no sound and they trail at a run. He never hunts them alone. There are always two and they are identical." The old Cuban finished the beer as his eyes took on a glaze.

"Don't go to sleep now". Osler's voice seemed to startle Dom Pedro and he sat the beer can down and continued.

"When they corner their prey, they do not bay or worry it. They simply kill it as quickly as they can … man or beast. An El Taino dog will weigh around 115 to 125 pounds and have no mercy in them."

Quietness enveloped the stuffy room as Rod Osler and Samuel Reyes digested the information from the old Cuban. Was it to be believed?

Rod Osler eyed the old man as he processed the story about the El-Taino dogs. Osler was a dyed-in-the-wool pit bulldog man. He believed that nothing could take the punishment meted out by a mature, battle tested pit bulldog. He well knew the killing ability of wolfs and hyenas and the like, but nothing had the bite power and the tenacity of the pit bulldog. He also knew that the wolf and other wild canids had survival mechanisms built into their psyche. Deep in the recesses of their brains was a 'quit-this-shit-get-outta-Dodge' button … frequently used. Not so pit bulldogs. They had only one accoutrement built into their psyche … don't quit and don't let go!

"What about Chino the man?" Osler was starting to worry about the arrival of the mythical Cuban mountain man, cum assassin. There was no way to read the intentions of Dr. Quentin Burgaard, III, and the Myrmon headmaster knew he was on shaky ground.

"Ah, Señor Osler. The man, Chino El-Taino, is a man of peace. He abhors guns and violence. He does not even own a gun and he only resorts to violence to protect his dogs – which he will to the death ... or his family. Whatever killing is done at his hand is done by two wolf-dogs and there is never a need for the coup de grace." Dom Pedro paused and stared at his feet as Roderick Osler mumbled something to Samuel and popped the top of another beer.

"What does he look like?' Osler's question seemed out of place given the drift of the previous dialogue.

"Que, Señor? What does he look like?" Dom Pedro's eyes registered vacant as he searched his memory for a vision of Chino El-Taino to describe to the Myrmon headmaster. "To his friends he looks like a movie star, a Tarzan. To his enemies he looks like Thanatos ... death!" Dom Pedro seemed to choke up as he described the Cuban mountain man. "One time a group of militia got drunk and decided to tame the Cuban devil dogs. They went to the El-Taino homestead and tried to talk Chino's wife into letting them play with the dogs. Of course she had to refuse, but they were drunk and went to the kennel. One bitch had just whelped and the militiamen forced their way into the whelping box and tried to play with the pups. Mama dog tore into them and they had to kill her. In the melee, three pups were stomped to death and the whelping box badly damaged." The old man paused as he wiped away the tears that had quietly leaked down his cheeks. "Chino found them at the local bar in the small mountain town just below his homestead. There were ten of them. Most were drunk but all were armed. Chino slipped into the bar and, almost casually, went man to man and slit their throats in a manner not to be believed. The proprietor said that he was so quiet and deliberate that the militiamen had no idea they were being slaughtered like the pigs they were. He killed them all! After, he hung the one in charge and quartered him like he does the wild boar. No force came to bear against him. You ask me what he looks like? I think you are better served by not knowing what Chino El-Taino looks like." The old man yawned and decided that he had talked enough about the Cuban assassin. He was tired and no longer feared for his life.

"Señor Rod. Chino El-Taino is my godson. I would like to go to bed now, thank you."

Roderick Osler exhaled a 'Goddam, son of a bitch,' as the impact of Dom Pedro's last words sank into his muddled brain … 'Goddam …'

●　●　●

Chapter TWELVE

Charlie was seriously conflicted. He had just hung up from talking to Dr. Quentin Burgaard, lll, and it seemed like the plans they had agreed on were changing by the minute. The good Doctor now wanted Charlie to deceive Elise Jones and deliver her to the Cordrerro kennel in Miami for a surprise vacation on Hoostra Island at Myrmon Academy. Charlie Sharp's involvement with Quentin Burgaard, lll, was going from just getting his feet wet to up to his neck in shit. From looking the other way, to abetting a dognapping, to murder, was a stretch the ambitious groom could not get his confused mind around.

Charles Sharp had been around horses all his life, starting as an exercise boy and horse breaker. His motto was that he would ride what you couldn't walk. And he could. While exposed to the sub-culture of dog and cock fighting common to all racehorse opera-tions, Charlie Sharp never got interested due to his lack of the two M's – machismo and money. True, he attended many such events simply to have something to do and someplace to go. When he took the job at VentureQuest Farm, he had known Clax O'Steen many years and was well aware of his obsession for both, especially dog fighting. His position at VentureQuest put him in the middle of the dog fighting culture and he went with Clax to many such events.

That was how he came to meet Dr. Cordrerro and the group of Cuban ex-patriots the good doctor had infiltrated. He was dumbfounded when he realized the extent of this sub-culture. Millions of dollars floated around at these events. He heard of two Humane Society investigators who suddenly disappeared – into the Everglades, it was said. Charles Sharp realized that if he was to achieve longevity at VentureQuest Farms, he had better develop an acute case of lockjaw.

And along came Dr. Quentin Burgaard, lll. What had been merely interesting and tingly suddenly became malignant and ominous. Charlie Sharp had been called up from the minors. He was now in the big leagues.

It was nothing to allow, and cover for, the spidery kid prowling the stables and the guy, Osler, with his black box magic fooling with HighAndMighty. Burgaard had promised him a management position at VentureQuest with the possibility of part ownership. Then, out of the blue, the good Doctor informed Charlie that everything was going down because Clax O'Steen was not cooperating and if something wasn't done pronto, the whole deal would collapse. Murdering the recalcitrant Irishman seemed like the thing to do – at the time. Now it seemed like the act of a crazy man.

The negotiations with the Jaxe estate for the purchase of the farm by the group covertly owned by Dr. Burgaard was going smoothly as Big Jaxe's widow was fond of Charlie Sharp and not too fond of lawyers, even her own. Charlie's thoughts were doing cartwheels in his grossly undereducated brain. 'What if Burgaard decides he is uncooperative?' Charlie had no proof of O'Steen's reluctance, only Dr. Burgaard's word, but if Charlie Sharp didn't comply with the latest request, there would be no doubt of his reluctance and he knew he would be toast.

He also knew that kidnapping was a federal offense, and as he dialed the phone a plan was slowly drifting through the fog of his mind. "Hello Cecile. Got some info for your niece about that horse she was interested in …"

· · ·

Skeets studied the darkness of the beach off the west side of Hoostra Island as Dugan's boat, Podzilla, rode the soft swells like a resting pelican. He had talked to Samson yesterday and still couldn't make the pieces fit. Charlie's involvement in Clax's assassination still didn't fit. Neither did the Cordrerro kennel or the taking of JunkYard. Skeets Kirby had little faith in coincidence and less in the fates. Someone or something was driving this drama and he felt that the answer was to be found on this island. His main concern was stopping the Miami assassinations and cutting off the head of whatever monster was responsible. All the rest was just window dressing and while he regretted the loss of JY, his focus was strictly Myrmon Academy.

"Be careful, Skeets. The extra security has dogs and don't seem to be on a standard schedule." Big Johnny Dugan's voice was just above a whisper as the reflective Kirby quietly slipped overboard in the knee-deep water. It was 2 am.

"What … oh. I'll be careful. I sure don't need to have dogs after me on a night like this." Skeets' mind was already halfway to the Myrmon buildings. His attempt to convince his partner to join him for this foray went nowhere once Elise's unexplained absence was put on the table. Skeets had waited until the moon was dark to call and when Sam put him on hold, knew he would have to go it alone.

"Don't forget to use the flare when you get back to the beach. That's the only way we'll be able to find you. If you have to run the beach after flaring, try to run clockwise so we can get to you without using the spotlight. Junior left the bulletproof boat covers at home. Just like a kid …" BJ's whisper trailed off as Skeets vanished in the grimy murk of the moonless night.

"Okay, Daddy. I'll remember." The voice floated out of no-where as Skeets Kirby's regimented mind went over the layout of the island and the main Myrmon building, just before he felt the water-packed beach sand's silky crunch under his bare feet. He also realized that Sam's impromptu visit to Miami had blown the lid off any stealth advantage they may have had. The word had spread and Skeets knew that he and Samson were marked and knew very little of their adversaries. This little night call could turn out a bigger surprise to the Skeeterman than to the bad guys. He chuckled as he carefully picked his way north toward the dim light of his target building. Thank God for the manicured grounds and flat terrain that allowed him sky lighting privileges even on this moonless night.

Skeets figured the Myrmon facility to be vulnerable due to its isolation and acceptance of outside students. Whatever, their security was probably in-house personnel with a smattering of local help – amateurish and easily compromised. Samson had given him a few names he was sure were not the honchos, but if he could access meaningful files he could identify positions and hierarchy and disrupt this nest of killers. The FBI had a special team waiting for his high sign but the presence of paying scions of wealthy Americans and Europeans made faulty intelligence unthinkable. The FBI guys were not an extraction team; they were seek and destroy. Their goal was to functionally disable all structures while avoiding any contact with personnel. Use force only if absolutely unavoidable. Skeets had to reconnoiter the school buildings, relay the intelligence to the team and get back to the beach alive. The island security was a horse of a different color. These were stone-cold pros and getting back to the beach may be the most difficult part of the entire operation.

'Oh how I miss my birddog buddy," He thought as he neared the first structure. 'He wouldn't miss a beat with these thugs and their guard dogs riding patrol around the island. Just stick his sniff-er in the breeze and play dodge-bad-critters all night. Wherefore art thou, my faithful friend' ... Skeets' brain fart was interrupted by a collision with a barely visible golf cart. Stifling his groan, he quickly dropped to all fours and felt his way to the back of the cart.

Thirty feet away was a doorway lit by a low intensity yellow bug light. It appeared to be the end of a hallway in what should be a dormitory, housing students and their faculty counselors. Several hundred yards east was the business office and Skeets' target. It was showing the same dull, yellow glow of a bug light. Both buildings showed a few dimly lighted windows but Skeets could detect no other lights or movement.

The Skeeterman knew the Academy was in recess and held no outside students on the premises, only full-time resident students and counselors. He had not been able to discover the connection between the full-time students and the seasonal influx of wealthy youngsters and the implication that the full-timers were actually killers-in-training just wouldn't compute in his mind.

Sideling to the door, Skeets tried the knob and found it unlocked. 'Something's not right,' he thought as he slowly opened it to allow a view of the darkened hallway. Most heavy outside doors had automatic locks so this door may be purposely unlocked. A thin beam of light outlined the bottom of the second door on the right of the hallway. Skeets retreated and quietly closed the door, approaching the room from the outside. The pulled shades of the window glowed an eerie golden hue and shadowy movement was evident on one side of the room. Adroitly pulling an enhanced hearing device from his belt pack, the Skeeterman placed the suction cupped instrument against the windowpane and expertly situated the earpieces.

"Ahh … ahh. Señor Little Three Fingers, you are quite the hombre." The feminine voice was barely audible but the intonation was crystal clear … Sex 101. The intent Skeets could only pick up snatches of the intimate conversation but interspersed with the earthy utterances was enough for him to do the two plus two equals four drill.

"Ahh, Señorita Donna, I must return to the main office within the hour or the good Dr. Cube will turn his computer onto me or feed me to Goar-dog." This last sentence was louder and signaled the end of the tryst.

Cruzo Dominguez was now 15 years old and could claim title to being the top Myrmidon in the Myrmex Terminus program. He was handpicked by Quentin Burgaard, lll to handle the Miami job and was heartless as a heart transplant donor. This would be his last round of security duty before the Cessna floatplane picked him up for transport to Miami. His dalliances with the volatile Donna Eye had become routine as his metamorphosis into a roué proceeded ahead of schedule. He had no pie-in-the-sky attitude about his future at Myrmon Academy, and poor Benito's fate was not on his radar should this last job be successful. No academy holiday and picnic for him. Cruzo Dominguez had other plans, whistling as he exited the building in the vaporous darkness and climbed into the green golf cart.

"Hi, young fellow. Mind if I hitch a ride." Cruzo Dominguez knew better than to turn his head as the razor edge of Skeets Kirby's knife licked the skin of his neck. Not speaking, he looked straight ahead and acted as if he was alone. "Hmmm ... what have we got here? A real live hero! Cat got your tongue?" As Skeets spoke, he moved the knifepoint to the angle of the boy's jaw and applied a little pressure.

"No, Señor Charles Kirby, unless you consider Señorita Donna Ileana a cat, in which case I have no tongue, but she is really just a little pussy so I have my tongue. And you Mr. Kirby, you have a tongue?"

"Ahh .... you know who I am! Stand up just a sec ..." As his surprised brain sifted the unexpected information, his business-like hands frisked the taciturn man-boy. "You're clean. Sit down and let's review the rules." Pricking the skin of Cruzo's neck as he slipped around to the passenger seat, Kirby continued. "What's your name? Give me straight answers or I may turn my part of this little chat over to my little buddy ... he conducts pretty sharp interviews, at times."

Cruzo interrupted. "Ahh, Señor, I have lived my whole life with a knife to my throat. A bigger knife than you prick me with now. My name is Cruzo ... Cruzo Dominguez and I am a student here."

The Skeeterman's mind was doing flip-flops as he tried to grasp the full impact of Cruzo Dominguez's pronouncement and stoicism. This kid had no fear of him or knife, didn't display fear-posture and Kirby's fine tuned sociopathic radar did not register any artifacts. This man-child was the real deal and, Skeets sensed, a very dangerous adversary ... regardless of his youth.

Sheathing the knife, Skeets sat back in the seat as he whispered. "I want to go to the main office and check out a few things. Want to be sure their bookkeeping is up to proper standards and such. Take me and act dumb. I'll just look and leave ... won't touch a feather on your little rooster head. Just remember that dumb and stupid are not the same. Avoid security, get me into the office, then to the beach, and I'm just a funny dream. Play stupid and I'm a nightmare ... know what I mean?"

Cruzo aimed the silent vehicle at the main building as he replied. "Sí, yes. I have no reason to stop you and no one has told me to kill you. I will do as you ask ... boss."

Kirby was quiet as the cart eased across the pitch-dark area toward the dimly lighted main building. This man-child was cold and very dangerous. Whoever was calling the shots sure knew what he was doing and the rumors about the calloused child-killers must be true. He wondered how much was known about him and Samson and how widespread it was. In any event, the advantage of anonymity was history and Skeets knew that Cruzo Dominguez would kill him in a heartbeat, given the chance ... but, Skeets was still Skeets, and this little job was going to get done. Regardless.

• • •

Quentin Burgaard, III, had a restless night. He knew this Miami job would wind up his little ball of yarn as regards Hoostra Island and his Myrmon Academy. He thought that if his VentureQuest deal went through, he could disappear, reinvent himself as a veteran horseman and live happily ever after. But, there were a few speedbumps and he was sorely pressed to keep them from becoming detours. Even though he had covered all contingencies, he still worried about the competency of his handpicked cohorts. His guarded faith in the Myrmon headmaster, Roderick Osler, had been rendered moot by Osler's obsession about dogfights and Samuel's recent out-of-the-blue conversation about his relationship with the headmaster and other bullshit minutiae, so out of context that Burgaard thought the Haitian back on drugs. He had acted concerned, but pleased, that Samuel had came to him and assured him that every thing was fine with Rod Osler and he should continue to work with him as before. Inwardly, the scientist was fuming. The spidery line in the floor of his Myrmidon operation had grown into a widening crack, thanks to the stupid kidnapping of a one-eyed pit bulldog!

Eastern light was barely visible as the restless Quentin Bugaard, III, walked to the gate of the enclosure confining the huge mastiff, Goar. "Come on, big boy, let's go for an early morn stroll. Do us both good." Applying the head halter and leash as he spoke, QB-3 walked through the gate and headed into the rising sun toward the southeast beach. As he walked he signaled security on his hand-held, informed them of his walk and asked to have the patrol car meet him on the beach.

The mastiff was on the short side of full maturity but his demeanor did not reflect it. He was massive, athletic and gifted with a disposition that could diaper a grizzly bear. Burgaard had to limit Armando's walks to occasional, and under no condition could any animal or young person be allowed near the canine beast. Burgaard also carried the pocket computer control with him in case he had to stop the recalcitrant dog. He had developed a morbid attachment to Goar, and inwardly laughed every time the dogfight guys lauded the pit bulldogs and the wolf-cross dogs or any other badass breed. His Goar dog would eat those wannabes for lunch and if prompted, their handlers could be dessert. The morbid delight caused by his ownership and control of the man-killer dog-beast coursed his vascular system like uber adrenalin. He could feel the hair on his neck stand as he thought about the fierce canine.

Turning slightly to his right as Goar hosed a small bush, the scientist was dumbstruck as a brilliant orange flare burst caught his attention. Someone was on the beach just a little west of him. Notifying security as he headed for the beach, the curly haired man stumbled as he felt for the 9mm Glock pistol in his waistband and tried to loose the mastiff at the same time.

Skeets popped the flare and strained to see the red and green bow lights of the Podzilla. He had spent more time than he anticipated going over the myriad files and letters in the office. He had hundreds of photos and he needed to get out of Dodge without getting them wet. Besides, he didn't feel up to a morning swim, especially while dodging automatic rifle fire. True to his word, he had let the stonehearted man-child go, knowing that it would cost him precious minutes ... totally out of character for the sociopathic operative. A morning fog was settling in and Skeets caught sight of bouncing headlights just off the beach, headed in his direction. The fog would make it all but impossible for the Podzilla crew to see him on the beach but he knew the fog would be in pockets and if he ran the beach, he had a chance of being seen.

Trotting north, the Skeeterman broke through the fog and with the day slowly wakening, saw the Podzilla up against a rare sandbar where the beach turned to rocks and scrubby wiregrass.

"Hallelujah!" The jubilant man was so distracted by his good fortune, he totally ignored the two men on the boat waving their arms, pointing, and shouting unintelligible words at him.

Goar's 180 pounds hit the Skeeterman from behind like a rolling boulder of hair, teeth, and bone. The force of the attack carried the mismatched pair into the water at the end of the sandy beach. Goar had grabbed for the stricken man's shoulder and got a mouthful of backpack that he instantly shook like a dishrag. Skeets reacted instantly by rolling to his back and putting his arms across his face. The Goar-beast immediately jumped astraddle the defensive man and grabbed both arms in his slavering mouth. Confused, Kirby wrapped his legs around the lithe dog's waist and squeezed as hard as he could, simultaneously twisting his body as to put the mastiff's head underwater.

The Dugan's watched from the Podzilla as if in a trance. Knowing they were helpless did little to ease their anguish as they watched the security vehicle slide to a stop and two short, swarthy men carrying semi-auto weapons exit on the run. The stocky man weaving his way up the beach waving a pistol and shouting, "Don't shoot him … don't shoot the dog!" did not even catch their eye as they gunned the 25 feet of fiberglass up to planing speed.

Kirby's arms were trapped in the dental strait jacket that was the huge beast's maw and the sharp dagger of pain was just starting to pierce the numbing fog of somatic shock as he struggled to drag himself to deeper water – 'his only hope of survival', he thought. The brute strength and weight of the mastiff were more than the disabled Skeeterman could handle as he turned to deeper water. His face went under and with his arms transfixed and useless, the euphoria of asphyxiation quickly removed all traces of pain or apprehension. Skeets couldn't see the winded man stop at the waterline and point a small, black object at the struggling pair and rapidly push several button-keys. He wasn't able to witness the huge mastiff give up his grievous grip on the barely struggling man, stagger to the shore, brace his shaking legs and vomit like a drunken sailor. Charles Skeets Kirby was drowning.

• • •

Samson had been back at the VentureQuest loft since midnight and still could not connect the dots about what seemed to be totally unconnected events. He had been unable to contact the Dugans, and Skeets, but knew they would get in touch when they could. He did know that he was going to the Bahamas and whatever came from that was going to be after he reclaimed his dog. He had notified the FBI about the Cordrerro involvement in the assassination attempt and with Skeets input he was certain they would abort the operation.

But, where was Elise? He had called and left a message earlier and it was going on noon and no returned call. He wanted to confront Charlie but was told that Charlie was out of town checking out some horses with a client and wouldn't be back for at least a week. And no, they did not have his itinerary. He was somewhere in South Florida. He would have to tie up these loose ends later since his flight to Nichols Town on Andros Island in the Grand Bahamas left the Ocala Airport in two hours and he was going to be on it. He knew where to start and he had hope that JY was still alive. The ringing of the phone interrupted his reverie.

"Samson, the bad guys got Skeets ..." Johnny Dugan's voice cracked as he relayed the bad news to the incredulous Sam Duff.

"You think he's alive?" Sam's voice was low and monotone as the young Dugan filled in the details and advised that they didn't hear any shots and the odds were that the Skeeterman was alive. "I'll be in Nichols Town before dark. Meet me there." A new dot had just been added to the plot chart.

• • •

Rod Osler sat with Raul and Samuel in Eula Mae's small dining room pulling on cold longnecks.

"You think the old Cuban will try get out of Dodge?" The Myrmon headmaster posed the question as if he were talking to himself. His two companions had a far away, trancelike stare, as Samuel answered.

"No, Señor Rod. He has nowhere to go and he misses that dirty old queer dog." The introspective Haitian took a cooling swig from the cold bottle.

"Where do you think those big dogs have gone. No one's seen them fly away and no boatman has reported any dog stowaways ..." Osler's capricious query was interrupted by Raul.

"The word around here is that there are a couple of vicious dogs back by Eula Mae's mango trees but nobody will go there. Even the stray dogs avoid it." Raul pulled on the longneck. "Only the little Che Che kid goes there. Some say he takes scraps to these vicious dogs. I don't know. Maybe so, maybe not."

Osler nodded. "How about it, Samuel? You hear anything like that. You maybe should go and check it out ... seems possible."

"No way Señor Rod, do I go where those bad dogs even may be. I know they do not like me and I for sure do not like them!" The Haitian's words did not seem in jest.

"Ha, ha, Samuel. I'm not going to order you to go. Chino El-Taino is on his way and his little to-do list includes a certain one-eyed pit bulldog and if it has company, too goddam bad. Those wolf-dogs of his will make short work of that patch-eyed son of a bitch and his queer friend if they are, in fact, still here." Rod Osler's lighthearted dismissal of the potent pit bulldogs brought a crooked smile to Raul Pena's face.

"Ah, Señor Rod, I thought no dog in the world could take the full measure of a battle tested pit bulldog. Were these not words I learned from you? I have never seen a wolf-dog such as you describe that belongs to this Chino fellow." Raul clenched his teeth as he hissed the name of the Cuban assassin. "I have seen this Dirty Dog with no balls in action, and I will not bet against him … but you will?"

"Raul, Raul. Get real. There will be no ring and no handlers. Pitbulls don't fight together like wolves do. That gelded son of a bitch tried to run out of the arena, and when those wolfies come there won't be anywhere for him to run, or no one to handle him and call time out. They will simply tear him to pieces and then get the other one if they can find him … and they will. Take it to the bank!" The headmaster was getting seriously worked up as he took a long draught of the rapidly warming beer. "In the arena, the pit bull probably would take the wolf-dog, but in the woods, the wolf will be the master because they are a product of the wild and the pit bull is artificial – man made."

Raul stared at an imaginary spot on the tablecloth as he spoke, slowly. "We will see. We will see … maybe."

Samuel's lips were clenched tighter than an asshole in a first parachute jump. He had no dog in this fight.

The three men walked in to the small dining area without looking around. The largest one, Big Johnny Dugan, plopped down at the small table and made room for the other two. Samson Duff and Johnny Dugan sat, and then the three covertly glanced around.

Rod Osler blanched as he eyed the three men. Samson Duff was here. Quentin Burgaard, III, had distributed photos of the two men he knew to be dangerous to their operation and here sat one of them. The other was wounded and a prisoner on Hoostra Island, and Osler was certain the one-eyed pit bull was on Andros Island.

"Guys, I've got to go." His voice barely a whisper, the Myrmon headmaster stood and dropped a fifty on the table and abruptly left the cramped dining room. Raul and Samuel knew something was wrong, but only sat and stared at the window as Rod Osler hurried from the small house and quickly gained the green golf cart.

Samson Duff was churning inside. As he passed the Myrmon headmaster he recognized his scent as that from the Cessna at the Cordrerro Kennel's hangar. This was the guy who was at VentureQuest when the stallion went off its rocker and was in the plane with JY. This was the guy that visited his loft apartment while he was gone. Here was the key to finding JunkYard. He could feel his face flush as the realization of JY being alive finally sank in.

"What's going on, Sam?" Big John's query fell on deaf ears as Samson's mind churned out all kinds of possibilities as to the whereabouts of his dog.

"Uh, what? Sorry. I just recognized the man that hauled ass when we sat down as the visitor at VentureQuest who may know something about JY's kidnapping. I need to have a little talk with him …" Sam's impatience was getting the best of him and Big Johnny Dugan well knew Sam Duff's explosive capabilities. But this wasn't Ocala, Florida and these Bahamians were peaceful, non-confrontational people and a Samson Duff style interrogation here and now could blow the entire operation.

"Samson, I arranged for Dave Rosen to meet us here. Let's get his take on this deal about Skeets' little problem and this guy your talking about. Dave may even know the gent and for sure Eula Mae knows him … he's most likely a regular and from the looks of his two companions, I'd say they might even be locals. And Eula Mae is like a sister to Dave." As Big Johnny finished speaking, a short, well-built middle-aged man approached their table. Dave Rosen was the tanned picture of health and the tank top did little to conceal his muscular build. Rosen was an accomplished SCUBA diver as well as one of the most proficient free divers in the Bahamas. He plied open water depths like most people plumb their backyard pools and since a speargun was illegal, his prowess with the Hawaiian sling while free-diving was legend.

"Oh, hi, Dave. Sit. Pull up a chair. That table can spare one ..." Just as Big Johnny motioned toward the table, its two occupants slid their chairs back and casually walked into the kitchen where they appeared to have a few words with Eula Mae before exiting through the kitchen door.

Samson intuitively liked Dave Rosen and told him of his dilemma and of his suspicion concerning the three men who had been at the other table. Dave said he casually knew one of the two who had remained and felt sure he could find out more from Eula Mae, which he would be more than glad to do.

"I'll drink to that!" Young Johnny raised his beer and four "cheers!' caused Eula Mae to stick her head into the small dining room.

• • •

Roderick Osler had been on the two-way radio for over an hour. He had left Eula Mae's dining room and went straight to the house. He knew that Raul and Samuel would be coming soon but he wanted to talk to QB-3 in private. The old Cuban, Dom Pedro, would be there but Osler didn't give a flip. He knew the old fella's days were numbered and hoped he would try to run off again.

"He's here. In Nichols Town. I saw him in Eula Mae's dining room. Had two big men with him." The Myrmon headmaster was breaking a sweat as he greeted Burgaard with the news. He knew nothing of Skeets Kirby's injuries and ultimate capture. The scientist was very guarded about what was happening and Osler was hesitant to check in too often since his embarrassing last meeting. Out of sight, out of mind ... he hoped!

"Good." Burgaard's voice almost quivered as it squirted out of the mic. "Get him out of town – out in the boonies and let Mr. Chino El-Taino earn his money. Maybe that stupid one-eyed dog will meet up with him and Chino can score a double. I don't want any connection to this, so be careful. Wherever he goes, El-Taino will find him so don't take any chances. This Sam Duff has quite a reputation so don't screw this up. Just get his ass lost in the woods. Then, get back to the academy and let's finish this little job for the Castros."

"Roger. I'll see you tomorrow night." The headmaster's voice sounded strong as he laid the mic on the table and saw Raul and Samuel coming through the rickety door.

"Señor Rod, the man who came in Eula Mae's was one of the guys Dr. Burgaard's looking for. Samuel and I stayed until the dive shop guy came." Raul paused as he opened the cooler and retrieved a beer. The house had no electricity but a generator supplied enough power to run the lights and appliances. Ice was always available in the myriad coolers occupying available space.

"I recognized him, Raul, and I just finished talking to the good doctor. Sit down and let's talk. That guy has to go – ASAP!" Osler drew his finger across his throat as the Haitian sat down on the sofa. "Samuel, can you get someone to watch this place and see that the old Cuban fart doesn't get away and spoil our party? Also, if by chance Duff shows up here, we'll need someone who can take care of him. This friend of yours use a gun?"

"Yes, sir, Mr. Rod. I can get that man. He don't have no gun, but he's tough and he can sure use a gun. He just don't have no gun." The Haitian's voice was vibrating from excitement at this breach in the perpetual ennui that was life on Andros Island.

"Now, Samuel, how far is it through the woods going north to Nichols Town?" Osler's query caught the excited man by surprise.

"Uh, I guess thirty miles at least. Tough going. Nobody in their right mind is going to walk from here to Nichols Town. Why do you ask?" Samuel's face showed total confusion.

"I need to know so I can cover all possibilities. This Sam Duff is sort of a superhuman and we have to cover all the bases. Dr.

Burgaard doesn't want any slipups." Osler's voice was persistent. "How far to the east before the mouth of the creek?"

"About a mile. But there is a trail. You know it." Samuel was freaking out. "Just go kill the son of a bitch and be done with it. What's the big deal?"

"We can't take a chance on being connected to his disappearance. Getting him to the house is a done deal and whatever happens after will be up to Mr. Chino El-Taino who should show up shortly after this Sam Duff fellow. Just be sure there's no way for him to get back to the sea basin except by foot." Osler motioned toward the creek. "Don't leave any of those little boats here, even the half-sunk ones. Get rid of them. Mr. Tough-Shit's going to get a note and he's going to come right here to get his pooch. Mr. Chino El-Taino and his two poodles are going to be right behind him ... end of story. Do your job and we'll put an end to this superman. Those El-Taino wolf-dogs don't read resumes." Rod Osler's words floated around the room like bubbles of doom. Suddenly, the beer tasted much better.

• • •

Sam entered the small dockside office and stood silently as the bulky Bahamian Customs agent finished stamping a bevy of passports collected from one of Dave Rosen's dive charters.

"Sit down, Mr. Duff, sit down." The high-pitched, singsong voice of the beefy official seemed woefully out of place, like King Kong aping a canary. "So, you don't have your passport. Okay, Mr. Duff, your U. S. driver's license will suffice, if you would be so kind. And Mr. Dave informed me that you might stay longer than his six days charter. Is that correct?"

Sam's suspicion antennae were stirring as he wondered why he had been singled out and called in. Dave and Big Johnny had both assured him that all he needed for legitimacy was some I.D and the sanctuary of the dive boat ... and he sure never said anything about being here more than the six days of the dive trip. "No sir. I'll only be here for the diving – why do you ask?"

Quietly the big man pushed back his chair, stood up and closed the door just off the end of his desk. Still mute, he reached across the desk and handed the curious Sam Duff a folded piece of paper.

Locking his eyes on the bland stare of the portly agent, Samson slowly reached out, took the note and in slow motion, stood up. Covertly glancing around the confining office he unfolded the note and read: 'I have a one-eyed pit bulldog. Take this note to Eula Mae's kitchen immediately. Do not delay or detour.'

Sam's heart skipped a beat as he tried to look nonchalant; he folded the note and slipped it into the pocket of the cut off jeans. He was wearing a tank top with the cutoffs and Key West sandals. A custom made folding knife adorned his fish decorated canvas belt. His gear, gun and accessories were hidden aboard the Podzilla and it was God knows where, refueling.

"I've got to go!" Sam opened the door as he spat out the words and exited the cramped office. He missed the beaming countenance consuming the florid face of the Customs agent as he gloated over the easiest $500 he never earned. Samson headed for Eula Mae's kitchen fast as his sandal clad feet would allow.

The excited man's suspicion antennae were fully deployed, and operational, but he knew he had no choice, so damn the torpedoes ... he had to find JunkYard.

• • •

JunkYard spent his days lazing near the mango trees back of Eula Mae's kitchen. He and the Havana dog had nestled deep into a growth of lantana bushes and the natural insect repellant provided them some relief from the myriad insects. The pungent lantana all but neutralized their sense of smell. Regularly, after dark, the pair of canines walked to the hidden landing beyond the mangos to search for any recognizable scent. On several occasions they had smelled the familiar spoor of the men they had escaped from and after pissing on the spot, would move on. Eula Mae left plenty of food scraps so the duo had no need to fool with the beer-can sized land crabs or the occasional iguana that happened to climb a mango tree.

The few island stray dogs that happened to wander by avoided the unlikely pair of pit bulldogs and no pack leader had yet emerged since the untimely demise of the German shepherd, Bonefish.

Eula Mae was scared to death of the two big dogs, though secretly she reveled in their presence since the strays were leaving her alone and she felt a twinge of power over their presence and truly believed they were dogs of destiny and somehow she was playing a large part in the fulfillment of this karma. The talented Bahamian cook believed in the Chickcharnie and the Lusca, allowing her metaphysical bent to be stimulated by the businesslike pit bulldogs.

On the occasion when Che Che brought the scraps and tried to befriend the dogs, JY would allow the small boy to approach and even pet him. Sucio Perro, wary of young boys, would avoid any overtures by the naïve little man.

• • •

Chapter THIRTEEN

Charles Kirby clenched his teeth as nurse Elise Jones removed the serum soaked bandages from his forearms and wrists. His chest hurt like hell with every shortened breath. He inwardly cursed the security guards for not being more proficient in artificial respiration. He cursed dogs more. Skeets Kirby had never had an affinity for man's best friend and his recent experience with the Goar-beast cemented this bias.

"Ah, does this hurt too much?" The pretty nurse's voice was oil on water to the beat-up, frustrated Skeeterman.

"Hell yes, it hurts. My whole frigging body hurts … if I have an idea pop up in my stupid head, the idea hurts! Far as I know the entire world hurts!" His own worst critic, the stoic operative could not yet fully comprehend his massive fuck-up. He had never been so careless and the slow acceptance of his foe's massive intellect and ability being superior to his and Samson's was gnawing at him like microscopic rats.

"You should be more charitable toward Dr. Burgaard. He saved your life. He's the only one that can control that beast of a dog and from what I can gather, those security guys were going to let you drown until he stopped them." Elise applied the antibiotic ointment to the grievous bite wounds on Skeets Kirby's forearms and started with the clean bandages. "You're lucky to be alive, Skeets."

"I know. And I'm not ungrateful. I just can't believe I let this happen." Kirby's inherent sociopathic ethos was unrelenting and the Skeeterman vowed he would get even.

Elise looked out the window into the encircling courtyard. The huge mastiff was lying in the shade of one of the few shrubby trees in the manicured yard. She had been warned not to go into the yard should the mastiff be there. So far, she had yet to look out the window and not see the slobbering beast.

Closing her eyes, the befuddled nurse subconsciously relived her nightmarish dilemma.

When she left Ocala with Charlie Sharp, she had no idea that they were not going to Pompano Beach to see a hunter-jumper that suited her neophyte ambition to ride and compete in equine hunter-jumper events. She wanted to surprise her Aunt, so no one knew of her little trip. She had not had a chance to tell Samson and she had all but stopped answering George Martinez when he left his canned messages. In fact, she had not even feigned surprise when Charlie drove all the way to Miami and ended up at that dog kennel. Charlie was nice as pie until he told her to get in the Cessna. Her Everglades experience was still fresh in her mind so she complained and threatened the three men whom she knew could make her board the little aircraft, but offered no resistance. She had no idea of motive.

"I'm your humble host, Quentin Burgaard. I trust your short journey wasn't unpleasant. The Bahamas are really beautiful this time of the year – they're beautiful any time of the year, really."

The solid built, curly headed, curly bearded man spoke in a most neutral monotone. "And, I guess you want to know why you are taking this impromptu vacation."

Elise sputtered as she spit out her objections to what seemed to her to be an insignificant kidnapping, or a huge mistake. "Who are you? Why am I here? My God, man, I don't know you ... you don't seem to be crazy, either. What's going on?"

"First, you will not be harmed. Second, I need you to convince a Mr. Samson H. Duff to visit this glorious little piece of real estate. Actually I needed a Mr. Charles Kirby also, but would you believe, he ups and visits on his own and is now a guest here ..."

The scientist's sentence was cut short by Elise's startled gasp. "Skeets is here? Skeets Kirby? What is ... how did ... what is he doing here?"

"At the moment he is trying to recover from a really bad dog bite and near drowning. Otherwise he is just a wayward tourist my puppy dog tried to bring home." Burgaard's voice had taken a sarcastic tone and his face was slowly turning to stone. I don't wish him to die – yet. I trust that you will feel charitable enough towards him to tend his wounds as I feel he is surviving the water overdose. Also, I really do not need your cooperation to entice Mr. Duff to join us. I have all I need – your seductive presence ... the man will come." The memory of the scientist's matter of fact pronouncement sent a shiver down the reminiscent woman's spine.

"Elise, help me with this water bottle. I can't do shit with my hands ... my fingers just don't listen to me anymore." Her patient's request for a drink of water broke her reverie and she quietly opened the plastic water container and held it to Skeets Kirby's mouth.

• • •

The 20 minutes it took Sam to reach Eula Mae's kitchen seemed like a week. The sandals kept shifting and causing him to stumble so he quickly removed them and arrived barefoot and winded. Sitting at a table was one of the men who had been there when he met the Dugans. Otherwise, the small dining room was empty. Proffering the note, Sam calmly sat down and pulled the sandals on his sandy feet.

"Let's go, man!" Sam spat the words as he finished putting on his footgear. The man stood, took the note and glanced at the writing, turned and walked rapidly through the kitchen and out the kitchen door. Eula Mae stood by her stove as if catatonic.

Heading away from the small house, the man, Samuel, walked briskly toward the stand of mango trees and veered to the small cove just before reaching them. Samson was lockstep with him. He could feel the hackles on his neck coming to attention as he furtively glanced in all directions. He simply could not comprehend how easily he was being manipulated. It was as if invisible strings were attached to his appendages and he had to abide their pull and direction. Whoever was sitting on the other side of this chessboard was more than qualified and he could only hope that his partner was still alive.

Gaining the white, sandy beach skirting the deathly quiet cove, Samuel stepped into a small aluminum skiff and motioned Sam to follow. The small outboard sparked to life and Samuel headed the tiny craft toward the main coastline and turned south.

The slight sea breeze beginning to come off the open water was barely causing a stir in the long weeds bordering the lantana thicket holding the two big pit bulldogs. The one-eyed one had his muscular head and neck resting on his forepaws with his good eye closed as if asleep. The larger, off-colored dog was stretched out on his side and was asleep, his massive rib cage rising and falling with each measured breath.

The sudden gust of wind slapped JunkYard's face like an electric whip. Instantly on his feet, he pushed his quivering nose into the wind as if it was the very breath of life. His sudden movement caused the Havana dog to sit up, yawn and start sniffing the air, just as JY took off at a dead run toward the hidden cove.

Reaching the beach, the excited pit bulldog searched the air currents to find the diluted scent of the man he had been waiting for ... Samson Hercules Duff! Running along the tiny inlet, he came to the beach and turned south following the rapidly degrading spoor carried by the lazy breeze. His master was there and he would follow until he was physically unable to do so. He had no way to know that it would be over 30 miles of some of the roughest coastline in the world before he would pick up the valued scent on terra firma. It did not matter.

JunkYard had smelled his destiny and only death could acquit him of this commission.

Two hundred yards behind, another pit bull succumbed to the fates as a shadowy Sucio Perro settled in stride and followed his friend.

• • •

Johnny Dugan eased the Podzilla up to the dock and Big Johnny tied off by the Customs office. "Wonder where he is?"

"Sure not on this dock and looks like Customs is closed for the day. Those guys only work when there's work and there's no boats here now." Big Johnny had climbed onto the dock and was walking toward the dirt path leading into Nichols Town where two men were tinkering with a small boat on the beach.

"You guys seen a tourist, cut-off jeans, well built, tank top ..." Identical blank stares answered Dugan's query and he turned back to the Podzilla. "He must be at Eula Mae's," He said as he carefully eased his bulk into the boat. "That's the only place he knows. Bet we find him there in the company of a cold beer ... and I could go for one, too."

"Ditto, big Poppa," Johnny replied as he moved the boat to a more preferred mooring spot. "Let's trot over there and see what Customs wanted with him."

Big Johnny's face was turning red as he answered Eula Mae's reply to his question about Sam. "What do you mean you haven't seen the guy. He had to have come here ... he doesn't know anywhere else to go." Taking a long pull on the longneck, the frustrated man turned to his son. "Something's going on here. Nobody knows nothing and the Customs shit had to be a scam of some kind."

"Mimi ... Mimi, 'de bad dogs gone, Mimi. Both bad dogs gone!" Little Che Che's excited voice caused the people in the little dining room to turn and focus on the stammering little boy.

Eula Mae's face froze as she grabbed her small grandson and shushed him as if he was a ventriloquist's dummy, simultaneously looking at Big Johnny Dugan and proclaiming, loudly, what big dogs? Boy, you know they's no big dogs 'round here anymore. They's all gone. Shut your mouth!" Too late!

"Goddam it, woman, what is that little shit talking about? What bad dogs. Tell me or I'm going to the authorities!" Big Johnny's voice crackled with the regnant authority of righteous indignation. "Don't lie to me! A man's life is at stake here. You want to murder a man?"

The gentle grandmother could take no more. Tearfully she related the story of the dogs and their sheltering and feeding of them. Now, they were gone and so was Samson. Eula Mae also told of the meeting earlier of Sam and Samuel and said that all she knew was that they left by boat. She told of Samuel's house and its location, as she had spent many nights there. She pleaded for them not to hold Samuel responsible, that he was a good man but in bad company. The Dugans listened, with an occasional nod or headshake as witness to Eula Mae's confession. There was no need for an interruption.

Walking back to the boat, Johnny Dugan's voice was choked as he said. "Dad, I think this little bit of intrigue is way above our pay grade. I'm for getting the hell out of Dodge and letting the FBI in on our little secret – before two of our best friends get fucking killed. Somebody has taken two of the smartest and baddest dudes on the goddam planet without breaking a sweat and I think we're on borrowed time if we hang our ass around these islands anymore."

"Son, we can't just up and go, and run out on Skeets and Sam. We can notify the authorities but let's not cut and run … yet." Big Johnny Dugan was seriously conflicted. He wanted no part of any intrigue that might get them killed. Yet, he couldn't run out on two of his best friends without finding out what was really going on. "Johnny, let's run down to that little house Eula Mae told us about. If Samson is anywhere in the frigging Bahamas, it's got to be that house."

"Okay, Poppa. Lay it on me." Johnny felt a lump rise, slowly, in his throat.

• • •

Samuel beached the aluminum skiff at the mouth of the creek and quickly stepped out. He had wanted to run the flat-bottomed skiff up the creek to the house but Osler had been adamant about having the marked man walk from the sea basin. Without a backward glance, the reluctant Haitian started up a narrow road leading into the dense greenery. The mute Samson Duff followed like a leashed dog.

Five miles up the coast, a small, nondescript boat was easing its way south. Aboard the boat were two large, brownish, medium coated dogs with beautiful wolf-like heads and dark muzzles. Their yellowish, bird-of-prey eyes were focused on the horizon as they sat, stone-like, in the bow of the small craft. They sported no collars and were unleashed. Both were intact males and when the wind danced in their fur, indistinct grayish white spots came and went like pastel strobe lights. The muscular, black-haired man guiding the lazy craft appeared to be talking to the big dogs – or to no one. He wore clothes made of buttery soft pigskin and carried a large, sheathed knife on his left side. No firearms were on the boat.

Thus came Chino El-Taino and his devil dogs.

• • •

Five miles south of Nichols Town, two pit bulldogs trotted down the beach, avoiding any human or animal they saw or smelled first. When unavoidable contact ensued, they immediately ran into the woods and skirted any obstacle, fixed or mobile, but their southward progress was not to be interrupted. The lead dog was the deep red of burnished mahogany, his muzzle and rear half of his tail jet black and possessed of only one eye. His companion was 10 or 15 pounds heavier and his brownish-blue, bleeding brindle coat was beyond casual description.

Thus came JunkYard and Sucio Perro.

• • •

The mute pair had travelled a mile on the path-like road when the Haitian stepped off to relieve himself, causing the trailing Samson to slow down and bypass him. Continuing a few yards, the anxious man turned and where Samuel had stopped was now only greenery – the man had vanished! Sam was dumbfounded! He had been set-up and led around like a lamb! His usual pro-active behavior was being so compromised by his desire to find his dog that he had totally disregarded the rules of this dangerous road that he and Skeets Kirby had chosen to travel.

Sam Duff realized that the mastermind behind this bizarre drama had figured out this little bit of psychology from the get-go and the realization that he had been fighting himself as well as the bad guys hit him like a well-placed sucker punch.

Refusing to give up the humbling sandals, Samson continued at a fast walk. His senses were completely tuned in and while he knew he could have trailed the errant Haitian, he also understood that JunkYard's life hung in the balance if the trail dead-ended. New ground seemed more promising and this path must lead somewhere.

Samuel winced while he backtracked to the skiff. He was supposed to break off just before the house and bring the local left to guard the old Cuban. Osler had repeatedly told the Haitian that he didn't want any locals caught up in this ... but Samuel was afraid of the tough looking Sam Duff. He also saw the folding knife attached to his belt and knew the trained operative wouldn't hesitate use it. This would call for an extra beer …

Sam came upon the little house with no warning. Suddenly, there it was. Pulling back into the bushes he tested the air and picked up fresh human spoor – male. No fresh dog smell so he carefully circled the wooden edifice and found nothing else. The afternoon was rapidly wasting as the adrenalized man suddenly noticed the relative darkness enveloping the shaded house. A sense of urgency welled up in him.

Hiding behind a shrub, he began to knock on the side of the house with a stick. Within 30 seconds a man appeared on the porch, holding a rifle and calling out to Samuel. "Samuel, that is you? Speak out, mon, speak out." Realizing that enveloping shadows compromised clear vision, the nervous fisherman pushed the door open with the rifle and cautiously cleared the two steps to the ground. He did not feel the razor sharp knife slice both jugular veins and one carotid. Staggering toward the creek and unable to vocalize, the unfortunate collapsed onto a shroud of his own blood.

Samson was already in the house, pushing the inside door open with the rifle barrel. Sitting quietly on a chair was a very old man with bowed head and tightly closed eyes. Samson sensed that there was no other human in the house and no dogs. "Wake up old man!" the rifle barrel pushed into his flinty midsection brought Dom Pedro back to the real world.

"Ah, Señor. I have been expecting you." Dom Pedro tried to stand as he spoke but Sam pushed him back in the chair.

"Yeah, you and half the male population of the Bahamas! You have 10 seconds to tell me why I shouldn't kill you … one … two …" Samson's count stopped as the nervous old Cuban pulled a red leather eye patch from his shirt and flipped it to the incredulous Samson Duff. "What the shit … where did you get this? Speak up!"

"Señor, give this tired old man a chance and I will tell you the story. I have been wondering when you would come." The darkening shadows verified the end of day and Sam stood the rifle in a corner and sat down on the tired sofa.

"It's dark in a few minutes and we can't go anywhere in the dark, so tell your story … and it better be good." The old Cuban glanced at the bloodstained folding knife sheath and shivered.

One hour and four cold beers later, Dom Pedro had brought the skeptical Sam Duff up to scratch on the fortunes and possible current status of his JunkYard, as well as his Dirty Dog, Chino El-Taino and his devil dogs, and everything he had gleaned from his eavesdropping on the bad guys' conversations.

The rifle Sam had brutally confiscated turned out to be a relic of the revolution and useless. Sam's face reddened when the flush of guilt coursed his body. Killing bothered him. Needless killing really bothered him!

Sam had given up the idea that Dom Pedro was a baddie. He took the old man at his word but could not quite accept his rendition of this man, Chino El-Taino, ergo the Cuban Assassin, and his ghost dogs. He also had a lot of trouble with the old man's casual recital of the bond between JY and this Dirty Dog of his. JunkYard would never permit another male dog to get anywhere near him unless stringently supervised. Dom Pedro did seem genuinely concerned and, given his leave, indicated he wanted to go immediately. Sam did not consider the old Cuban a threat … but?

"Not possible, old fellow. We'll go first thing in the morning, when we can see, and if the boogieman and his puppies show, we'll have a better chance. I'm a light sleeper, so if you wake me, you're dead."

At the mouth of the creek, a small boat beached and a man and two dogs went ashore. The man erected a crude shelter, started a small fire, made coffee and ate. The two dogs, unfettered, ate their food and curled up by the fire.

Thus landed Chino El-Taino and his ghost dogs.

Ten miles north of the mouth of the creek, two mud-splattered, foot sore pit bulldogs swam and clawed their way across another tidal creek on their destiny driven pilgrimage.

On came JunkYard and Sucio Perro.

•　•　•

Quentin Burgaard, III, sat at his desk and wondered if he had done the right thing by letting the badass Skeets Kirby live. He had desperately wanted a worthy candidate for his computer controlled implant and when the Skeeterman showed, he just couldn't resist. Nor could he resist implanting the dark haired nurse. Now he needed the fickle fates to provide the appropriate scenario, and with his indomitable help felt sure they would. Kirby's dog bite wounds were severe and the bacteriologist knew that without aggressive treatment and antibiotics he could lose use of his arms, or worse – lose his arms. With the expertise and dedication demonstrated by the nurse, he felt no need to call in a Cuban doctor and he did not want to give the incorrigible Kirby any opening that would allow him to retaliate. Quentin Burgaard, III, well knew that paybacks were hell!

• • •

The sun was trying to pierce the scudding summer clouds while the dark haired man drank his coffee and studied the pictures of the two men he was paid to kill. He knew that one of them was only a mile away and he was in no rush. His two hard-wired companions didn't give a dog turd about time and never complained about doing the lion's share of the work.

Samson woke with a nagging sense of urgency and again quizzed Dom Pedro about the best way to get back to Nichols Town.

"Señor Duff. We must go the shortest way. Chino's wolf-dogs will track us no matter. We must go to the sea basin and get a boat … quickly. The path takes us there. We must go!" The scared man's voice trembled like a wet kitten.

"I don't give a rat's ass about this Chino and his dogs. I just need to get back to where my dog may be. I'm fed up with this island and this scary movie shit. Let's go!" Sam adjusted his sandals and started down the darkly shaded path, the nervous Dom Pedro on his heels.

Chino El-Taino washed his coffee cup, rolled up his sparse accoutrements and placed them in the small boat. Walking to the head of the path, he whistled sharply and both dogs trotted to him with their ears up. Picking up a branch, he stirred the trail until the dogs started sniffing the stirred ground. Increasing the action of the branch while slowly walking the path, the entranced man intoned a chant-like "Kill! Kill! Kill!" Raising his voice as he scratched the ground, he began shouting and whipping the ground. The Cuban Assassin was working his killer dogs into a crazed frenzy.

Wraithlike, the ghost dogs of Chino El-Taino set about their gory pursuit and were soon out of sight. Chino sat on a stump. He did not need to hurry as he knew the terrain and had been to the little house a few years ago. His assignment was in good hands even if they were fur-covered. Again he looked at Sam Duff's picture – this time he smiled.

A quarter mile north of the sea basin, two dogs trotting down the grass edge of the beach stopped, and as one, put their noses into the increasing breeze driven by a high-pressure ridge pushing the scudding clouds. The lead dog, one-eyed, tested the wind like an experienced English Pointer before breaking into a dead run as he angled into the woods. The larger dog hesitated for a split second more of testing the air before he took to the woods at a dead run.

JunkYard had caught the wind driven scent of Samson Duff along with the familiar smell of the house where he was held captive. He also caught the spoor of strange dogs, increasing his sense of urgency and danger. Faster came the one eyed dog!

On his heels came the Havana dog, crashing through the bushes like a furry rocket. He had caught the scent of his savior, Dom Pedro, as well as the strange dog spoor. His experiences with a life of vagrancy made him double wary of strange dogs, especially when they threatened anything he cared for … and he cared for the old Cuban. Faster came the Dirty Dog!

The lead ghost dog hit Samson before he could react, biting at his thigh, causing the surprised man to spin away and hit the old Cuban like an NFL linebacker before sprawling into the thick underbrush. The second wolf-dog slashed at his body while he cowered deeper into the protective greenery. The killer dogs had the wind in their faces and were on the pair before Samson got their scent, making it impossible to get to his belt knife.

Dom Pedro had burrowed into a thicket next to a huge tree trunk and rolled into a fetal position with his arms shielding his face. Both dogs were attacking Samson as if Dom Pedro wasn't there. Only able to bite through the encircling greenery, the ghost dogs of Chino El-Taino could only worry the tender flesh of the bayed up man, but the increasing flow of blood was stimulating the two beasts to the point of insanity. Sam still couldn't reach his folding knife and both arms were pinned by the restrictive bushes. Samson Duff was helpless.

At the sea basin, the muscular, dark haired man methodically looped a short length of rope around his neck and, looking up at the brightening sun, started up the path. Methodically came Chino El-Taino!

Sam knew better than to shout for help as that would only encourage these killer dogs and their presence assured the appearance of the Cuban Assassin. He did not know of Dom Pedro's whereabouts or status. Since both dogs were worrying him, he thought the old man must be alive, at least

JunkYard hit the nearest wolf-dog with the force of a bowling ball shot from a cannon. This was not a defensive maneuver, a warning, or a get out of my territory disclaimer. The one-eyed pit bulldog was driven by deadly intent and as he clamped the surprised ghost dog's shoulder in his vice grip jaws, a whimper of pain escaped the slavering jaws of the caught beast as he desperately slashed at the muscular body of the worked up JunkYard. Ripping JY's skin like scissors gone mad, the wolf-dog tried to pull apart from the smaller dog and in so doing exposed his throat by extending his neck. In a flash the pit bull loosed his hold and clamped to the bottom of the stricken beast's throat. No sound ensued as the 125 pound ghost dog came face to face with the destiny of his name. With every death quiver, the one-eyed dog's hold tightened …

Within a few seconds of JY's attack, the Havana dog rocketed onto the other wolf-dog and with the experience of a street fighter went for the snapping dog's head, clamping from top to bottom with his lower canines just under the jaw and his upper ones deep in the top of the beast's head. Sucio Perro's weight forced the ghost dog to the ground and he expired within minutes.

Sam extricated himself from his green armor and inventoried the myriad lacerations on his arms and legs. He was smeared with blood but okay. Looking around, he helped Dom Pedro to his feet and then surveyed the gory scene. The Cuban seemed unable to speak. Sam looked at JunkYard and mumbled a "thank you, God." He knew better than to approach his pit bulldog under these conditions and it would be up the dog to decide when enough was enough.

Dom Pedro regained his voice and walked to the Havana dog and spoke in a quiet tone. "Ah, Sucio Perro, you returned. And just in time." At the words the huge dog loosed his hold on the dead dog and slowly walked to the old man, licked his hand and lay at his feet while Dom Pedro stroked him and wiped away the tears squirreling down his wrinkled old cheeks.

Suddenly, JY gave up the ghost dog's carcass and stood, a spine tingling snarl emanating from deep inside. Sam swung around as if bee-stung to face the black haired man standing quietly in the shadows. "Where are my dogs?" The voice was strong and very clear. Sam noticed the covert move to un-sheath the Bowie-like knife carried on his belt and squared his blood-caked body as he palmed his folding knife. "Where are my dogs?" Again he asked, and moved to the center of the path out of the shadows. JunkYard had moved beside Sam and a toothy rictus adorned his face.

"They are dead, mi hijo de Dios! They are dead." Sam turned to see the old Cuban walk up behind him and speak to the strange man. At his side strode the Havana dog, his bristles up and showing a full lip curl. He made no sound.

"Tio Dom Pedro! What is it you do here?" As he spoke he sheathed the knife and stared at the nearest dead dog. "It is my dog?"

The old man approached the Cuban Assassin and placed his hand on his shoulder." They are your dogs. These two dogs killed them to protect the bloody man and me."

Sam stared in disbelief as he returned the folding knife to its sheath. The strange man's eyelids were blinking very rapidly and he seemed to be entranced or in a mild state of shock - Dom Pedro knew him.

"No, Tio Dom, no dogs could kill my dogs. Who killed my dogs?" The enormity of what he was seeing could not penetrate the ego driven wall of invincibility Chino El-Taino had erected around these unusual wolf-like beasts. What lay in full view, before him and his God, was just not possible! It was to be a while before the gate of denial opened enough to allow the healing flow of tears ...

Glancing in Sam's direction, Dom Pedro whispered into the anguished man's ear. "Let us go to the house and tend to the wounds on the man and his dog. There are medical supplies there, and we can make our plans about your dogs. I will return and bring them to the house ..."

"No, Tio Dom. I will bring them ... they are my dogs." Walking to his dead dogs as he spoke, the sturdy man, eyes yet to be dampened, shouldered both carcasses and staggered up the path.

Dom Pedro looked at Sam, shrugged his shoulders and started after the humbled man. He realized Sam needed immediate medical attention and JY had many skin gashes that needed suturing. Sucio Perro was unscathed, as was he, and he knew there were plenty of medical supplies at the house, including sutures and antiseptic.

• • •

As the conversing men approached the dock where the Podzilla was moored, Johnny suddenly grabbed his Dad by the arm. "Dad, look! What going on with our boat?"

"Damn! Didn't know there were that many Customs agents in the entire Bahamas!" BJ's reference was really overstated as he eyed the three Custom agents dockside talking to another agent aboard the sleek fishing craft. "Let's see what this shit is all about."

"Hi. I go with this boat. How may I help you gentlemen?" Johnny Dugan's cheery greeting did nothing to change the cat shit-on-upper-lip grimace that seemed standard equipment on these Bahamian officials.

The agent in the boat looked up and said. "We have reason to believe that this boat may be involved in the transport of illegal substances. We have searched it and found evidence to support this charge. We also found a handgun which is prohibited unless by special permit." The agent was very precise with his elocution and while he spoke, both Dugans noticed the tactical deployment of the dockside agents.

"I have a permit for the gun and I can assure you any evidence of any contraband you may think you have, is absolutely false!" Johnny's face seemed to enlarge with each higher pitched word.

Climbing to the dock, the Customs agent ignored Johnny's invective and headed for the tiny office a few doors up the dock. "Come with me. I have a few questions to ask and forms for you to sign." Opening the office door, he entered without looking back as Johnny and BJ Dugan followed.

Spread out on the desk was Samson's backpack with his knife, pistol and assorted items vital to his mission. The agent asked Johnny to please close the door and sat down behind the desk.

"Big Johnny's antennae were rising. "Okay, what's the big fucking deal? Why are you nosing around our little fishing boat like a dog looking for a bone?"

"Gentlemen, gentlemen. We have a job to do and we were advised in regards to your boat, the Podzilla, and it may be an overreaction; however, I am obligated to investigate every such incident and I can assure you that your visit to Andros Island will end on a pleasant note." While he spoke he shuffled papers and laid out two officious looking forms. "I found no evidence to support the allegations and if you will read and sign these forms, I will be happy to release your boat … however, I'm afraid the handgun will have to stay until we can establish its proper permitting." Avoiding eye contact with the incredulous Dugans, the agent continued.

"Once proper ownership is established, we will arrange return of the weapon to it's rightful owner – say about 2 or 3 weeks. Sign and you are free to go and enjoy the bounty of our great fishing."

Johnny Dugan looked at his chuckling father. "See, I told you we need to get the hell out of Dodge!" Standing as he spit out the words, Johnny stepped to the end of the desk. "Where do I sign?"

"You not going to read it?" BJ's comical question was answered by the rapid scrolling of the pen as his son signed the two forms, straightened up and waited as the Customs agent separated the forms and handed the antsy man his copies.

Back in the boat, the two men replaced Sam's gear, minus the pistol, and idled away from the dock. "Dad, we need to get our ass south and see if Samson is at that house – pronto. If he isn't, the Podzilla is heading to the good old USA. Enough is enough!"

• • •

Roderick Osler was deeply concerned as he and Raul docked the Mako and decided to walk to the house for their meeting with Quentin Burgaard, III.

Raul Pena's mind was not as confused. His boss and he had come to kill the overbearing scientist … period and end of story. Their meeting with Samuel yesterday evening at the tiki hut bar in Coakley Town at Fresh Creek, just north of the sea basin and creek leading to Samuel's house, had started innocently with the Haitian's lively description of setting up the gullible owner of the one-eyed pit bulldog. And how he had seen the small boat carrying the Cuban Assassin and his ghost dogs and how that sight brought up the big goose bumps all over his body. And how he had hidden the small skiff and tried to find a spot on the trail so he could watch the fabled wolf-dogs in action, but fear overcame him and he hid in the boat until he heard the savage fighting, at which time he snuck to the house to see his fisherman friend and maybe free Dom Pedro as he really did like the old Cuban.

Rod Osler chuckled as he swigged his vodka and tonic. "Come on, Samuel, slow down so we can understand you."

Samuel, drinking his favorite beer, stopped with his mouth open. "Uh, uh Señor Rod, I am telling the truth! Let me go on."

A pensive Raul Pena, cradling his Cuba libre, chimed in. "Go on, man. Finish."

"And when I snuck back, nobody was there so I look in the yard and just by the porch was my friend, with his throat cut ear to ear. I was afraid to go inside but I went on to the porch and peeked inside. Empty. No one there." Samuel paused as he caught his breath. A sudden change seemed to overcome him as he continued. "Then, I heard a noise and I hid by the creek where I could see the trail as it came to the house. There walked the old Cuban with his queer dog, followed by the patch-eye dog and his man, covered in blood." The Haitian's voice was getting quieter and quieter as he recounted this part of his adventure. Leaning over the table, Samuel motioned the spellbound men to lean closer. His voice became a hoarse whisper. "Last came Chino El-Taino with a dead ghost dog on each shoulder. He staggered like a drunk man and his eyes were not seeing!" Abruptly sitting up in his chair, Samuel drained his beer and finished the saga. "I ran!"

Rod Osler sat back and stared at the thatched ceiling. If what Samuel said was true, Sam Duff was alive and Quentin Burgaard, III, would be furious. It would be Osler's fault due to his appetite for those stupid pit bull dogs and failure to do what he should be doing. QB-3, he knew, would brook no excuse.... And he had none.

"Raul, old buddy, we have to kill Dr. Burgaard." Osler's words drifted around the table like a radioactive fart. Samuel and Raul Pena both pushed their chairs back and stared at the Myrmon headmaster like his hair was on fire.

Samuel was the first to speak. "Señor Osler. I think I will return to Haiti for a while. I have family I have not seen for many months and I need to find another job for the racing season. I will let you know ..." Pushing his chair back, the solemn Samuel gained the door without looking back.

"Well Raul, I guess that leaves you and me." Rod Osler's words seemed almost a plea as he drained his glass and high-fived the waitress for another.

"Ah, Señor Rod, I agree. Dr. Burgaard will not let this go. We either kill him or he will kill us. Where can we hide from such a man?" The Latin machismo knew the answer to that question only too well!

Quentin Burgaard, III, was on the phone when Rod Osler and Raul Pena entered the cluttered office and found unoccupied chairs. They could not know that he was hearing the story of Chino El-Taino's colossal failure against Sam Duff and the patch-eyed pit bulldog. Choking back the rising bile of righteous indignation, the scientist abruptly hung up the phone and greeted the two men. Locking eyes with his visitors, he deftly opened a flat, black, TV remote sized object and pushed it to the center of his desk, assured no one had noticed.

"Quentin, we got here as quick as we could. It was blowing a bit when we left Andros but the Mako made it okay" Osler's voice sported a business-like edge.

"Okay, Rod ... Raul. So, how did it go? Chino do his job and the man and his dog are history?" Burgaard's voice carried an icy edge that could chill a margarita.

"Uh, ah ... everything went just fine, Quentin. Just fine." The Myrmon headmaster could see Raul Pena flinch and set his mouth like he did when they argued. He also knew there was a better than even chance the scientist knew of the Chino fiasco and was baiting them. Slyly glancing around, Osler saw no sigh of Armando or the big mastiff.

"So." Burgaard said. "Did El -Taino get his dead puppies back to Cuba?"

Raul Pena sprang from the chair knocking it backwards, a snub-nosed .38 cal pistol in his shaking hand. Rod Osler was only a half jerk-step behind him, brandishing a .45 cal. semi-automatic Colt. "Quentin, you sly old fox ... I thought you knew!" Osler's voice was a deeper timbre and a certain calm seemed to possess him as he pointed the pistol at the grinning QB-3. "No hard feelings, boss. Raul and I decided to hand in our resignations and felt you would understand a little hot lead way more than a tearful goodbye. No hard feelings, compadre?"

"Naw, Roderick … Raul." As he spoke, staring both men in the eye, his left hand was feeling the flat buttons on the small remote. "You guys do what you think you have to, although I would be happy to accept written resignations. Your way of resigning gives new meaning to the term 'job termination' and sure makes it difficult for me to do exit interviews to find out why you're leaving."

"Shoot him Osler, shoot the son of a bitch before he talks you out of it!" Raul Pena's whole body was shaking as he urged his cohort to action. Pena was deathly afraid of Quentin Burgaard, III, and possessed no killer instinct. Neither man noticed QB-3's fingertips flit across the flat keys.

Roderick Osler's gun began wavering and a strange, detached look spread across his tanned face as Burgaard began to speak, very softly. "Come on Rod. You don't want to shoot me! I'm your friend." The wavering gun-hand of the electronically hypnotized man began to lower and a quizzical stare replaced the initial trance-like gape. "Raul is the one who betrayed you, old buddy." The scientist's words were flowing like warm honey. "He's the one you should eliminate, not me!"

"Shoot! For God's sake Señor Rod, shoot!" Raul had turned toward the conflicted headmaster and started to back toward the door, his bone-dry mouth and dilating pupils a witness to the depth of his fear.

Osler's first shot hit the terrified Raul Pena in the shoulder, spinning him and slamming his body, chest first, into the closed door. The next three slugs peppered his back and stifled his gurgling "Madre de Dios …" Raul Pena's eyes were 'fixed in the stare of death' even as he slid down the blood-splattered door.

The piercing smell of burning gunfire filled the small room as Roderick Osler lowered the gun and looked at the quivering body of Raul Pena – a man he admired and considered his best friend.

Again Dr. Cube fingered the keys on the flat remote and spoke, this time sharply. "What the fuck did you do, Rod? You fucking crazy? Raul was your best friend … your man! Is that the way you treat your best friend?" Burgaard was screaming. "…. Just shoot the fucking life out of him!"

At these words, Roderick Osler slumped in the chair and hung his head in his free hand, letting the .45 dangle as his clinched eyes welled tears and child-like sobs struggled out his slack lips.

Again Dr. Cube's fingertips caressed the remote's keys and again warm honey oozed from his mouth. "Rod. I'm going to have to call the police. Man, I don't want to but you know I have to. Why did you have to go and murder your best friend in cold blood? You know, he was planning a surprise birthday party for you next week and I understand he managed to get you one of those Nugget pups you are so crazy about … couldn't wait to give it to you." Roderick Osler looked up through wet, dead eyes and with an animal-like groan, pushed the Colt's barrel far into his mouth and pulled the trigger.

"Armando. Get in here … have a little mess to clean up. And you may need help." Quentin Burgaard, III, dropped the intercom mic and chuckled out loud as he stroked the small, flat remote.

• • •

Chapter FOURTEEN

Charles Kirby paced the small room like a rat seeking escape. His forearms were healing but he did not have much use of his fingers. His stilted conversations with the dark haired Elise Jones were less frequent. He had warned her from the start that the premises were wired and any conversation had to be casual, but the trusting nurse could not seem to remember. Just yesterday she had asked him when he thought the FBI would come. His reply, until he calmed down, scorched her ears and sent her into a daylong pout, with her emergence coming about 2 hours ago.

Skeets knew he could not parry Burgaard's knowledge of electronics and his uncanny use of psychology on his employees, his man-eater dog, and his captives, including one Charles Kirby. For the first time in his professional life, the Skeeterman was feeling the ice-cold finger of intimidation as, minus lubrication, it breached the perfect circle of his ass.

He knew he would have to get to the beach if he was to have any chance of escape. Elise was definitely a chink in that armor, but he did not feel her life at risk as long as she played by the curly haired crazy man's rules. For this reason he resisted any conversation regarding a possible escape. Also, Skeets Kirby feared the huge mastiff more than anything, or anyone, on this God forsaken island. With no weapon and limited use of his hands, the Skeeterman knew he would be just another meal for the made-in-hell beast. These revelations put escape on the bench and rescue in at quarterback. And rescue always meant waiting … a word banished from the Skeeterman's lexicon many moons ago. Skeets Kirby hated to wait – on anything!

"Penny for your thoughts." Elise's voice pierced Skeets concentration like an ice pick thrust. "I hope you've figured a way off this island and maybe the reason for me being here. You just wait until I get my hands on that Charlie Sharp guy!"

Kirby felt the deep frustration of his co-captive and really didn't have a clue about the whys and wherefores of her captivity. "Honey, I guess Doctor Weird-O snagged you for bait to get Samson to come here. From what I gather, he's ready for anything or anyone and somehow knew that Sam and I were onto him … God knows how."

"Do you think Sam will come? You think he even knows we're here … that I'm here?" Elise's voice was breaking as she finished the sentence.

Putting a shushing finger to his lips and whispering, the perplexed man replied for the umpteenth time. "I don't know! But I do know that if Sam is alive he will come and if he doesn't know you're here, I guarantee he will know it way before he rescues you … take it to the bank!" With that, the Skeeterman cut his finger across his throat and turned away from the unsettled nurse with a barely perceptible "Shush!"

• • •

"Roderick and Raul are gone! Done! Dead! That goddam screwed-up scientist killed them both!" Donna Eye's startling disclosure caught the two men like a crotch delivered sucker punch.

"What the hell you talking about ..." Bud York's reply sounded strangely naïve for a man who had been around the horn.

"He shot both of them. Cruzo had to help Armando clean up and feed the big fish. Gone ... like they never were. Cruzo told me last night ... swore to it." Donna Ileana Villareal broke the news like a Greek bride breaks a wineglass.

Harrie Smithcors' pasty face could not get any whiter even as his shocked brain tried to catch up with Donna Eye's pronouncement. He was suspicious when the Brazilian hottie curtly asked for his presence in her room that evening. It had to be business because Harrie Smithcors hated Donna Eye. He had been expecting something to break since Doctor Burgaard had declared a hiatus in order to remodel aging facilities and retool the curricula to attract even more spoiled brats. He had been hard pressed to keep Toby with him, as all other Myrmidon candidates were sent to other facilities and no plans had been forthcoming. His suspicions went mainstream when no starting dates were announced for the putative makeover. The retained staff consisted of him, Donna Ileana, Bud York, Armando and Cruzo Dominguez. The young Cruzo had proved to be very able physically, and precocious in the anti-social arts so necessary for success in the Myrmidon program. "What shall we do. I have no place I can go ... and I have Toby to look after. He has no one but me." Harrie's plaintive thinking out loud caused the other two to stop and stare at the unraveling dog-bone of a man.

No one on the Myrmon Academy staff really liked the obtrusive Director of Student Activities, but all realized the weird expertise he brought to the table, so even the Brazilian Redhead sucked up her dislike and worked with him ...

Donna Eye hated Harrie Smithcors!

"You think you have a problem, Harrie? You could probably slip into the Miami area with your wormy, dark-eyed puppy and no one would cock an eye, but I can't go anywhere near there. I can't go back to Canada and I doubt I could get by in Cuba ... maybe." Bud York had worn out his welcome in most of the civilized world with his very conventional expertise in physical fitness combined with a very unconventional appetite in training pubescent young men. His gift always turned to gaff and persona non grata had become his mantra. "What about you Donna?"

Cruzo Dominuguez' face showed no emotion as he listened at the window to the stilted conversations. This wasn't the first time he had eavesdropped on impromptu meetings of the Myrmon staff. Cruzo knew the dorm rooms were bugged and he assumed the staff members were aware of this but the gist of their talk didn't reflect it.

"I think I'll fly into Miami and disappear in Little Havana." Donna Eye's comment raised the eyebrows of Harrie Smithcors.

"And how will that be accomplished? Bat wings … broom?" Smithcors' cynical words brought a fleeting smile to Bud York's face, simultaneous to a blossom of fire in the tempestuous Redhead's countenance.

Cruzo shook his head and stifled a deep laugh. This deadly serious meeting of the three conspirators was rapidly turning into a soap opera and God help them if the good Dr. Cube got wind of it.

The former Havana street urchin fingered the razor sharp, butterfly handled shiv he kept hidden inside his pants. The six-inch dagger was gifted to him by Armando, even though the bandy-legged Brazilian knew it was against Myrmon policy for any personnel or student to possess a weapon. The creative little .22's were only handled during instruction or usage. Everything else was simulated.

Cruzo Dominguez, with his mutilated hand, wistful good looks and devil-may-care duplicitous attitude was a hard pup to keep off the porch and Armando had taken to the waif at first sight, finding him bright and capable; he mentored him like a son.

Armando Montedinegre was a short, quiet man with a neutral demeanor and shallow emotions. He disliked violence of any kind and suffered any injured or sick animal – but people were a different ilk. Quentin Burgaard, III,'s meek gofer was, in fact, an accomplished knife fighter and not afraid of any man nor burdened by empathy when faced by a man with a knife in his hand. He never overtly owned this facet of his life and was happy to put it behind him when he came to work for the Myrmon Academy and Dr. Burgaard.

His forced relationship with the callous Havana throwaway street urchin, Cruzo Dominguez, slowly revived long dead memories of his dysfunctional childhood and in trying to suppress a rising paternal instinct inadvertently mentored the recalcitrant child-prisoner of circumstance.

After a few months, young Cruzo was exposed to knives as weapons and his ex-knife fighter mentor reveled in sharing his macabre avocation with the eager Myrmex Terminus student.

With a flick of his wrist, Cruzo could retract the paired handles to expose the thin, six inches long, razor sharp blade. The stolid Brazilian had taught him the vulnerable areas of a man's body where the thin, razor sharp blade could penetrate, painlessly, causing uncontrollable hemorrhage and unavoidable death; the preferred method used by miscreant knife fighters to dispatch an opponent or assassinate a hoodooed victim.

The three-fingered Myrmex Terminus student was an avid pupil and practiced diligently with his newfound toy.

· · ·

Samson awoke from a stupor-like sleep looking like he had been in a fight with a sewing machine and emerged second best. His body ached and all visible skin was a patchwork of skin sutures or antiseptic stain. JunkYard sidled up to him as he rose from the jury-rigged sleeping mat.

"Man, JunkYard, you look worse than I do!" Sam laughed as he surveyed the myriad stitched areas on the smooth skin of the stoic dog. Chino El-Taino's ghost dog had gotten in a few licks of his own before succumbing to the battle tested pit bulldog and the old Cuban had done a first class job of cleaning and suturing the many wounds; ditto for Samson's wounds.

"Okay Samson, what's the plan?" Big Johnny Dugan was sitting on the ratty sofa as he rubbed his sleep numbed eyes.

Sam's reply was interrupted by Dom Pedro's measured voice. "He is gone, Señor Duff. Chino and his dead dogs are gone. We will see no more of Chino El-Taino and his ghost dogs. One can only trust that he accepts the peace he has paid such a dear price for. God go with him."

Sam's eyes narrowed as he answered the elder Dugan. "I need to get to that goddam Hoostra Island ASAP! I feel that Skeets is still alive and I mean to get his ass out ... in one piece."

Unnoticed by the three men, Dom Pedro quietly slipped out the front door, the Havana dog his shadow.

Sam continued. "I want to be on that beach at sunset and you two can man the boat."

"What about your wounds?" Johnny Dugan spoke as he noticed Samson's stilted gait as he walked to the water jug.

"Don't worry about me – I'm fine, once I get up a head of steam ..." Sam's voice cracked like a calving glacier as he tried to lift the water jug to his mouth.

"Bullshit, man!" BJ.'s booming retort to Sam's obvious pain caused JY to raise his head. "You can't do this rescue shit if you can't raise you arms. We need help ... big-time!"

"Cool it, big man. I'll be fine." Samson's measured response was interrupted as the old Cuban returned with a bundle of thick, dark green serrated leaves.

"Ah, Señor Duff. I have found the aloe plant and I will apply its wonderful nectar to your skin and in a few hours you will not be so uncomfortable; also to the one eyed warrior who serves you so gallantly." As he spoke, the old man was splitting the meaty leaves lengthwise, freeing the clear, gel-like sap.

"I want to be on that beach at sunset!" Sam blurted out the words like a military command and considered the subject closed as Dom Pedro began applying the unctuous balm.

● ● ●

Cruzo approached the small office just as the sun was setting. Armando would have just fed the monstrous Goar and the onerous mastiff would be locked in the small feeding area wolfing down the many pounds of fresh offal his warped master took the pains to procure and keep bloody fresh for the man-eating beast.

Armando had to tediously record every ounce of food the Goar-dog chowed down, and any behavior he considered unusual. Also, since Kirby and Elise had appeared on the scene, the squat Brazilian had been assigned their overseer and jailer.

Not the least resentful, or aggressive, the mild mannered gofer entered into conversation with the prisoners at their behest. To him they were more disgruntled guest than incarcerated hostage-prisoner. Guided by this rationalization, Armando Montedinegre was quite the affable host – except he would not give them their leave. He was as non-judgmental as he was loyal ... to Quentin Burgaard, III.

Also, his relationship with the throwaway Havana street urchin had blossomed into a father-son dynamic resulting in his life being more pleasant and definitely more rewarding. He loved the dispassionate man-child as his own and treasured every moment with him.

Cruzo tapped lightly on the door, opening it as he did. Palmed in his right hand was the handle of his shiv, its blade flat against his wrist, pointing up his skinny arm. The ex-urchin hardly weighed over 120 pounds but was strong as wire and very coordinated.

Armando glanced up as the door opened and broke into a full facial grin. "Ah, meu amigo jovem! I did not know you were coming!" Pushing back from the small table used as a desk, he stepped toward the silent youth with arms extended to hug the three-fingered Myrmidon. Still mute, Cruzo Dominguez stepped into the arms of the only person on earth that loved him and deftly plunged the shiv to the hilt at the base of the stunned man's neck, just behind his collarbone and into the top of a healthy, beating heart. The quick as a blink side-to-side motion of the blade's handle insured the laceration of the top of the trusting man's major cardiac arteries along with a section of his windpipe.

Even as he hugged the boy, he knew he had received a fatal blow. Cruzo had pulled back as he removed the shiv and stood, without speaking, as the mortal discomfort in Armando's chest was reflected in his face. Seeing the bloody shiv in Cruzo's hand drove the stricken man's voice to a high pitch. "What have you done! Meu homenzinho ... what is this you have done to me!" His fear-driven voice was weakening and bloody saliva flecked his lips as life-blood rapidly filled his chest cavity.

"Ah, I have killed you Señor Armando. It is as you taught me." At Cruzo's reply, Armando staggered to his chair and fell into it, barely managing to grab the table and stay upright as he sat down.

"But why ... why? I taught you, I loved you like my son ..." every blood-stained word birthed more confusion and disbelief. "You ... repay my trust and love ... with this!" Blood dribbled down his chin as his lips slackened.

"Ah, Señor Padre, I do love you. Señorita Donna Ileana and Señor Harrie have taught me in school how to love and I have practiced until I did love you. I am a very good student." Cruzo's face showed no emotion, voicing his love mantra as if reading it.

Armando's face was ashy white and his head lolled as if supported by a neck turned to rubber. Barely able to speak, the dying Brazilian could only manage a "Why?"

"I want to leave this place. I need the man and woman to help me leave and it had to be tonight. No one can know when or where I go or they will find me and kill me." The Myrmex Terminus student's child-like motive was interrupted when the dying man coughed up a huge blood clot and tried to answer.

"I ... would have ... given them ... to you ... for the asking. You are ... without a soul. God have mercy on you ..." Armando Montedinegre's head leaned forward onto the table as the life force abandoned his violated body. He did not hear three fingered Cruzo Dominguez's parting words. "Ah, amigo, I did think of it but I did not trust you."

● ● ●

"Something's not right, Skeets." Elise's voice carried a hint of concern as she tried to look out the partially obscured window. "That huge dog has been fed but is still penned up, and I haven't seen or heard anything from the little man guarding us."

"I know. I've been trying to figure it out but so far nothing jumps out at me. I haven't heard any strange noises or seen any different people going or coming but something sure seems different." Skeets continued his hand exercises as he spoke. His hands were improving rapidly and the dog bite wounds were healing and seemed to be free of infection.

The silent opening of the door caught both hostages by surprise. Skeets sensed something and turned to the door just as Cruzo Dominguez stepped into the room.

"Ah, Señor and Señorita. Very nice to see you again, especially you, Señor Kirby." Cruzo's words popped from his lips like ice cubes. "And I think we have some unfinished business, no?" Facing the motionless Kirby, the three-fingered Myrmidon slowly pulled Skeets' knife from his belt. "Ah, what a nice blade!" Walking up to the stoic operative, he placed the deadly instrument against his neck. The Skeeterman never blinked as the warped man-child nicked his neck. "Now we will see who responds to the blade the best – you or me!"

Adjusting Skeets' tactical backpack for his small frame, Cruzo motioned the pair to the rear door and into the utility electric cart used in the maintenance of the grounds. The rear seat was replaced with an open bed filled with various tools, ropes, and had a rigid pipe bar across its width to be used for pulling or as a stationary tie-off. Prodding Elise into the driver's seat, the three-fingered killer slid in beside her and motioned for Skeets to get in. "Ah, Señor, the pretty one will drive and if anything goes wrong, she will be suddenly not so pretty. Put your hands on the dash, and if you move them or if she does not drive to please me, well, I think these knife will have to do a little more work ... comprende?"

Cruzo had decided that if he got to the beach and released a flare, a boat would come. He felt confident that he could finagle a ride and escape this island prison without fear of being followed. He knew that no Myrmex Terminus student ever left the island alive. There was no Myrmex Terminus alumni club. His early deprivation and sociopathic education left no room for sympathy or nuanced thought. All he had to do was get to the beach without being seen and release a flare. Any variation of that theme meant failure or death ... period!

The moonlight cast eerie shadows as Cruzo guided Elise away from the beach toward the rugged area north of the buildings. He knew he couldn't escape the security if he went straight to the water. The utility cart was equipped with armored tires and could handle the jagged moonscape, rife with blowholes and ragged depressions that could cut a person to ribbons if they fell into one and tried to climb out. The rocky knoll north of the buildings was the result of a large gash in the carbonate shelf at the water's edge resulting in a deep depression in the lime-rock strata, extending inward for several hundred yards and resulting in the formation of many caves and lateral tubes with some opening, like manmade wells, on the ragged surface. Given the necessary weather conditions, these blowholes could rhythmically spew sea foam, seawater, or just blow air. A few were so situated that at the peak of propitious tide-wind-wave height, they could spew tons of seawater that returned to the hole with unbelievable force. Cruzo knew he was tempting the fates with this circuitous route to the beach but believed it to be the only way he could safely get there ... and nothing else mattered to his clueless, shriveled psyche.

He knew he could avoid security and anyone who may be following although he did not expect to be followed. He could dispose of the two hostages, hit the beach near where Skeets had been taken, release the flare and the rest would be history. No witnesses and no trail. The treacherous man-child smiled as Elise cautiously navigated the malignant terrain.

Skeets sat as if turned to stone. He had come to realize that the three-fingered boy was a trained assassin with most of the skills he would expect of his FBI counterparts. He knew he could take him, even with damaged hands, but he would not be able to put the bastard down with out some harm to the innocent nurse. Not an option. His hands were glued to the utility cart's uncluttered dash as it swayed and bounced through the moonlit scrub.

• • •

Johnny Dugan eased the Mako until the bow touched the sand of the beach. Two shadows silently exited the craft and disappeared into the darkness within seconds of the boats silent departure to an advantageous anchoring point.

Sam headed straight for the main building, checking the air currents for human or canine spoor to avoid whatever security may be in place. He glanced up as the rising moon slowly threatened the inky darkness. The full moon would be up soon and Samson wanted to get Skeets and get back to the beach ASAP. He felt confident his friend was still among the living, although he may be hurt. His own wounds were easing with each step and JY, trotting alongside, seemed normal.

Approaching an outbuilding several hundred yards from his target, Samson picked up a strong dog odor. JunkYard had stopped and was testing the air currents, his hackles rising along his spine and neck. The swirling air caused Samson to turn toward the building and slowly circle it while testing the capricious wind. 'Must be some sort of dog kennel,' he thought as he turned back toward the main building. As he did, a sudden gust of wind hit him in the face and the big man gasped as if he had just taken a low blow from King Kong! That sudden gust was laden with unidentifiable odors, but two were unmistakable – Skeets Kirby and Elise Jones!

Sam groaned as he sank to his knees and reached for JY. How could Elise be here? No wonder he couldn't reach her … these bastards had kidnapped her and nobody knew it until now. Speaking softly to the nervous pit bulldog, he set him to heel and started toward the building. Dim lights were visible from two rooms and as he approached, a large dog could be seen in a small, fenced off part of the yard. Ignoring him, Sam quietly approached the door of the lighted room and saw that it was ajar. The smell of death was overpowering as he quietly entered and saw the body of Armando Montedinegre slumped over the table, as if asleep. JunkYard slipped by the table and stood next to the inner door, nervously sniffing the bottom of the wooden barrier. Sam sidled to the door and tried the knob; it was unlocked and the reassuring scent of Skeets and Elise wafted up from the bottom as he slowly opened it. The room was empty with no signs of struggle or injury. The other recent scent, a young male, intermingled with the hostages, was unfamiliar to the perturbed Samson. Following the scent trail to the rear door, Samson stepped outside just as the moon made its expected appearance. He quickly discovered where the three had entered the electric cart, and with a large lump forming in his throat, set out on their trail, all thoughts of rescuing his pal replaced by his desire to find his love safe and unharmed. He had no idea of who the third person was or if his friends were actually in danger, but he was certainly going to find out.

• • •

Quentin Burgaard, III, slammed the intercom phone down for the second time in ten minutes. Where was that Armando when you needed him? QB3 had wanted to take Goar for a walk this night because the moon would be full and both mastiff and man were restless on full moon nights. His bugging device had not been working properly these past few days and he had not been able to monitor the conversations at the small outbuilding, relying on Armando for any pieces of info regarding the two hostages. 'Oh, well.' He thought. 'I might just as well go get the beast as sit here and help my ulcers grow.' Stuffing his 9mm semi-auto handgun into his pocket along with his computer remote, the Brillo bearded scientist set out to pick up Goar.

He had decided to erase the two hostages whether Duff showed up or not. His operation was in trouble, as the Miami deal had to be postponed, much to the chagrin of the Cuban Connection. He knew if he didn't act proactively, his unheralded disappearance was a certainty and Armando's ill-disguised distaste for aiding in the disposal of Osler and Pena's bodies bode ill for the future of

Myrmon Academy. If Duff showed up, so much the better, charity not being a prominent aspect of the bitter scientist's rare attack of moral largesse. Killing the ubiquitous Samson Duff would be icing on the cake!

Nearing the side of the building, Burgaard heard labored breathing and scratching sounds. Turning the corner of the fenced yard he saw the mastiff digging at the bottom of the fence and groaning like he had just experienced coitus interruptus. Dirt was slung everywhere, but the wire footing installed for such occasions was doing its job and the huge beast was miserably frustrated. Knowing that Goar should not be confined in the small area, the suspicious man ran to the front door and burst in, even though he found the door slightly open. One glance at the bandy legged Brazilian slumped over the table caused the 9mm pistol to appear in his hand as if by magic. Stumbling through the other rooms, Quentin Burgaard, III, knew the other shoe had fallen … 'but who?', he thought. 'Who could do this?'

Telling himself to calm down, QB-3 retrieved the planted listening devices and tried to make sense of the scratchy recordings. The only one he could understand was Armando talking to someone he seemed to know. The stranger's voice was not clear enough to allow identification but the Brazilian referred to the stranger as 'meu amigo jovem', Portugese for 'my young friend', a term he had often heard Armando use to describe the Myrmex Terminus student, frequently sent to help him – Cruzo Dominguez.

'…. But no. This couldn't be the work of one of the Myrmidon.' He thought as he searched the outside for anything he could find that seemed out of place. "Has to be that asshole friend of Kirby's and the stupid girl." Burgaard was speaking out loud as he scurried around the perimeter. "Duff must have sneaked in and rescued his friends … killed poor Armando … but who penned Goar?" Pausing to mull over this little factoid pushed the harried scientist into an introspection mode, slowing him down enough to allow his scientific training to re-surface.

'No one but Armando or me could have put that fucking dog in that corner lock-up.' QB-3's thoughts were lining up like ducklings following mama duck. 'Couldn't have been Duff … or Cruzo.

Unless Armando was killed before he could turn him out after he fed him. Killed? How the hell was Armando killed? Better find out ...' Slowed by the necessity of logic, Burgaard dutifully revisited the slumped body of his once faithful servant.

Carefully examining the small stab wound at the base of Armando's neck, QB-3 completely ruled out Samson Duff. Whoever administered this fatal stab was Armando's friend and very skilled with a shiv ... neither stuck to Kirby's co-operative. And, there was no way Kirby could have pulled this off since he only had limited use of his hands. Also, who besides himself and the Brazilian knew when Goar was fed and that he was confined while he ate? Burgaard had set the time of death around the mastiff's feeding time and came to the conclusion that the only plausible suspect had to be three-fingered Cruzo Domingo!

Quentin Burgaard, III, was a genius, with an upper crust education in medical arts and bacteriology, obsessively self taught in anatomy and physiology, and capable of grasping any theory proposed by anyone from planet earth. Taking Dr. Cube for a fool was neither easy task nor laughing matter, as such a perpetrator would discover.

Cruzo and the hostages would have to be on foot or in an Academy cart. The moon was high enough to light up the landscape and Burgaard laughed as he realized the only escape for the treacherous Myrmidon and his companions would be the beach which meant he and Goar beast could have a say in that. Grabbing the nylon leash, the jubilant scientist surged through the fence gate and expertly affixed it to the heavy leather collar adorning Goar's neck. He had never seen the huge dog so agitated. Whatever happened here must have struck a raw nerve in the mastiff ... and, 'maybe' QB-3 thought, 'this dog will track whoever just left and save me some time. He sure wants to get to something – real bad!'

Goar had never smelled a dog scent such as JunkYard's. His presence in Goar's territory was not to be tolerated and the agitated beast could not rest until he had at this arrogant interloper. The strange man and the people in the house meant nothing to him in light of the strange pit bulldog and until he got to him, nothing else could register.

Goar took off like a four wheel drive power wagon, pulling the cursing Dr. Cube to the ground and causing a two minute rodeo as he brought the beast under control.

"Slow down, you cheeky bastard! I'm going to let you have whatever you find, just I want to be there when you do!" Straining like an overloaded ox, the mastiff headed north into the moonlit no-man's-land, away from the beach. Burgaard noticed the direction as well as the dog's conviction. "What the hell, shithead, nobody's going to run that way unless they're crazier than you seem to be! Head for the beach!" QB-3's shouts were being challenged by the rumbling emanating from deep in the bowels of the moonscape-like ground. He knew that the moon, wind and tides were optimal for the many underground passages to fill with force-driven sea-water, racing to the nearest opening in the labyrinth of caves and tunnels carved by eons of its unintended landscaping. Some open blowholes could spew salt water with seismic force into the air like behemoth stone whales magically aroused. The underground tunnel prepped as an escape route in his office was connected to this network and at times like this would be filled and if not for the pressure hatch securing the opening, would have converted his office to driftwood. He damn sure wasn't going for a dog walk in that god-forsaken piece of real estate. With great difficulty, the pre-determined dog-beast was slowed, turned and headed toward the beach.

• • •

Chapter FIFTEEN

The struggling electric utility cart seemed to pick up speed, as if Elise found level ground in the difficult going or had become suicidal. Skeets, with his hands on the dash, knew that couldn't be the case and intuitively braced his self. The silent machine stopped as if hitting a wall. Even at a relatively slow speed, the results were dramatic: Elise Jones fled the driver's seat like it was afire. Cruzo slammed into the dash, simultaneous with the Skeeterman grabbing his shoulder and head butting him with the force of a rutting goat, arms and hands benumbed by the adrenalin surge. Three Fingers dropped the knife as he tried to recover his balance and deal with the mind-numbing effect of the head butt. Skeets expertly kicked the slightly built assassin to the ground, slipped behind the steering wheel and stepped on it.

Cruzo staggered to his feet and surveyed the moonlit emptiness. Shrugging his shoulders, the diminutive killer, after looking in vain for the knife, adjusted Skeets' backpack and headed for the beach. Incapable of abstract thought, the sociopathic myrmidon smiled as he contemplated his escape. In his one-track mind, nothing had changed.

• • •

Sam had no trouble following the cart. Arriving at the spot where Elise had fled the vehicle caused the determined man to stop and look around. JY paused after sniffing the small area, then without a sound, headed north into the eerie gloom. Finishing his search, Samson determined that Elise had left the cart alone as well as the strange third party, each going a different way. JunkYard had wasted no time taking after the anxious beauty. 'Skeets has gone on in the cart so he must be all right.' Samson thought. 'The strange guy headed for the beach – alone, and JY is hot after Elise, bless his pit bull heart …'. These thoughts bounced around in his mind as he took off after the cart, knowing it couldn't be far ahead, hollering Skeets name as he went.

Within five minutes he came upon the electric vehicle with a front wheel securely trapped in a deep gash in the crinkled ground. He had run through several gusts of cold, wind blown sea spray and his tactical clothes were damp. A cold chill coursed his body.

"How's it going, old man." Sam's greeting was met with a stoic face and a terse reply.

"About frigging time you got here! What in hell have you been doing … never mind! Your precious apparently got fed up with captive lifestyle and took matters in her own hand. Locked up the brakes and really slammed the kid … bailed out and then took the wrong fork. Ran north away from the beach and right to that mess of ground holes and blowholes. Get your ass in gear and find her or you may be checking the lovelorn columns in the Ocala newspaper when we get back." Skeets motioned to the chagrined Samson as he spoke and the two quickly set the cart's tire on solid ground.

"I know, I know, old pal, but JY should be with her by now and she couldn't be in better hands …" Sam knew, even as the words slid from his clenched lips, that the love of his life was in a very dangerous area and as competent as the loyal pit bulldog was, he wasn't human. "I'm going back and pick up her trail. Follow my light as fast as you can. She may need both of us before this night is over." His last words trailed as he started on the back track with the focus of a bloodhound. His flashlight swung from his belt, taunting the bouncy vehicle that followed.

• • •

Cruzo Dominguez felt relief as he left the rugged lime rock up-croppings behind and aimed for the beach. The moonlit night made for easy walking and his head was no longer throbbing. The sudden glare of headlights caught him completely off-guard and the flinty "Please, stop little man and turn around," caused cold goose bumps to cover his lean body as he shaded his eyes from the sight-robbing headlights. This security guard was not Hispanic and Cruzo did not recognize his voice. He knew many of the security personnel but realized they changed frequently; he also knew each vehicle had a guard dog.

"Ah, Señor. I am a student at the Academy and I am doing a night hike as part of a school project. You should have been informed of this ... no?" As he spoke, the myrmidon slowly loosened the backpack and let it hang from his left hip. The handle of his shiv nestled in his right palm as the guard approached him.

"I have had no such information, young man ... so let's see some ID." The guard, carrying a large, tactical flashlight, kept his back to the glaring headlights forcing Cruzo to blindly comply.

"Ah, Señor. I cannot see. My school papers are in the back-pack." As he spoke, the three-fingered killer-child proffered the tactical pouch by extending his left arm, with the pack, toward the impassive guard while shading his eyes with his forearm. Placing the flashlight under his left arm, the security guard reached for the pack and as he pulled it toward his body, Cruzo Dominguez pushed the shiv into his chest just below the breastbone and into the liver, expertly shifting it side to side before the stricken man knew anything had happened.

Stepping away from the ravaged man, Cruzo smiled. "Ah, I see you have found my ID! Good, now I can be on my way." Wiping his knife and picking up the flashlight, Cruzo ignored the gasping security guard as he fell to his knees, his unseeing eyes fixed in a death stare reflecting utter disbelief.

Walking to the electric security vehicle, the Myrmidon turned off the lights and gazed at the German shepherd tethered from a harness to the back seat. The dog wore a wire mesh muzzle and had quietly watched the brutal assassination but was emitting a low growl since Cruzo had neared the vehicle. The three-fingered Myrmidon had no regard for any animal, especially dogs. Life on the streets put him in direct competition with animals and the canine proved to be the most formidable. He considered this meeting with the dog, under these circumstances, to be a gift from his fairy godmother – bless her soul!

The dog's choke chain, hanging on a hook by the driver's door, could tow a truck and the nylon leash was like steel cable. Avoiding the snarling beast, Cruzo deftly looped the choke chain over the agitated dog's head, ran the end of the leash between the seat top and the bar edging the seat top and tied it securely to the bottom strut holding the seat. Moving to the passenger side, the sociopathic man-child cut the short leash to the harness, freeing him. With one huge effort, the pent-up German shepherd lunged across the seat at Cruzo's proffered throat, inches short, as the anchored leash would not allow his leap to be completed. He hung by the neck while he tried vainly to find the ground with his rear legs. No such luck this day … he was effectively hung by the neck until dead.

Retrieving the backpack, the ebullient assassin started for the beach. Looking back, he laughed out loud as the writhing German shepherd terminated his life, swathed in his own excrement. His escape plan was still on schedule.

• • •

Sam had no trouble backtracking the electric cart and quickly picked up Elise and JY's spoor. The shadowy moonlight slowed his steady trot and the rocky terrain worsened as he went north. He hoped Skeets could get the utility vehicle through this moth-eaten crap. The hissing of escaping air and seawater became omnipresent and he realized that he was entering a very unstable area and slowed to a nervous walk. Standing upright, the anxious man searched the swirling air currents frantically before understanding that the ground scent was the only way he could find them ... albeit the slowest. The wind had picked up considerably and Samson knew from his detailed preparation for this Bahamas soiree that the myriad fissures and blowholes in this particular area were unusual and dangerous.

Dropping to the ground, Sam looked back the way he came and, thankfully, sky-lighted the workhorse electric vehicle – a move that saved his life.

Rising to his knees, Samson caught an overpowering whiff of JY's scent mixed with a trace of Elise. Turning his face to the fresh wind gust he crawled toward its source, which seemed to be a glimmering shadow a few yards ahead. Scudding clouds suddenly erased the glimmering dark spot as the quivering man reached the edge of a geometrically correct blowhole - fixing to erupt. Feeling the edge and having the pressure driven wind hit his face caused Samson to roll sideways, the oyster bar-like ground chewing his tactical clothes like razor wire. The hissing of escaping air was rapidly being replaced by a distant rumbling resembling an approaching freight train.

Frantically retrieving his flashlight, the frustrated Samson clawed his way to the edge of the blowhole, and in the face of overpowering scent from Elise and JY, illuminated the most chilling scene he had ever seen – no real life episode or unspeakable nightmare approached the made-in-hell scenario brought to light by the powerful beam of the tactical flashlight.

Directly beneath him, six or seven feet below the rim, on a small shelf-like ledge, lay the loves of his life. Elise was lying face down with her left arm hanging loosely over the ledge. Her body appeared completely soaked with her beautiful dark hair matted like seaweed. The right side of her body appeared to be tight against the sidewall of the blowhole, and Sam's deep concern at the morbid scene totally blocked his mind from the reality of what was unfolding before him. His agile brain was deep into possible rescue scenarios before he shined the light, again, on the unexplainable dark lump covering most of the stricken nurse's back. The sight of Elise in these dire circumstances caused the highly disciplined operative to totally dump his 'cool'. The rumbling was nearing unbearable pitch with the escaping air reaching wind-tunnel status as the benumbed man shouted with all his might … "JunkYard! JunkYard! My God, it's my dog! It's my dog!"

His body suddenly racked with trembling as the sharp edge of somatic shock touched his psyche. Biting his tongue and taking forced breaths, Samson concentrated on the improbable scene below. Elise was wearing English-made jodhpur riding breeches with a plain saddle leather belt. Her blouse was ripped across the back but Samson saw no blood or visible wound; a running shoe clung to her right foot – her left, bare. He had yet to see movement.

Straddling the semiconscious Elise Jones, legs planted like oak trees on either side of her prostrate body, a wad of jodhpur and belt locked in steel-trap jaws, was 75 pounds of bone, muscle and determination … with no 'off' switch!

Sam only had time for this spectral phantasmagoria to register in his numbed brain before the freight train rush of seawater hit the bottom of the blowhole and tons of the salty stuff regurgitated up the irregular tube, smashed into the bottom of the ledge holding Elise and JunkYard, caromed around and ejaculated into the moonlit sky. Samson tried to duck away from the lip but was too slow and the force of the erupted water pushed him back with the authority of ten fire hoses.

Burying his face in his bloody hands, the awe-struck Samson Hercules Duff could only manage a throaty, "Oh … my … God!"

• • •

Quentin Burgaard, III, tried to keep his eager mastiff headed toward the beach but the obstreperous beast wanted to turn back to the north no matter what the irritated scientist said or did. "Damn you, you stupid asshole. I'm going to trade you for a poodle. At least I'll be able to lead it!" He was clueless about real canine behavior but knew way too much about canine – and human – physiology. He never considered the world-apart differences of the inner workings of the dog mind, only how to manipulate their neuro-chemical systems and thereby change the way they reacted. It was in no way a behavior modification method, merely a sea change in their internal balances.

Dr. Cube grimaced as he recalled his exasperating discussions with Rod Osler, God rest his soul, about the sheer courage of the pit bulldogs the late Myrmon headmaster obsessed about. Burgaard was too cerebral to accept raw courage at face value – in animal or man. He knew, without doubt, that any animal had a built in survivor mechanism that had to kick in before the animals' life force became irretrievable when faced with mortal danger. Physical strength and intimidation were real, as was weakness and lack of size. There was no frigging way a 75 or 80 pound pit bulldog, or any dog that size, could beat up on his mastiff ... no frigging way! True, some dogs did possess a raw courage beyond expectations but so did some individual men and these select individuals, canine or human, were called 'heroes' by the ordinary. But this phenomenon, to be realized, always depended on circumstances. Events and circumstances made heroes, not the other way around. Heroes could never be manufactured - only uncovered, discovered or recognized. Who or what dog was ever fully tested in daily life? When was a heroic act a planned event?

These ponderous questions had been circling the errant scientist's mind like vultures over road kill, but he had never totally convinced himself of their validity. To him, smart was strength, strength was strength, and smart strength was heroic. The intent of these attributes, good or bad, contributed nothing toward this interpretation: Ergo, he, Quentin Burgaard, III, was a hero and the vicious, strong mastiff, as well.

That a staged dogfight allows fulminate display of this characteristic was something the brilliant scientist never argued – only that a large, fierce beast could chew up a smaller, fierce beast … elementary, my dear Watson! That somewhere inside the brain of a dog, every dog, was an off switch that under the right circumstances would turn on and cause the animal to quit the fight … period! To save his life!

'Too bad,' Quentin thought, 'that I could never get through to that thickheaded Osler … just as well. Seeing Goar tear up his precious pit bulldogs may have been bad for his health and given him a heart attack.'

The scudding clouds caused sudden darkness and Quentin Burgaard's wandering thoughts came skidding home. "Let's go, asshole! I need to get to the beach and clear this mess up. Hopefully, it'll mean a little exercise for you." Reluctantly, the willful beast conceded to the head halter and headed for the beach.

It was several hours before sun-up as the pair sauntered through the moonlit darkness. Goar now seemed more dedicated to the task, a fact Burgaard mistakenly attributed to the maturing of the beast along with his half-hearted training sessions. It was impossible for the massive intellect of QB-3 to understand the simple cause-and-effect mentality exhibited by the canine.

A sudden wind gust hit the side of Goar's face causing him to spin around. Emitting a warning growl, the headstrong dog pulled his surprised owner to the east like a canine bulldozer. His forceful pull was not to be denied, so QB-3 went with the flow rather than be pulled down or cede his hard-won control of the leashed animal. Fifty steps and the fetid smell enveloping the curious scientist almost had him retching as he made out the shadow that was the security guard's vehicle. Deciding to chance his flashlight, Burgaard shadowed the beam with his hand and took in the macabre scene of the dead German shepherd hanging from the back seat, covered in his own feces and urine.

Goar ran to the dead dog, eagerly sniffed a few chosen areas, lifted his huge back leg and pissed on the remains. Vigorously scratching the ground, the stimulated beast tried to pull the quizzical Burgaard toward the beach, as if on a track.

"Get back here!" Jerking the leash with all his bulk, QB-3 managed to turn the dog's head and regain some control. "We're going to find out what the hell happened here, asshole! So cool your jets and calm the hell down!"

Tying the heavy leash to the vehicle, Burgaard quickly searched the area, finding the dead guard and expertly establishing the cause of his untimely demise. "Cruzo. It has to be that three-fingered little bastard!" QB-3 was fuming. How did this ungrateful, throwaway street urchin get the balls to go against Dr. Quentin Burgaard, III? Where did he learn to use a shiv? He had to be taught those techniques and he had to have the trust of the dead men to be able to assassinate them in such a fashion.

Calming down, he shuddered as his mind wandered against the possibility of Cruzo Dominguez coming into his office, unannounced, and getting close enough to stick him with what had to be a palmed shiv. 'My God,' he thought, 'He's way ahead of the Myrmex Terminus training. Somewhere along the line he got his PhD in Assassination 101!' Deep in Quentin Burgaard, III's, cluttered mind, a microscopic bubble of moral conscience began to rise, pushing through the sociopathic scum of his psyche. 'I can't turn that cold-hearted kid loose in the world! What the fuck have I done with this stupid Myrmon Academy and these blood thirsty Cubans I'm in bed with?'

QB-3 knew his introspective relapse was rehearsed, and with whatever soothing salve it coated his psyche, was as artificial as Cruzo Dominguez' professed love for Armando Montedinegre. Myrmon Academy alumni were not intended to join any society; however, the reason driving that policy was entirely self-serving and political. It had nothing to do with moral gyroscope or wind-driven compassion. Simply put, they were throwaway human beings – totally disposable!

QB-3 was more determined than ever to intercept the three fingered Myrmidon – to hell with aborting his escape – abort him! Retrieving the sentry's night vision binoculars, Burgaard and the antsy canine set a course for the beach with the mastiff following Cruzo's scent-track like an experienced Bloodhound. The good Dr. Cube had no idea – he thought Goar had suddenly gotten with the program. Topping the last ridge before the beach, Burgaard was startled to see a bright orange flare light up the southern sky. It couldn't be more than half a mile from the willful duo.

Steadying himself against a stunted tree, he searched the beach in that direction. After a few seconds of acclimatization, he could make out a figure on the beach near where the flare had to have originated. Indistinct as it appeared, it had to be Cruzo Dominguez. This was a new wrinkle. Who could he be signaling? Was this some bigger plot and he, Quentin Burgaard, III, merely a pawn on his own chessboard? The Cubans? Chills ran his body like fleas on a skinny dog. It was still a few hours until he would be able to see. Working their way to within 300 yards of the person on the beach, Quentin Burgaard, III, and the mastiff-beast, Goar, settled down for the most important intermission in their ill-gotten lives: The curtain for the main act was only hours from going up!

• • •

Skeets appeared out of the eerie gloom as the errant water returned to its bowels. "You okay? Speak to me!" His anxious words trailed off as Samson appeared by the driver's door.

"Skeets, she ... Elise ... and JunkYard ... are in that blowhole." The exhausted man quickly briefed his buddy on the situation. I can't get to them except by reaching down with my upper body, if I can wedge my feet in the rim rocks to keep from falling on them ... there is no room on that ledge! Elise seems to be lying next to the wall but I think JY's got her anchored and is pulling her to the wall as hard as he can. I can see his neck muscles working but he can't move. If that erupting water catches any of her body surface, they're gone!" Skeets heard the shiver in his pal's voice. He knew the eruptions probably had not peaked, so time was against them.

While talking, the frustrated Samson rifled through the utility box in the bed of the maintenance vehicle, found some ski rope and started pulling it out.

"You going to get a rope on her?" Skeets' question tailed as Samson interjected:

"No! Can't. Can't get to her and I think I can only get to JunkYard's head or back. Skeets, we have to do this now – that hole may blow anytime …" Sam's anxiety was written across his squinted eyes and clenched lips. The Skeeterman had never seen his pal so distraught.

Samson Hercules Duff had never been so distraught!

His voice a monotone, Samson Duff approached the edge of the hole, careful not to trip or knock loose rocks into the menacing hole. Easing his head over the rim, he was pleased to feel the downdraft created by the retreating water column. He knew he had a little time before Momma Nature's water cannon locked and reloaded.

The opening appeared to be seven or eight feet wide, circular and possessed of a lip. Samson realized he could not get the rope over any part of Elise or JY. Even if that were a possibility, he would not be able to pull them clear of the lip and too much tension on the rescue rope could result in damage to them worse than death. Staring down at the stricken pair, he realized the breeze was coming up the tube and a low rumbling could be felt through the limerock ground. Samson Hercules Duff experienced the cold breath of death's bright Angel as the two greatest treasures in his life lay, just out of his reach, and only minutes from extinction. The rumbling was almost palpable.

Returning to the vehicle, he locked eyes with the indomitable Skeets Kirby. The Skeeterman had never seen the focus or resolve shining through his pal's eyes like this - laser beams from hell. He spoke first. "What you want me to … ?"

"Shut the fuck up! Just listen, goddammit. I know your arms and hands are kaput, so don't bullshit me about what you can do. I'm going to tie the end of this rope to the crossbar above the bumper…. I'm taking the free end with me into that hole. Don't want any slack in this goddam line, so I'll take it out. You don't touch this rope!

"How will I know when to pull …" Skeets voice sounded hollow as Sam cut him off again.

"Just listen, dammit! You don't pull anything! I'm out of time. Do as I fucking say! Back up to here and when the hell hole erupts and you see water coming out the top, step on the gas like you're a drag racer, and don't stop until you feel weight on the rope. Just … fucking do it!" Sam disappeared into the gloom as the Skeeterman tried to process the scattershot information spewed at him by a man unraveling. The grotto noises were intensifying and the rope was lying loose. The come and go moonlight added to this surreal nightmare as Skeets Kirby chillingly realized he could be losing his best, maybe only, friends in his world. He shivered as the rope silently tightened.

Sam's tactical clothes were steely tough, but the scalloped moonscape had treated them badly, exposing many of the healing dog bite wounds resulting in chronic bleeding of these unprotected parts. The up-swelling demon rushing to claim his loved ones created a rumble he would hear in his dreams for the rest of his life.

Leaving his fanny pack in place, Sam took his Randall knife and looped the thong securely over his hand. What he was about to do would take every ounce of his trained body and iron will. Failure was not on his radar as he slithered to the hole and went head first over the rim. The ski rope was in his teeth with seven or eight feet hanging free. Grabbing the tag end, he placed it in his mouth to leave about four feet of double line to the bight, as the free end. Dangling from his waist, he knew he had to find a hand support before he committed his soon to be overbalanced body, and the only possibility was JunkYard's sturdy back. Unable to monitor the victims, Samson overbalanced and slid down until both hands felt the steel-like back of JunkYard. His feet found a crack in the rim-rock and he curled his toes inside the tough tactical shoes with all the force he could muster, making flesh-like grappling hooks with his contorted feet … giving no voice to the sudden, intense pain.

Suddenly able to look into JY's eye, Sam could see the ice-cold fire running to the depths of this magnificent beast, a fire that screamed: 'Everything's under control and Miss Elise is never going off this ledge … period!'

Sam could feel the increasing updraft and the low rumble was swelling to freight train crescendo. Expertly, he grabbed the neck skin of the JunkYard dog, scruffing him like a bitch carrying a pup. "God forgive me!" he cried, as he deftly slipped the Randall through the skin below his grasp and expertly stabbed through the tough skin and connective tissue covering the dog's impressive neck muscles, ran his index and middle fingers through the inch wide gash as he withdrew the knife, hooked the bight in the rope with these fingers and quickly pulled the double strands of rope through the bloody gash. The thewy dog never flinched, never blinked. Samson could feel the increasing updraft and the rumbling was now a roar. Elise had not moved, but the anxious man thought he heard a moan when he placed his hands on JY's back.

He had fashioned a living, bloody collar from the stoic pit bulldog's neck fascia and skin and if Sam's plan was to work, JY would be the clamp holding the precious female cargo, and his impromptu collar the lifting device - with Samson acting the human float.

Letting the knife hang from the thong, Sam ran his left hand through the bight, grabbed the double strands with his fingers and began wrapping the slack around his opened hand like a bull rider getting set for the chute to pop open. Salty spray was bouncing up the tube with a ton of angry seawater chasing it as the pertinacious Sam Duff wrapped away the remaining line slack, and gripped the wadded rope as if a live diamondback's head.

As the water column neared, Samson waited until it caromed off the bottom of the ledge before unlocking his numbed toes and contorting his body, dragging the semi-conscious nurse with the locked–on JunkYard into position to expose their combined body surface to the full force of the eruption. Like a loosened champagne cork, the hapless trio swooshed ten feet into the air as Skeets Kirby pushed the utility vehicle to its limit, landing them five feet clear of the hellish blowhole, with JunkYard still firmly attached to Elise Jones' belt and breeches.

Dawn was breaking as the perturbed Kirby reached the sodden players in this Shakespearean drama from the netherworld. Samson was freeing his hand and trying to turn Elise's face toward him while JunkYard's hold on her clothing and belt was as tenacious as when first applied, preventing the distressed woman from being turned to her side or back.

"Skeets, I've got to get JY out of his hold. See how Elise is while I see if he will respond to me. Try to keep her from groaning or speaking loudly, and for God's sake, don't make any loud noises." Samson was only too aware that any noise, especially from him, or loud, could cause the gallant dog to tighten his hold ... if that was even possible. He could see Elise breathing and there was no water oozing from her mouth or nostrils.

Tears ran down his face as he quietly stroked the rock-hard head of the warrior dog, letting his hand slide gingerly across the mutilated neck, bloody fluid a silent reminder of the gashes and the only testament of their presence. Sam suddenly became aware that JY's steely gaze had locked on his two eyes, guilt filled as they were. He saw: No regret. No resentment. No remorse. Only the dead honest fulfillment of his pit bulldog destiny and the uncompromised protection of those he loved.

"She's hypothermic, Sam, we've got to warm her up, pronto! I don't think she has any serious injury but if we don't get her some heat it won't matter. We need to wrap her, especially her head ..." Skeets was at the utility vehicle pulling out everything that could be used to cover the chilled woman. "We need to get her to a hospital, old hoss, so loosen that canine sky-hook of yours and let's get the hell out of Dodge!"

Softly stroking the hard-wired pit bulldog's shoulder, Sam noted JY's eye following the movement of his hand and felt the slight softening of his taut muscles. Struggling for time, Sam thought he might be able to reorient the stark discipline of the resolute dog. Exposing one of the myriad bite wounds on his forearm, Samson positioned it under JunkYard's nose, and was rewarded with instant softening of the dog's body. His inquisitive nose began a search of Samson's arm and his eye lost its ice-like, empty stare. Letting go his hold, the intrepid beast rose from his guardian position over the semi-conscious Elise Jones, vigorously shook his bruised body, scratched the rocky ground with bloody front feet, moved to Samson's side and began licking the wounds on his arm ... his tongue, warm and gentle as puppy breath.

Samson Hercules Duff could not disavow his tears.

• • •

Chapter SIXTEEN

The brilliant orange flare shattered the predawn darkness with the regnant authority of a lightning bolt.

"He made it Dad! Sam's back ... let's get him!" The excited voice of Johnny Dugan cut the warm, humid air like a hot knife.

Focusing his 7x50's, BJ Dugan mumbled. "Whoa, big boy, Sam's flares were bright red, not orange. That's Skeets' flare ... something's not right. Samson made a point to tell me he carried red flares and Kirby toted orange ones" Putting the binoculars down, Big Johnny turned to his son. "Wake that old Cuban and let's ease along the beach. I can't see shit in this gloom."

"I am awake, Señor Dugan. Do not delay your mission for us. Mr. Sucio Perro and I stand ready to help in any way." As he spoke, a muscular head rose at his knees, displaying the yawn of a caged animal. "Ah, yes, my canine friend seems to need some action ... good. Let's be off!"

Johnny fired up the motor and slipped to within 50 yards of the beach. He judged the flare launch to be less than half a mile from their position. Dawn was fast approaching and he wanted to finish this pick-up before good daylight. They had not seen any sign of life for several hours, not even those of the security patrol that ran the beach almost on the hour. Nor could they see his lifeless body or that of his German shepherd. They also could not see the stocky, curly-bearded man peering through high tech night vision binoculars at the beach, in general; them, in particular.

As hard as it was for him to comprehend, Quentin Burgaard, III, didn't have a shot at dealing the hand about to be played, but he also didn't bluff … easily. Whoever dealt this fucking mess on his island had better be ready to call, and God help them if it was a bluff! Shifting his view further up the beach, he could barely make out a small figure walking slowly toward the boat.

'Has to be that little three-fingered shit head,' he thought. Judging the intervening distance between the urchin and the boat, and allowing for terrain, QB-3 maneuvered the eerily complacent mastiff to a small up-cropping with an unobstructed view of the beach … and requested two cards from the dealer … whomever!

Cruzo Dominguez could barely make out the boat as he walked the beach. It had to be there because of his flare. Now, he had to be extra careful. Escape was just around the corner! All he had was Skeets Kirby's backpack and his bloodied shiv. He realized that all the skills learned at Myrmex Terminus would be needed to make this chicken fly. Like rubbing a lucky charm, the Myrmidon palmed the shiv and felt his heart rate slow – Cruzo was ready for the next chapter.

"I can make him out now. Hmmm, seems to be a small man, or a child. Whoever, it's a little person." BJ's voice dropped to a mumble as he studied the approaching figure. "Sure not Kirby, or Duff … son, I think we have a problem."

The idling boat moving toward the walking figure was narrowing the gap rapidly. "What you think we should do. Don't have a clue who that could be." Johnny Dugan pushed the throttles into neutral as the blurry figure silently morphed into a small boy waving his arm at the boat. "What you think, Papa San, let's give him a hug, pat him on the back-side and send him back home?" The younger Dugan chuckled as he caught the dead serious gaze of Big Johnny.

"Hey, man, we saddled this horse, so now we have to ride the son of a bitch. Let's see who this young man is ..." BJ had lowered the binoculars and was studying Cruzo when the drifting boat touched bottom and stopped. The shore breeze was gusting and Cruzo, seeing the boat stop, headed for the water's edge, the grounded boat still over 50 yards away.

The low, throaty rumble from the Havana dog filled the boat like a subpoena from the netherworld. "What the hell ..." Johnny Dugan stepped back as he sought the source of the most threatening sound he had ever heard. He could feel the hair on his neck snap to attention and the cold sensation of rising goose bumps. "What's his problem?"

Dom Pedro had been standing quietly at the bow of the boat watching the approaching figure. Something about it seemed eerily familiar, swirling around the blurry edge of his memory. At the Dirty Dog's warning, the perceptive old man wet his finger, raised it above his head to verify the wind direction. "Ah, Mr. Sucio Perro, you know more than we do about this stranger. What is it you know?"

Dawn's light idled as a light fog descended in pockets along the beach. Cruzo Dominguez reached the water as Dom Pedro spoke softly to the Dugans. "Señors, let me speak with this child before we make any decisions. He appears Cuban and probably speaks small English. Please allow me this." I will leave the dog here, please." Moving to the bow, Dom Pedro tied a mooring line around the Havana dog's thick neck, eliciting another chilling growl. "Patience. You grumble like a volcano, mi Sucio Perro. I will be back very shortly. Do not embarrass this old man."

Stepping overboard at the stern, the curious old Cuban waded the length of the sandbar, forded the chest –deep trough guarding the shore and walked slowly toward the emulous, three-fingered, ex-Havana street urchin.

Cruzo saw the old man depart the boat and stopped. He had no idea how he should act, so he decided to wait and see what would happen. He also did not see the lithe shadow that departed over the bow of the boat after efficiently chewing through the tethering mooring line like a stick of licorice. Massaging the bloodied shiv with the palm of his hand, Cruzo's mind remained calm as he awaited his fate.

"What are they doing?" Johnny Dugan peered into the opaque air, straining to get a clear view of the old man. Big Johnny grunted as he tried to adjust the focus on the binoculars to better see the beach. "Hear that splash a few minutes ago? Johnny's voice hinted of concern.

"What splash?" BJ replied.

"That goddam dog's gone … overboard. Headed for shore going the other way." Johnny's voice hinted of relief.

"Well, I'll be damn! I guess the old fart just lost his dog. Shouldn't have tied him up like that … too fucking bad." Turning back to his binoculars, the senior Dugan muttered, "Wish I had a frigging gun!"

Quentin Burgaard, III, watched as the beach scene unfolded. He saw the man leave the boat, watched as Cruzo hesitated, and wondered what it was that jumped from the bow of the boat to swim, vigorously, to the beach opposite the man's approach. The spotty fog neutralized the high tech binoculars but the querulous scientist thought the thing was an animal of some sort. He did not think it was a person, but he couldn't be sure since it looked big enough to be a human. He didn't give a shit. His hand was looking better every minute.

As Dom Pedro neared the Myrmidon man-child, he noticed the disfigured hand. The old Cuban was well aware of the legend of Hoostra Island and the Myrmidon Academy. He knew that some of the shanghaied street urchins were rumored to be going to the Myrmon Academy and were never seen again. He also recalled his awkward conversation with the urchin, Julio, when he was looking for the Dirty Dog.

"Ah, Señor Cruzo. And how are you this fine morning. It is a nice day for a stroll on this beautiful beach, is it not." Dom Pedro smiled and extended his hand as if to touch the smallish man-child. "Is your friend Julio with you or do you take your pleasure alone?" Dom Pedro was playing his long shot and not looking back.

Cruzo Dominguez was stunned. Who was this old man and how could he, or anyone, know of Julio and Cruzo? For the first time since the Myrmidon had planned his escape, doubts appeared in his psyche like maggots in sun-ripened meat. Cruzo knew immediately that the old man had to go ... and quickly. He had no doubt that he could wheedle the men on the boat to take him away if the old fart didn't screw it up; perfectly clear in his mind.

Cruzo glanced toward the interior and caught a glimpse of a small thicket of stunted trees a few hundred yards off the beach. The patchy fog was starting to lift but visibility was still iffy. "Señor, you seem to know me but I have no recollection of our meeting. I am interested in how this can be ... if you would excuse me, I have to relieve myself. Would you be so kind as to accompany me to those trees while we talk and provide me with some discussion as to how you came to know my name and that of my friend." Turning toward the trees as he spoke, Cruzo Dominguez squeezed the palmed shiv and became aware of his sweat soaked hand.

Quentin Burgaard, III, had been watching the inopportune meeting and wondered who the wizened old man was. Whoever he was, he seemed to know the three-fingered Myrmidon. The men on the boat seemed as interested in the meeting as QB-3. Maybe they didn't know who Cruzo Dominguez was, and maybe this wasn't all planned out. Maybe this entire cluster-fuck episode was the result of unintended consequences. Burgaard was working on a full house!

Nearing the small copse, the duplicitous man-child stumbled and fell into the grass with a child-like groan. Taken by surprise, old Dom Pedro rushed to aid the stricken boy, extending his hand as he approached. Rolling to his side, Cruzo had clear aim at the old Cuban's crotch and femoral artery. One quick jab, two or three wiggles and the old fart was history – silent history ... end of problem!

The force that hit the conniving Cruzo had no comprehension. As his knife wielding hand set to deliver its fatal blow, 85 pounds of vengeance driven bone and muscle hit him, catching his hand in midair and with the force of a leviathan vice, crushed his forearm and straddled him like a demon from hell. No sound escaped the mouth of Sucio Perro. No growling, no snarling, only deadly efficient dismemberment of what once was Cruzo Dominguez.

QB-3 couldn't understand what he was seeing. Where did the big dog come from? Is that what jumped from the boat? What happened to the old man? What happened to Cruzo? All he could see now was the old man trying to get the dog to come with him; did the dog kill Cruzo? What in hell was going on? Enough was enough! Quentin Burgaard, III, was going to end this soap opera shit and find out what the hell was happening.

The radiant burst of red in the murky sky over his left shoulder rendered the red-bearded observer speechless with the realization that Kirby and Duff had to be alive, and were probably headed for the beach and the waiting boat.

Quentin Burgaard, III, loosed Goar.

Johnny Dugan was having a fit to go ashore and find out what happened to the old Cuban. "But Dad, what if it's a trap? We can't see shit from here and it's only a few hundred yards to those trees … let me go. I'll get right on back!"

"Grow up, Junior. This boat is our only ticket out of here, and Sam's and Skeets', too. Big Johnny's words almost collided with the red burst trying to burn a hole in the dingy sky. "Look! Goddammit look! That's Sam's flare! He's alive and I bet a buck old Skeets is with him. He's telling us to wait … keep your ass on this boat and get ready. Something fixing to happen and we better as hell be ready!" The big man was so excited he had to lower the binoculars. "Listen up, Johnny boy. Samson confided to me that a special FBI unit is going to drop in on this operation some time this morning - soon as the weather allows. Don't know when, or where, but he told me we better be gone before the fireworks start 'cause they're not supposed to know what we've been doing, or even that we're here. This Academy from hell is going down and this team is to take no prisoners and Samson has to extract Skeets and get back so we can sail off into the sunset … alive! Get your ass in gear and be ready!"

Dom Pedro finally calmed the Havana dog and headed for the beach as fast as his bony legs allowed. He shivered as he remembered the bloodied knife dropping from the mangled hand of the three-fingered former urchin. For sure, Mr. Sucio Perro saved his wrinkled old hide … he had no idea of danger from the frail looking man-child. Over a hundred yards from the beach, the wizened old Cuban still had no idea of danger as 180 pounds of ornery dog meat closed on him at a dead run. Too preoccupied to notice the flare, Dom Pedro fixed his gaze on the gently bobbing boat and bee-lined for the beach, the Havana dog trotting in his shadow.

"What's that?" Johnny asked, as he pointed at the running mastiff, closing fast on Dom Pedro and his dog.

BJ Dugan aimed the 7x50's at the huge dog and whistled under his breath. "Son, that's gotta' be the biggest damn dog I've ever seen!" Scanning the surrounding area, Dugan spotted QB-3 as he topped the last small ridge before the beach. "There's a man standing on that little hill overlooking the beach, and I think he's connected to that God-awful dog lighting a shuck for the old Cuban. Don't know what's going down but we've got to stay put 'till Sam gets here ... he's on his way!"

Dom Pedro saw the Goar-dog two jumps before the beast was on him, and never saw the blur that leaped past him like a shadow come to life. The Dirty Dog hit the charging mastiff like a battering ram, causing the two beasts to rise to their hind legs and spar like two boxers, their savage biting a blur of tooth, skin and blood. Sucio Perro was fighting to get a hold on the much larger mastiff while Goar was not able to upend the sturdy pit bulldog, roll him to his back and tear his throat out as he did with every dog he had ever killed. The size and strength of Goar was such that Sucio Perro could not get a hold, and every slashing bite from the powerful warrior dogs ripped skin and flesh.

Quentin Burgaard, III, stopped so he could appreciate the full scope of the warring dogs. He had no idea who the other dog was or where it came from, but he recognized it as a pit bulldog and that Rod Osler had to have been involved in its presence on Hoostra Island. Digesting the size differential between the combatants and gloating inwardly at the vicious frontal assault launched by his Goar, the sanctimonious scientist chuckled as he thought. 'Now Roderick, old boy, Mr. Goar-dog is fixing to show you how to make minced dog-meat out of one of your invincible pit bulldogs! I trust you've settled in hell long enough to know how to work the TV's. Don't want you to miss this one!'

As Burgaard's ego sunbathed in the glow of his big dog's putative superiority, the besieged mastiff was not quite as confident, as his meaningless skin slashes and impotent air bites did nothing to deter the rock solid, hard biting machine paying absolutely no attention to Goar-beast's best efforts to rend him asunder. Lacking the experience of real opposition, the hurting mastiff sought to reposition himself and get relief from the bone crushing power of the Havana dog – a serious mistake since the Dirty Dog had yet to find a solid hold.

Backing down and away, Goar turned to flank his nemesis and bowl the smaller dog over, to expose his belly for the slashing teeth of the 180 pound behemoth.

Dr. Cube had moved closer and was so engrossed in the battle he totally disregarded the old Cuban, and the boat, with its two highly suspicious occupants. He was as close to an epiphany in his misspent life as he would ever be, and did nothing to conceal his presence, or pleasure.

Dom Pedro was also engrossed in the mesmerizing dance of destruction being staged, without benefit of choreography, by the canine warriors. He was overwhelmed by the timeless loyalty of his beloved Sucio Perro, and near tears as he watched the fearless pit bulldog absorb the horrendous, slashing attack of Goar; without so much as a blink of his eye. His busy jaws issued no sound. His stout legs gave no ground. He was a warrior … and he was at work!

The Halloween mask-like effect of the mutilating lip trimming surgery had turned the once beautiful black masked mastiff into a toothy, dog monster from some slimy underworld. His fierce grin struck fear in any man that could bear to stare … few could. Sucio Perro knew no such constraint.

The wise old Cuban knew he had to remain silent, that any show of excitement or loud talk, especially shouting, would heighten the pit bulldog's efforts even as that seemed impossible – a fact the Goar beast was to learn … the hard way! Dom Pedro could not imagine his beloved Dirty Dog prevailing over such a huge and ferocious beast. Tears were rolling down his wrinkled face as he watched his champion defend him in what had to be a losing effort. He, Dom Pedro, could not desert the gallant dog. Whatever the outcome, Sucio Perro's destiny would be his, as well. He turned his back to the boat.

Johnny Dugan watched in awe, the unfolding Greek tragedy playing out just off the beach. "Dad, let me go help the old man. Those dogs could kill him! Why doesn't he run back to the boat?"

"Son, that's the dog he brought on board. That dog is protecting him and there's no way he's going to leave that mutt, so cool it and let's hope he can get the job done; that Sam and Skeets get here ASAP and we get our little asses out of here!" BJ Dugan focused his binoculars on the weaving bulk of Quentin Burgaard, III.

The instant Goar backed and turned, the biggest mistake of his unfortunate life, the Havana dog ducked under and hit his left elbow with hydraulic force and locked on. The mastiff's left leg was immobilized and the 85 pounds suddenly swelled to 300. The position effectively immobilized Goar and rendered Dirty Dog impossible to bite with any force. In trying to pull away, the stricken mastiff quickly realized that every effort he made was met with an increasing bite force that he could no longer tolerate. None of the gaping wounds on his adversary seemed to have any visible effect and the burning eyes of the pit bulldog would boil water.

Adrenalin was deserting the huge dog's body like cave bats at dusk. Quentin Burgaard, III's mastiff suddenly wanted a change of scenery, preferably one with a dog free lounge! Howling and shaking his head, Goar tried to drag his burden by sheer force, but the stout dog was too savvy to allow such a maneuver.

When Dr. Cube saw the mastiff make his move, he figured it was over for the pit bulldog. As the play developed and the Havana dog locked on and held, Burgaard took that to be a sign of him quitting, since he stopped slashing and ripping at the huge mastiff. Hearing his dog squalling like a banshee and trying to pull away caused the bearded Doctor's face to redden, as he realized Goar's efforts were totally focused on escape – he had thrown in the towel!

Screaming like a man possessed, Burgaard headed for the battling dogs as fast as his stubby bulk would allow. Oblivious to his surroundings, he palmed the small black remote and within 50 yards stopped and began rapidly hitting the various keys, his eyes darting like water bugs.

"I'll show you, you goddam asshole pit bullpoodle!" QB-3 was screaming as his fingers played the keyboard like a phantom piano virtuoso. Hitting the enter key caused the besieged mastiff to roar like an injured lion, shake his head and start bucking like a strapped bull. Rearing with maniacal force, the Goar beast ripped his caught elbow free of the merciless jaws of the Havana Dog, rendering his elbow useless, arterial blood spurting like artesian wells. The hard-won freedom exposed the head of Sucio Perro for a split second and the artificially stimulated dog slashed down and ripped the left side of his adversary's skull like a gear driven biting machine.

At the sudden change in the fight dynamic, the Havana dog instantly shifted his head to go for the exposed throat of the deranged Goar, the combined force of the change of direction enough to cause the entire left side of Sucio Perro's head to be ripped from the bone; his ear, muscles and part of his facial nerve were rendered free of their attachments.

With the expeditious efficiency of a striking rattlesnake, the mutilated pit bulldog locked on the exposed throat of the robotic mastiff.

Quentin Burgaard, III, bathed in the toxic sweat of his own denial, yet mesmerized by this battle of canine warriors, could not comprehend how the dirty looking pit bulldog could still be alive, much less have a death grip on his invincible mastiff. Goar's struggle for life-giving air could be plainly heard, and no manipulation of the keyboard made a difference.

There was no sound from Sucio Perro. With each agonizing breath of the suffocating mastiff, the emotionless jaws of his adversary tightened. Apocalypse!

Screaming aimlessly, the frazzled scientist dropped the keyboard remote, pulled his handgun and ran for the struggling dogs. "I'll show you, you miserable son of a bitch!" Everything else in his world was white noise. His only mission was to kill the mordant pit bulldog that had the arrogant temerity to somehow best his Goar-beast. His frustration morphed to hypnotic trance, and was so overwhelming he failed to notice the approaching objects in the clearing eastern sky.

"No-no-no!" The high-pitched scream of the here-to-fore ignored Dom Pedro sundered the highly charged morning air like a thunderbolt as he slammed into the gun hand of the slaughtering Quentin Burgaard, III. Grabbing the arm, the wiry old Cuban started scratching and biting at the entranced man's head and neck.

QB-3 had no idea what had attacked him; he had no idea where he was. Instinctively throwing the buzzing attacker off, he stepped back and viewed the two dogs. Goar's eyes were glazing as life-force departed his violated body, evicted by the inexorable pressure of the Havana dog's inclement jaws. The pit bulldog's head was partially hidden by the bulk of the dying mastiff, with only the left side exposed, a gory rearrangement of his anatomy. Unrecognizable. That he lived could not be determined visually.

His mental clarity rapidly returning, Burgaard considered both canine warriors dead and the wizened old man sprawled in the weeds merely a pest. Looking for the pistol, he became aware of the 'wup-wup-wup' of the approaching helicopters, one nearing the beach, while the other headed inland. The pulsed synchrony of the rotors mimed the rhythmic beating of vengeful hearts and heralded the only real fear in the warped, ego-driven genius – violent death!

Intentions disappeared as a single purpose commandeered his clearing mind - Dr. Cube headed for his office at a run.

Big Johnny Dugan took in the drama playing out on shore and when the choppers were spotted, lowered his binoculars. "Johnny, I see a vehicle coming from the direction of the last red flare … gotta be Sam … maybe Skeets. Go help the old Cuban. I think his dog may be dead. This little ball of yarn is fixing to wind up!"

Departing the boat with the pent up energy of a caged tiger, Big Johnny Dugan's namesake shot back, "Thank God, old man. Any thing for action … this has been the most boring, least productive, most fucked up fishing trip I've ever been suckered into …"

• • •

Epilogue

Sam and Skeets reached the beach just after the FBI chopper landed. Elise Jones had started shivering and was responding to questions as she and Skeets were loaded into the helicopter to be airlifted to the Naval Hospital in Key West. Samson declined, and told Skeets that he and the Dugans would meet them in Key West the next evening.

As the chopper took off, Big Johnny, Samson, and JunkYard went to help Johnny and Dom Pedro.

The old Cuban and the young Dugan could not separate the two canine combatants even though they believed the Havana dog was alive. Dom Pedro was trying to pry open the mouth of his beloved Sucio Perro when JunkYard arrived and started sniffing the mastiff's carcass. Reaching the locked on jaws of the battered Havana dog, the fateful JY stopped sniffing and started licking the grievous wounds on the pit bulldog's head, causing the old Cuban to step back. Barely perceptible, the massive jaws of Sucio Perro loosened and the mighty head relaxed against the body of the once invincible Goar-beast.

Seeing that he was alive, the men carried him to the boat, knowing that his injuries may well prove fatal.

The FBI team completely destroyed the Academy buildings with no confrontations. In the dormitory they found the bludgeoned body of a red haired female with her throat cut. Hanging in the dorm's office was the bodies of a gangly man and a young boy with jet-black hair; both naked and hanging from the same noose – dead. Otherwise, the buildings were deserted, except for the body of one Armando Montedinegre, in a small, stand-alone house: All burned in the ensuing conflagration.

Bud York was never seen again.

Quentin Burgaard, III, was never found. The tunnel running under his office to the ocean was searched, but only SCUBA gear found. No sign indicating his demise or injury was discovered, and no body. He is considered – presumed – to be alive.

Samuel and his cousins act as if Quentin Burgaard, III, and Roderick Osler never existed. The tenor of the activities at Eula Mae's homey little kitchen, and around the mango trees, continues as before; she gets less visits from stray dogs.

Chino El-Taino, the Cuban Assassin, returned to his mountain home and never again hunted men. The prevailing wisdom proclaims him a reclusive hunter – of pigs – with dogs only remotely resembling his former, feared Ghost dogs. The brooding Palladin transitioned from Cuban Legend to Caribbean Myth during the remainder of his life, and his death at age 91 was never officially recorded.

Elise's Aunt Cecile decided to purchase VentureQuest Farm as an investment. In so doing, she tried to locate Charlie Sharp. Her hired investigator traced him to South Miami and the Cordrerro Kennels, and the possibility that he was aboard a Cordrerro seaplane that reported a passenger falling from the plane while over the Florida Everglades. Police reports confirm the incident but the identity of the unfortunate passenger remains unknown.

Samson and Elise moved into the main house, while Skeets Kirby stayed in the loft apartment. Skeets recovered full use of his hands and was finally able to ignore the ragged scars adorning his forearms, like macabre tattoos.

JunkYard had the run of the farm, but could always be found in the shadow of the beauteous new matron of VentureQuest farm. Elise Jones and a patch-eyed pit bulldog, answering to JunkYard, were inseparable.

Permission became absolutely a must for strangers to approach the dark-haired mistress of the thoroughbred farm ... and not from Samson Duff!

• • •

It was three months since JunkYard saved Elise's life, and she was fully recovered. Samson's myriad gashes and punctures had healed without complications, and the one-eyed pit bulldog's wounds and feet had healed. His grievous neck wound had to have Penrose drains for ten days, but had healed with minimal scarring.

The glaring sun was high overhead as the four people climbed out of the Podzilla, riding lazily against the ratty Customs' dock on North Andros Island at Nichols Town. All were dressed in shorts and wore sandals, except the four-legged, burnished red dog with a crimson eye-patch where his left eye once lived.

The leisurely stroll to Eula Mae's kitchen took all of thirty minutes and Big Johnny Dugan was the first to speak. "Well, Sam old chap. I'll bet this visit is a little less stressful than the last one! Especially since the one you were seeking now trots along at your side."

Sam Duff laughed as he recalled his previous, anxious visit. "Yea, man, that was a nightmare. Not only that, I didn't know Elise was on that stinking little island ... only found out when I got there. How's about those little green apples?"

Eula Mae was expecting her visitors and had saved tables for them. As they entered, several locals abandoned their tables and sauntered out the door. Sam and Elise entered first, and quickly spotted the wizened old man sitting alone at the oilskin- covered table by the small window. At his feet lay a muscular pit bulldog with a droopy left eyelid, a large defect in the musculature of his head, topped off by a nub of a left ear; a coat color that defied description ... he just appeared to be dirty.

"Ah, Señor Dugan, Señor Duff, and young Johnny. What a pleasure for this old man to greet you once again ... and under these most pleasant circumstances. And who is the beautiful young lady?" Dom Pedro's face reflected his heartfelt pleasure at meeting his compatriots under these more pleasant circumstances. "Please do me the honor of joining Señor Sucio Perro, and yours truly, for a cold beer ... please."

Samson noticed the veiled scrutiny of the unperturbed dog as he introduced Elise. He also realized the pit bulldog perfection demonstrated by this noble dog's body and felt a strong attraction. His dog-scent evoked no aura of strangeness ... some peculiar familiarity he couldn't pin down – almost magnetic. He also noticed that JunkYard acknowledged the big dog's presence but did nothing to evoke challenge ... he acted like they were old friends.

Pulling up extra chairs, they crowded around the old Cuban, coercing the Havana dog to move. Soundlessly, he moved to the wall and with a stifled grunt, laid down beside JunkYard, causing Samson to swallow his comment, "Wait a min..." as neither dog batted an eyelid. "I'll be dammed! Never seen JunkYard cozy up with another dog, especially a male. What's going on?"

"Ah, Señor Duff, your Seeing Eye Dog sees more than we realize. We three had tough going during our time of tribulation, when my Sucio Perro also acted the friend – which he never does. Ah, maybe they knew each other – in another life ... maybe coursing through the strong veins of Señor JunkYard, claiming kinship, giving nourishment to his magnificent body, and being much more than just a coincidence, ... is Havana Blood!"

THE END

Made in the USA
Charleston, SC
10 May 2015